Praise for the Victor McCain thrillers

The Hand of God

"With plenty of tense moments and a bold and lively wit, *The Hand of God* is a wild and crazy ride that sets a new standard for thrillers, supernatural or otherwise. Victor McCain has my vote for badass of the year."

--Chris Brown, author of Necromancer

"This would make one freaking good movie. Bloody, paranormal, noir, and funny…"

--Jamie Lee Scott, USA Today Bestselling
author of the Gotcha detective series

The Watchers

"After reading *The Hand of God*, Tony Acree's outstanding debut novel in the Victor McCain thriller series, I could hardly wait for the follow-up, but I was worried. How could Mr. Acree top the incredible story that pitted God against Satan, greed against good, and combine humor with the deepest tragedies known to man? A tall order, indeed.

My angst was wasted. *The Watchers*, Mr. Acree's second novel in the series, was exhilarating, thought-provoking, and best of all, extraordinarily entertaining.

It takes a rare talent to create a compelling, thoughtful, and immensely enjoyable work of fiction. But to create one that does all of these things plus imagining believable supernatural characters, insight into the thoughts and deeds of God and Satan, puts Tony Acree in the rarefied atmosphere of elite authors.

I look forward to reading *The Speaker*. I have complete confidence that it will be a journey well taken."

--Bill Noel, author of the popular Folly
Beach Mystery series

The Speaker

ALSO BY TONY ACREE

———————

The Hand of God

The Watchers

The Speaker

By

Tony Acree

Printed in the United States of America

ISBN: 1-942212-02-X
ISBN-13: 978-1-942212-02-7

Hydra Publications
1310 Meadowridge Trail
Goshen, KY 40026

www.hydrapublications.com

The Speaker

CHAPTER ONE

Eduardo kept watch out the front window while Congressman Owen Grenville committed suicide. True, the congressman was not doing so willingly, but in the end it would be suicide, nonetheless.

Outside all was quiet in this upscale section of Georgetown, not far from the university. A row of town homes crouched on each side of the street, occasionally illuminated by the light from a wan street lamp. It was a bit before ten p.m. at the end of July, the night warm and pleasant. Activity was starting to wind down, the sidewalks now mostly empty as residents settled in for the night.

Eduardo turned from the Norman Rockwell view out the window to take in the macabre scene inside this particular town house: Congressman Grenville stood on a dining room chair, a hangman's noose fit snuggly around his neck with the other end tied to the wooden balcony railing above his head, while tears cut a path down the wrinkled folds of his aging cheeks.

Standing in front of him was a woman holding in one hand an iPad, turned in such a way the congressman could watch what was on the screen, and in the other hand she held a gun down at her side. About five and a half feet tall, with a ballerina's build and long black hair cascading down to the small of her back, the woman was the picture of beauty.

Deadly beauty, Eduardo thought. For six years they were partners in death, hired assassins known for pulling off the perfect murders, the ones people never suspected were murderers at all. They charged exorbitant amounts of money for their services, but those in need paid. There was no one better than them.

He called her Donut because they could not pass a Krispy Kreme donut shop without stopping to buy a dozen for her to eat. It was her one and only vice, as far he knew. How she managed to keep her slim figure Eduardo had no clue, but she did. From time to time, they spent evenings in bed together and he knew her body was flawless.

She was the one who gave him the name Eduardo, saying his olive complexion reminded her of a Latin lover from her past she was forced to kill after he became too clingy. Neither knew the other's real name, nor likely ever would.

His reverie was broken when he heard the congressman plead, "Please, don't do this. You can't do this to me. You can't."

A pudgy man with only a hint of hair circling a bald head covered in sweat, the congressman cut a pitiful figure as he begged for his life. Known as a party firebrand, he would stand for hours in the well of the House of Representatives, taking on any and all who stood in his way as he climbed the ladder of the party hierarchy.

Eduardo was sure he never pictured in his wildest dreams his life ending in anything but personal glory and power. Life could really be a kick in the teeth.

"Congressman, you've seen what both my partner and I look like," Donut said, "and either way, in the next five minutes, you will be dead. The only question is will your wife and daughter join you."

The congressman's eyes darted back to the iPad where a video feed showed a view of his wife and teenaged daughter sitting on a couch watching television. The camera had a clear shot through a patio door in their suburban South Carolina home.

"The man operating the camera also has a high-powered rifle. It's five minutes to ten and if I haven't called to tell him to stand down by ten o'clock, he will put a bullet through the head of your daughter first, and then your wife. Kick the chair out of the way, congressman, and your wife and daughter live. Don't, and they die and we kill you another way. It's all up to you."

Donut turned the iPad off and tossed it onto a nearby couch, waiting. Eduardo knew from experience she hoped the congressman missed the ten p.m. deadline. Donut loved killing people. She got off on the mayhem and destruction it caused in the lives of the victim's families.

As for himself, he was in it for the money. And the challenge. Killing people in ways which went undetected was an incredible high for Eduardo. He considered the two of them artists. They didn't paint on a canvass like Da Vinci or work with marble like Michelangelo to make beautiful statues. Their art came in the form of murders which required great creativity and precision. Tonight, a suicide was preferable, but the client wanted him dead, in whatever way they wanted.

The congressman swallowed hard a couple of times, his Adam's apple bobbing against the tightness of the noose. "I'm in line to become the next Speaker of the House. I have very powerful friends. If you do this, there is no place you will be able to hide."

"And you have very powerful enemies, it seems, hence why we are here. Tick-tock, tick-tock." She pulled a phone from her pocket and waved it at the congressman.

His shoulders slumped in defeat. "You swear you will let them live?"

"I swear it," said Donut. She glanced at the phone's screen and said, "Three minutes, congressman."

The Congressman straightened and hate filled his gaze. Eduardo had to hand it to the little man, he finally looked like the man who struck fear into the hearts of his rivals in the House. "I'll see you in Hell, bitch."

And with a kick of his foot, he knocked the chair backwards to the ground. The fall was only a few feet, but gravity did the rest, with the congressman's feet kicking back and forth mere inches from the ground as the noose strangled him to death. Fingers scrabbled for purchase, as he tried to loosen the rope, but without success.

Donut smiled, waved the phone at Grenville, and then slipped it back into her pocket. Grenville reached out towards her in what might have been a pleading gesture, but Eduardo couldn't be sure.

Soon his efforts grew feeble, then stopped all together as the noose cut off the blood flow to his carotid artery. Eduardo knew it would take another ten to twenty minutes for the congressman to die and they would wait until they knew for sure the job was completed.

Donut picked up the iPad from the couch, walked over to stand next to him, dropping the iPad into a bag on the floor near the window, her disgust evident. "O.K. You win the bet. I thought for sure he wouldn't kill himself to save his family."

Eduardo laughed. "No biggie. I had a fifty-fifty shot at winning. But it does mean you get to do the driving tonight. The dumb-ass died not even knowing the iPad video was shot two nights ago. The power of suggestion. That was cruel, though, waving the phone at him."

"Perception is reality," she agreed. "I didn't like him. He was the one who lead the effort to kill the Equal Pay bill for women in the last Congress. Besides, he earned those last few minutes of torture when he called me a bitch."

When they were sure Grenville was dead, Eduardo pulled out a phone, took a picture of the congressman to send to their client later that night, assuring the rest of their fee would be placed into an offshore account for them the next morning.

He picked up the bag and they left the congressman's town home, leaving no trace of their visit behind. They quickly walked the three blocks to their car, with Donut sliding in behind the wheel, while he tossed the bag in the seat behind him, hopped in the passenger seat and hit the recline button.

She pulled slowly down the darkened street, while he closed his eyes and tried to get some sleep. They would be on the road for many hours as they drove to their next job and he wanted to be well-rested so he could watch the news coverage the next day.

The suicide of Congressman Grenville would be national news. And though the next murder wouldn't be as newsworthy, in the end, it would be the one to bring a nation to its knees.

CHAPTER TWO

God, I hate running. Especially when it's for my life. When you're six and a half feet tall and weigh nearly two-hundred and eighty pounds, running is right up there with water torture and being forced to watch a *Bachelor* rerun marathon.

Yet here I was, sprinting through the woods in the mountains of North Carolina, faster than I'd ever run before. Then again, I'd never gone running while being chased by a monster. If I had, I would have lost a lot more weight.

I resisted the urge to look over my shoulder and concentrated on making sure I didn't trip on a rock or tree root and fall on my face, which would be fatal if a nightmare pounced on my back.

The plan nearly worked to perfection, right up until the moment it didn't. A few weeks earlier, I learned about a man in these mountains raising hellhounds. Seems he found out it was more profitable to create monsters for Satanists than it was to create moonshine from several stills for the locals.

Down at the end of a deep holler, Thornton Hopper built special dog runs made of thick steel beams, strong enough to hold the hounds. Think of St. Bernard's, then double the size and replace the lovable face with a snarling mass of razor sharp teeth and you get the picture.

Thornton kept three hellhounds at any one time. A male and female for breeding and one pup. When hellhounds give birth, they usually did so four at a time, but then one of the pups will kill the other three in an ultimate battle of the fittest. The three losers become the winner's first meal.

In the current training cycle, the pup was nearly a year old. I'd faced one like him the year before in the Bluegrass state and was lucky to still be alive to talk about it. Taking on three of them at close range was not something I cared to do.

But as the Hand of God, God's bounty hunter on earth, ridding the planet of creatures like the hellhounds came with the job description. The ones who came before me, I'm sure, had no choice but to get up close and personal and then do what was needed. Me? I came up with a plan using modern technology more likely to ensure I'd live another day or two.

After watching a *60 Minutes* episode about personal drones, I envisioned many ways I could put them to use. I did some research and then ordered one at a cost of about thirty thousand dollars, mere chump change when you consider I stole thirty-million dollars from the Church of the Light Reclaimed, a bunch of Satan-loving idiots. This one came equipped with a high resolution camera which allowed me to do some aerial surveillance with little danger to myself.

I spent several days in the hot July heat on the ridge overlooking the holler, with my drone hovering high over the kennels using it to watch Hopper care for and train the hounds. With him, they were incredibly docile and obedient. With others? Not so much. On the second day of my stakeout, Hopper and two friends set loose five pit bulls into the cage with the young hellhound. The men then sat in folding lawn chairs, relaxing and drinking Budweiser to watch the show.

In less time than you can say, "Holy crap" the five pit bulls were dead. The young hellhound moved with an agility and speed only a supernatural creature could possess.

And while Junior destroyed his lesser rivals, mom and pop hellhound sat peacefully watching and waiting. When the carnage was over, their son picked up a dead pit bull and dropped one near the bars of his parents' cages, offering each a share of the spoils of battle.

Hopper and his friends high-fived each other, clearly enjoying the massacre. My guess is they also cheered when someone stole candy from a baby. Watching the slaughter, even from a distance, turned my stomach.

I kept tabs at night and learned the area around Hopper's double-wide trailer was surrounded by light sensors, bathing the area in bright light any time someone or something came near the cages, which was a rare event. Even the animals of the holler gave the hellhounds a wide berth.

I felt I could get close enough to take out Hopper and then kill the hounds in their cages, despite his precautions, but I wanted to try something else and this gave me the opportunity to use the drone for something other than surveillance.

I drove back to Louisville for a day and spent the time modifying the drone. The drone was made to handle a load of up to five pounds and came with clamps to hold several items.

In each clamp I put a dummy grenade and then pulled the pins. The pressure from the clamps proved strong enough to keep the grenade spools from flying off.

I then flew my drone up about sixty feet and hit the release control for each clamp. The grenades dropped quickly to the ground, and the spools came off the moment the grenade cleared the clamps. I had the option of releasing them all at once or one at a time.

With a weight of fourteen ounces each, I could drop four grenades at a time with the use of the drone, taking out targets from a discreet distance, much like the U.S. military does. Modern technology sure does make our lives a lot easier. It also opens up scary doors warped minds can step through to create havoc on those they choose to target...warped minds like mine.

With my machine of destruction tested and ready to go, I returned to North Carolina. Early in the morning, I climbed the ridge above Hopper's house, getting into position as the sun climbed slowly over the mountains.

I enjoyed the fresh air and slightly cooler temperatures at this elevation. I pulled a flask from my pocket and took a deep swig of Fireball Whiskey, feeling the burn down my throat.

I put the flask away and used the remote controls to lift the drone to head height, reached into my duffle and carefully took out four M67 grenades. The uncle of one of my cohorts in hunting down the forces of evil, fellow bounty hunter, Winston Reynolds, is associated with many of the militias around a good portion of the country. If you're looking for black market military grade equipment, he's your go-to man. Procuring several M67 grenades proved to be no problem.

I set each grenade in place, tapped a few buttons and

closed the clamps. I then pulled the pins and managed not to blow myself up in the process. Score one for the good guys. The grenades hung suspended below the drone, dangerous fruit waiting for their drop of destruction.

I sent the drone flying high into the air, then down the ridge to hover over the cages of the hellhounds. When the little drone closed in on the first of the three cages, the hounds looked up, then came to their feet.

The drone came with a camera only and no microphone, so I couldn't hear their reaction, but I could see it. Teeth pulled back into snarls letting me know they didn't care for the drone's approach.

When I judged the drone was about thirty feet overhead, I punched the control to drop the first grenade. I watched as the grenade spool came off, the grenade bouncing off one of the metal bars, before landing in the cage with Junior.

The hound pounced, snapping up the grenade in its massive jaws right as the Composition B explosives lit, sending out the metal casing of the grenade in thousands of pieces and destroying Junior's head.

I quickly moved the drone over mom's cage and repeated the process. Instead of attacking the grenade, she tried to move away into a far part of her cage. Seems these nightmares were smarter than your average hound and she was trying to avoid baby boy's fate.

But she couldn't move far enough and when the grenade exploded, so did a huge portion of one of her back legs. She howled in rage and I could hear her easily from my position on the ridge.

She drug herself into a corner of the cage trying to get away from my flying machine of death. I nosed the drone over to where she lay and dropped the third of my four grenades. When the dust cleared from the detonation, mom lay twitching in death.

Before I could position the drone to take out dad hellhound, Hopper came running out of his double-wide in his underwear, shotgun to his shoulder. I saw him take aim at my drone and before I could move it or drop the next grenade, he blew it out of the sky, and the camera screen went dark.

Crap.

I threw the controller into my duffle, yanked the bag over my shoulder and took off at a quick shuffle down the ridge. When I hit level ground, I broke into a run, back where I'd parked my car. I could hear the one hellhound let out a howl which sent a chill down my spine because I could tell he was on the move.

I could only imagine what the other people living in the area thought hearing his battle cry echoing through the holler. I'm sure there would be stories for generations about the monsters of Jackson County, North Carolina.

Sweat beaded out on my forehead as I tried to release my inner Usain Bolt. I heard the hellhound crash up the ridge, plowing through underbrush to my former position. He must have picked up my scent as he began moving down the ridge, his bellows of rage getting closer as he battered down the side of the mountain like a deadly boulder.

I broke into a clearing and hit it at a full out sprint. My car, a Ford Flex, was parked behind an abandoned church. I guess the parishioners found other churches and left this one to rot away. Perhaps they sensed the evil lurking in the area. Who knows?

The hellhound burst into the clearing and I looked over my shoulder, knowing I shouldn't. The hound was huge and chewing up the distance between us. I tore my gaze away from my quickly approaching doom and focused on trying to keep from becoming a late morning snack.

With extra motivation, my feet flew over the ground and with a final jump, I dove through the open front doors of the church, turning onto my back, gun in my hand, sending a stream of lead at the hellhound as he crashed into the side of the church, rattling the entire building. Not that bullets would do much damage. I knew this from past experience. It's like shooting an elephant with a pellet gun. All I managed to do was piss it off even more.

There are very few perks to being the Hand of God. One of them, however, was as long as I'm in a church, I can't be touched by creatures spawned from the depths of hell. I am safe from harm and no hellhound can touch me, as long as I don't step back outside.

That didn't stop him, however, from pacing back and forth in the area in front of the door, his yellow eyes fixed on where I escaped within. Good thing I left the doors open when I left for the morning's mission. I could hear his deep growling and smell his foul stench from behind the church doors.

I moved out of site of the hound and started to put on the rest of my gear. Outside, I heard the roar of an ATV and glanced out a dirty window, watching as Hopper rolled up, coming to a stop a bit behind the hellhound.

The man's gut arrived a few minutes before he did. Stepping off the ATV the machine's shocks let out a sigh of relief. I know I shouldn't throw stones at glass houses, but this man's stomach was frickin' huge.

He held the shotgun loosely in his hand, walking up and scratching the hellhound behind one huge floppy ear. He'd gotten dressed in a hurry, his boot laces untied and his hair sticking up in all directions with a bad case of bed head.

"I don't know who y'all are or where yer from. But if y'all come out now then I'll be sure to blow yer damn head off before I let Biggin' here get atcha."

I continued to make my preparations and wondered if Hopper was under the same restrictions about entering a church as the hound. I was still new at this whole divine retribution gig and wasn't sure of all the ins and outs.

It's all on-the-job-training, with death being the ultimate penalty if you fail. I got the job when the previous Hand of God, Dominic Montoya, died at the hands of my brother, Mikey. Losing my own soul in the process, I'd been working every day since to punch my own ticket to the pearly gates. The jury was still out on if I'm going to make it or not.

"Y'all hear me? Hey, asshole. Who do ya think you are coming out to my neck of the woods and attackin' what's mine? Y'all got no right to be doin' such."

"I have every right," I yelled back. "I'm with animal control and it seems you failed to get tags for your hounds and the county found you in violation of county ordinance BR549. You were sent several warning notices and your failure to comply moved the ball into my court."

"What the hell you been smokin'? I ain't never seen no

notices. And ole' Robbie Crabtree is the damn dog catcher and he spends all his days drunker than a skunk, so yer fulla shit."

"You're not the first person to tell me that, surprisingly enough. But I do know something you might be interested in."

"Oh? And what the hell might that be?"

"Do you know what hellhounds fear more than anything on earth?"

Hopper snorted long and loud. "Mr., hellhounds ain't afraid of anythin' or any one."

"You're wrong," I said, stepping into the open doorway. "They're afraid of fire."

I bet Thornton Hopper never thought he'd see a flamethrower and the look on his face before I pulled the trigger was priceless. In quick succession I saw confusion, realization and then fear.

Flamethrowers first came into use during World War I to clear trenches in up close and personal fighting in Europe. By the end of World War II they were being mounted to armored vehicles, which is a lot safer than having all the fuel strapped to your back. More than a few men died when the flamethrower would take a bullet to the tank and explode.

I was wearing a modified version of the M9 used during Vietnam. There were three tanks, two for the petroleum gel, and one for compressed air. When you squeeze the back trigger, compressed air mixes with the gel, forcing the mixture through the hose. Pulling the front trigger sets off the igniter and when the gel passes over it, you get a steady stream of fire in a bloom large enough to cover a Mac truck.

I learned over the last few months creatures spawned from the depths of Hell, feared fire more than anything. Satan once gave me a glimpse of what an eternity would be like in Hell, with my body nailed to the wall as flames engulfed me. A mirror was across from me so I could watch the whole thing happen. My body literally melted away. From time to time, I still wake up in the middle of the night, my bed sheets soaked in sweat, dreaming about it.

With safety goggles protecting my eyes and the memory of my brief trip to Hell in my mind, I pulled both triggers and fire roared out of the hose. Hopper yelled something and started to raise his gun, but never made it. The fire raced over the hellhound and engulfed them both, Hopper's screams mixed with the howls of the hellhound.

Hopper took a couple of steps, turning in a circle and fell face first to the ground. The hellhound tried moving away, but I kept pace, never letting up on the trigger and soon he also lay still on the ground. I didn't stop until the last spurt of flame died away, the fuel tank empty.

I reached over my shoulder and cranked open the pressure valve, letting out the last of the compressed air, then hit the quick release buttons on the harness and slid the flamethrower off my shoulders.

The entire area in front of the church was charred black from my attack but the surrounding trees remained untouched and I said a silent prayer the rest of the holler wasn't on fire.

I went inside, snatched up my duffle, unlocked the Ford and tossed it in the trunk. I decided to change later when I stopped for the night. I waited until the flamethrower nozzle cooled enough for me to pack it away, and then hopped into the Ford and slowly drove down the dirt path to the main drag.

The smell of burnt flesh road heavy on the air and I swore I could still smell it even after I was long gone from the torched remains of Hopper and the hellhound.

I wondered if I would have trouble sleeping when I stopped for the night. I knew I would, but not because of the image of Hopper and the hound burning to death in the fire, but because of a woman with bonfire red hair.

CHAPTER THREE

I called it quits south of Knoxville, Tennessee and checked myself into a two-bit motel next to an even seedier dive bar named The Mason Jar. After paying for my room, I didn't bother to take my stuff inside and headed straight for the bar.

I shouldered open the door and stepped inside. The smell of beer and cigarette smoke assaulted my senses, accompanied by the murmur of quiet conversations which all stopped the moment I made my entrance.

The room was narrow and long, a shotgun design with an old wood-style bar down one side and booths down the other. The back of the room featured a pool table and dart board, but neither was being used. To say the lighting was dim would be an understatement.

I ignored the stares and made my way to the bar. A bartender so thin he could use a food sponsor, with the requisite dirty towel thrown over his shoulder, walked over to greet me.

He rested his hands on the bar, his face a mixture of boredom and weariness. "What'll you have, Mr.?"

"Moonshine. Lots of it."

"What flavor?"

"What flavor? Moonshine. You know, White Lightning. Rotgut, Hooch. I want the real stuff."

Back when I was younger, one of my great uncles used to make his own moonshine and always gave dad a couple of gallons of the stuff. One day I asked my dad to borrow twenty dollars and he said he'd make me a deal. He poured about an inch of clear liquid into a glass and said, "Drink this in one shot and you won't have to pay me back."

Snickering, I picked up the glass and downed it in one

swallow. "That wasn't so—" and before I could say another word, the moonshine hit bottom and set fire to my insides. I turned on the water faucet, sticking my mouth under it trying to gulp down enough water to put out the wildfire raging in my gut.

My father, laughing, said, "That's the hardest twenty dollars you will ever earn." And he was right.

"We have all kinds of flavors: blackberry, peach, apple, cinnamon, cherry. All kinds."

"What the hell? Is this a Starbucks? Just give me a damn glass of moonshine. I don't care what flavor it is," I snarled. I could feel anger boiling its way to the surface. This had been happening more often in recent months. I knew the bartender was only doing his job, but I didn't give a rat's ass.

Raising his hands in surrender, the man turned and pulled a bottle from under the counter, set out a glass and poured several fingers. The label named it Old Smokey. When he started to put the bottle away, I grabbed his wrist, took the bottle from him and filled the glass three quarters of the way up, then handed it back.

"I'll run a tab. I'll need more when this is done." Without waiting for his reply, I snatched my drink, turned and made my way to a booth in the corner and away from the other patrons.

I heard some angry mumbles, but ignored them and began to take long pulls of the moonshine. From the taste, the bartender chose cinnamon. Considering my newly acquired taste for Fireball Cinnamon Whiskey, it fit. I began to wonder if my whole life would be full of fire. My mind thought about Thornton Hopper's blackened body, the smoke rising lazily into the air. But not for long.

The moonshine did what it was supposed to do and hit my system like a hard jab to the mid-section. I'd found myself drinking more and more lately, trying to get the memories to go away.

When I wasn't killing monsters in real life, I tried to slay others from my memories. Despite my best efforts, my mind always drifted to her. I played, over and over, the scene when I pulled out a gun and shot Samantha Tyler, the only woman I've ever truly loved.

My love life was very complicated.

I shot her in order to save her life....and to drive out the demon lodged in her head. But it didn't make it any easier to pull the trigger or live with the fallout afterwards.

After the shooting, I managed to get her to a hospital, but she nearly died. The morning after her surgery, she was moved to a rehab facility. When I plugged her, I shot her in the hip, doing a ton of damage and her rehab was still on-going.

Now months have passed since the shooting and I've heard nothing from her. Nada. Nothing. Not a peep.

Brother Joshua, the man who tells me where to go and who to kill, coordinated Samantha's care. When I asked to see her, Joshua told me she "needed time to sort things out" and would contact me when she was ready.

But now it's been nearly five months and she hasn't picked up the phone and tried to contact me and it was eating me up inside. More than this moonshine ever could.

The TV over the bar was tuned to Fox News and I could read the headline: **Congressman Commits Suicide.** I squinted trying to read the man's name and suffered a moment of disappointment when the name was not Cyrus Tyler, Samantha's dad. I went back to my drink, thinking of the old joke, "What do you call a hundred politicians at the bottom of the ocean? A good start."

Music played in the background and I finally caught the lyrics, realizing the song playing was *The Devil Went Down to Georgia* by Charlie Daniels. The song took on a whole new meaning for me and I knew the Johnny of this song was an idiot.

According to the song, Satan offered Johnny a fiddle of gold if he won a fiddling contest, but Satan got his soul if he lost. If you know Satan is real, why take the chance? Arrogance, that's why. The same thing which doomed me. I believed I could save my brother's soul, despite all the evidence showing my brother was going to Hell no matter what I did. Risking your soul for gold proved Johnny was a frickin' idiot. Trying to save Mikey proved I was one.

I downed the last of the fiery liquid and it rocked me like a speeding train. I slammed the glass down on the table much harder than I planned, shattering it. I became light-headed and plopped my arms down onto the shards of broken glass, ignoring the pain, then rested my head on my arms for a moment.

The bartender began yelling at me, but I ignored him and welcomed the sweet feeling of oblivion, finding it hard to think about Samantha or anything else. The only thought pushing through the haze? Get another drink.

I don't know how long I stayed light-headed, but when I raised my head to contemplate walking over to the bar and put action to the thought, I noticed I was no longer alone.

A woman just this side of pretty stared back at me. Hair, black and cut to shoulder length, framed a thin face and eyes the color of arctic ice. I blinked several times to make sure she was not a figment of my imagination. Yep. Still there.

"You are bleeding."

I have an ear for accents and the lilt in her voice suggested a European origin. It took a moment for her words to hit home. I looked down at my hand and saw there was a slash along the bottom of my palm, blood dripping over the table and across the broken glass.

The stranger pulled a couple of napkins out of a holder, turned my hand over and placed them against the wound, holding my hand between hers, pressing down, trying to stop the bleeding.

Her touch was warm and in my head, the way she held my hand felt intimate, familiar. Like the touch of an old lover. Despite being dead ass drunk, I knew we'd never met. Her eyes were not the kind you would ever forget. A mixture of intelligence and humor danced together in their depths.

I rolled my tongue, trying to lose the cotton mouth. When I could finally get a word out, I glanced over at the bartender. "I need some more Old Smokey."

The woman shook her head. "Coffee. Black. Nothing else."

I yanked my hand from between hers, the bloody napkins stuck to my hand. "Look, Lady. I don't need you to babysit me. I'm not in the mood for coffee. Thanks for your help. But you can move your ass somewhere else."

The words came out harsh, but I didn't really give a flyin' flip. I didn't need female companionship. At least not hers, no matter how pretty.

She got up and went to the bar, talking to the bartender in a tone low enough where I couldn't hear what she said. I watched her and admitted to the red-blooded American male inside me the part of her I couldn't see before looked pretty damn good.

She wore a purple skirt down to mid-thigh and black knee high boots. The skirt hung around a figure which began to get a response from the part of my body south of the border.

With week after week passing with no word from Samantha, my friends suggested I should move on. Let my hair down, have some fun. I'd resisted the idea, sure Samantha would come around. This woman made me wonder if I should take their advice. I tore my gaze away, working hard to get the carnal thoughts out of my head.

A few moments later, the woman returned, carrying a tray with a cup and a steaming pot of black coffee. She slid the tray in front of me, and sat down.

"Lady, when I tell you to leave me the hell alone, I mean leave me the hell alone. Can't you take a hint?"

She didn't answer right away. Instead, she picked up the pot, poured the coffee into a cup and placed it in front of me with the pot beside it. She then took a few more napkins out of the holder and brushed the broken glass onto the tray. Once finished, she sat the tray next to her on the seat.

The aroma from the coffee made it to my nose, but I resisted the urge to pick it up and take a drink. I peeled the bloody napkins off my hand, the blood flow now stopped. I wadded up the napkins and tossed them onto the table.

Looking into the eyes of this woman I said, "This is the last time I'm going to tell you. Leave. Now." I tried to put as much malice as possible into my words, wanting to drive her away. Even the biggest bad asses tended to leave me alone when I got angry, but this woman seemed unaffected by my growing irritation.

After a moment, she replied, "I think there is something you should know before I do."

"Oh? And what pearls of wisdom do you wish to share? Do you know the cure for cancer? The secret to ending world hunger? Maybe you know if Paul McCartney really was the Walrus?"

She laughed and damn if it didn't sound beautiful. "No. What I know is more immediate and pertains only to you."

"Then speak your piece and move on." I grumbled. My brain wanted her to leave. My body wanted her to stay and I wasn't sure which would win if she hung around much longer.

"In a few minutes three men will come in here and kill you." She smiled sweetly and waited to see what my reaction would be.

I thought for a moment or two. Then I picked up the coffee and began to drink.

CHAPTER FOUR

I downed the first cup, the hot coffee burn bringing my senses back to life. I picked up the pot, my hand shaking slightly and poured another, this time drinking in steady sips.

"Why should I believe you? Who are you, anyway?"

She pursed her lips. "I am the woman they hire to come inside to seduce you and to get you drunk. You already beat me to the whole 'getting drunk' part."

"And what about the seduction? Still planning to give it a try? And why didn't you call them in when you found me passed out on the table?"

She tilted her head to the side, seeming to examine me like someone seeing a strange creature for the first time and trying to figure out what it might be. Or if she should kill it.

"Maybe I like you," she shrugged.

I laughed. "Lady, you don't know me. And very few who do know me like me. Try again. Why not?" I polished off the coffee and poured one more, the caffeine racing into my blood stream, battling the moonshine for domination.

"Maybe I not like them. Does it really matter? Having said that, I'm going back outside and tell them you are in here, drunk. Perhaps they will still kill you. They have good chance."

I smiled, but there was no warmth. "You do, do you? Care to make a wager?"

She stood up and looked down at me. "If you die, there is no way for you to pay. Not much of a bet when one cannot pay. I can only lose."

"Fair enough. I guess I will have to satisfy myself with your shock and surprise when I walk out the door. I do have another question for you. How did they know I was here? I didn't even know I was going to stop here."

"They follow you here from North Carolina. When you killed the trainer, they knew who they were looking for and there are only so many ways out of the mountains. They have been following you for hours, waiting for you to stop."

She turned and headed for the exit. Before she got there, I shouted, "What's your name?"

She paused, one hand on the door. "Elizabeth." She pushed her way outside and disappeared from view, the door swinging closed behind her.

I briefly considered checking for the rear exit and making a run for it. But only briefly. Running from hellhounds was one thing. Running from two legged attackers, however, wasn't an option. With the dark mood I was in, I wanted someone to pound on and it seemed fate would provide several in short order.

I slumped back over the table, resting my head on my arms. This time keeping a watch on the front door. I didn't have to wait long as three men entered the bar, sized up things and headed straight to my table.

I picked up my head, swaying a bit. "Hey, bartender. I need more moonshine over here. Chop, chop. Let's get moving."

The bartender didn't move an inch, watching as the men approached me. The men were all on the large size. Two were in decent shape, the other evidently loved mamma's cooking a bit too much.

They stopped next to my booth, blocking my view of the bartender. "Hey, fellas. Mind moving your asses out of the way? I'm trying to get another drink."

The one who loved the home cooking said, "You've been cut off. That was our sister you just tried to put the moves on and we ain't happy about it. I think we need to teach you a lesson about being a gentleman. Ain't that right boys?"

The other two nodded and began to clench and unclench their fists, anxious to get it on.

"You are one lyin' son of a bitch. There's no way she was your sister. Too good looking. If you had a sister, she would have to be one butt ugly woman if she was related to you. You're so ugly when you were a kid I bet you ran through the ugly forest and hit every tree." Oldie but a goody.

I guess I pissed him off. He snarled something and reached for me. I grabbed the coffee pot and threw the half-full pot into his face, the still hot liquid scalding his eyes.

He screamed, his fingers clawing his face and I turned sideways in the booth and kicked him hard in the crotch, adding injury to insult. His two buddies moved him out the way and tried to jump me as I slid out of the booth.

Wielding the pot as a weapon I swung it hard right into the side of the head of one of them. His knees shook for a moment, then buckled and he collapsed to the floor.

The only one left didn't back down, catching me with a good right to the chin. I slipped with the blow and dropped the coffee pot to try and catch my fall on the edge of the pool table.

Then the unexpected happened. A couple of the locals, evidently not caring for my earlier behavior, joined in the fight. If I'd only needed to face one more attacker, I would have made short work of the fight and strolled out into the night a happy man.

Now three more joined in and the four of them forced me back and onto the pool table, pressing my face into the red felt, blows raining down around my head and my mid-section. I bellowed like a cornered bull and fought back. I found a loose pool ball, wrapped one large paw around it and then used it to pound one of my attackers in the head, over and over. It only took a few seconds and then there were three.

I tried sitting up, but one of the locals broke a pool cue across my shoulders, the pain nearly sending me down for the count. One thing I learned from my father, don't fight fair when your life is on the line. I managed to get a fist full of his hair with the other hand and pulled the man's face close to me. I bit down savagely onto the man's nose, twisting my face back and forth like an angry dog.

The man screamed and tried to push himself away. I let go and shoved him hard. Now there were two. I spit part of the man's nose into the face of my original attacker and managed to throw him and the other guy off me. I rolled backwards across and then off the pool table, slamming into the dart board.

I grabbed a couple of darts out of the board, then ripped

the board off the wall and threw it at the two men who circled the pool table, looking for their next chance to attack.

When the men ducked, I put a dart in each hand, the sharp end sticking out through my knuckles, holding them like they teach women to hold their car keys in self-defense classes.

The local yokel decided discretion would be the better part of valor and turned and ran for the door. The remaining man, one of the three who planned to kill me, slid a switch blade out of his pocket and snicked it open.

With a yell he charged me, stabbing low, surprising me. I expected a more measured approach, not a kamikaze attack. I danced sideways, but the move worked better in my head than in practice, with my reflexes slowed by the remnants of the moonshine and the knife connected.

The blade pushed deep and I could feel it scrape a rib, the pain roaring across my nervous system. The analytical part of my brain admonished me for being sloppy, for taking my opponent for granted. The animal part of my brain demanded a reaction.

I brought my fists together hard on each side of the man's head, right behind each ear and buried the sharp point of the darts into his skull, then lifted up, taking the man off the ground.

The man let go of the knife, still stuck into my side and grabbed my wrists, but after a moment his fingers went slack and I let him slide to the ground. I watched him for a moment, then tossed both darts into his chest, each sticking in about a quarter inch from each other. Triple twenties.

I yanked the knife out of my side and nearly collapsed, a wave of nausea hitting me hard. I leaned on the pool table for a moment, waiting for the feeling to pass and scanned the room for more threats, but the battle was over. The two men who came in with the dead man, were still laying on the floor. Everyone else exited the bar, running for cover.

The bartender held a phone to his head, but did not appear to be talking to anyone. If he called the police, I needed to hit the road, and quickly.

I tossed the knife onto the pool table, took a couple of steps and nearly fainted, but gathered myself and headed for the door. I pushed it open and stepped into the warm, muggy night air. I fumbled in my pockets for my keys and could feel my shirt sticking to my side as the blood flowed from the wound.

When I finally managed to pull the keys out, I dropped them on the ground. Cursing, I bent over to pick them up, but kept on going, finding myself lying on the ground. I rolled over, staring up at the stars, becoming incredibly tired.

The last thing I thought, before darkness overtook me, was "well, this sucks."

CHAPTER FIVE

Eduardo watched doctor Alfred Michaels dive into one end of his Olympic length swimming pool, neatly cutting the water. He dove deep, then surfaced and started what would be the first of fifty laps. The pool lights lit the water from above and below, the warm Pennsylvania air making it a perfect night for a swim. The house, a four bedroom colonial, sat off U.S. 30, a few blocks off the Main Line in the western suburbs of Philadelphia.

Michaels put himself through med school at Dartmouth on a swimming scholarship where he graduated top of his class from the Geisel School of Medicine. While in school he medaled in the World Championships and briefly flirted with trying out for the Summer Olympics. A specialist in the hundred meter free style, he decided the extra hours it would take to make the Olympics would put too much stress on his school work.

After completing six laps, he stopped and took a long drink from the glass of scotch sitting at the edge of the pool, then flipped back into the water, heading for the other end.

Eduardo knew this was his regular routine, having watched the good doctor over the last few nights hit the pool after long hours at the Hospital of the University of Pennsylvania. The doc loved swimming and loved his scotch and found a way to combine the two of them. Twice divorced with no kids, swimming and a good scotch whiskey were his only passions.

Eduardo also knew something else. Doctor Michaels suffered from anxiety and kept a stash of Valium at home in case of attacks. An illegal stash, not that Eduardo was judging him. A man's gotta do what a man's gotta do to feel normal.

Donut found the plastic baggie full of pills in the bottom of a dresser drawer, underneath the neatly folded pairs of argyle socks in his bedroom during a reconnaissance mission inside the house. She climbed a tree overhanging the back of his house, then moved, hand over hand, down a branch until dropping onto the roof and entered through an unlocked upstairs window.

Michaels kept a detailed diary about cases and his own battle with anxiety. He lived in fear of his colleagues finding out about his mental issues, which only added to the anxiety. Recently, he needed to take Valium to get through a speech at a conference on the latest innovations in joint replacements.

Eduardo gave Michaels another lap, then stepped from his hiding place in the shrubs, moving quickly to the glass of scotch, emptying three crushed Valiums from the doc's stash into the cut crystal and stirred it quickly with a latex gloved finger. He was back in his hiding spot before Michaels made the turn and kick to return.

He watched and when Michaels finished lap twelve, he stopped and took a large drink of the whiskey, flipped and was gone. He did the same on laps eighteen and twenty-four, draining the last of the scotch, his movements becoming slow and clumsy.

He fell back into the water, but this time he did not turn for the other end, instead, tried to tread water. Eduardo left his concealment and walked to the pool. Doctor Michaels went under and then resurfaced, reaching for the rail of the ladder to climb out.

He made it about half way up when Eduardo put a hand on his head and pushed him back into the pool, Michaels landing with a large splash. Michaels broke the surface one last time, shouting to Eduardo for help, only to slip below again. He watched as Michaels floundered below the surface of the water, clearly disoriented, until the last of the air bubbles raced for the surface. A few minutes later, his body floated up and joined them.

Eduardo picked up the glass by the rim, went inside to the kitchen, washed the inside of the glass completely and then poured a few splashes, enough to cover the bottom of the glass, from a bottle of Bowmore Devil's Cask setting on the wet bar in his living room. Eduardo was a Glenlivet man himself, but again, who was he to judge?

He walked to the pool and put the glass down in the same spot he picked it up, then pulled out his phone, snapped a photo of the floating form of Michaels and left.

*****

Brad Stiles pulled the Lincoln Town Car over to the side of the road when the phone in his pocket beeped. He slid the phone out of his sports coat pocket, and glanced at the texted photo of a man floating in a pool. Putting the phone away, he put on his car's signal, and merged back into the Belt Line traffic. Later he would delete the text and then smash the phone to bits, discarding the pieces into different trash cans around Washington D.C.

He glanced in the rearview mirror at the man sitting in the seat behind him. Dark brown hair going gray at the temples, Congressman Cyrus Tyler looked more fit than most men half his sixty years. Dressed in a blue blazer and khakis, they were on their way to a private dinner at the home of a well-connected lobbyist. Fundraising for members of the House took place twenty-four hours a day, seven days a week.

A former Marine, Brad kept himself in even better shape than the congressman. His hair shaved in the classic jarhead style, flat top with the hair on the sides and back cut short, sat on a head which seemed not to be connected to any neck, and appeared to rest upon his shoulders. He needed to have his suits custom made to be able feel comfortable as the congressman's occasional driver and fixer, and to hide the gun in the holster under his left arm.

Tyler met his gaze and Brad nodded slightly.

*****

Tyler smiled and then returned to reading a draft of an immigration bill his party hoped to push through following the August recess. In his current position as the Majority Leader of the U.S. House of Representatives, it was his job to schedule when pieces of legislation would, if ever, get brought before the House for a vote. The latest draft of his party's immigration bill would piss off a lot of people on the other side of the aisle, which suited him just fine. Tyler knew the bill would never get beyond the Democratic controlled Senate, but he didn't want it to pass, being in favor of the status quo. The longer the country raged over the immigration debate, the more chaos would reign.

Tyler found it hard to concentrate on the bill, however, and after a moment tossed it into his suitcase on the seat beside him, closing the lid. With the doctor's death, another part of the puzzle snapped into place. He spent the remainder of the trip to the fundraiser thinking about what would happen in the next few days. All his planning came down to a simple lunch, already scheduled. Then it would be time to move on to phase two.

Tyler knew a secret few others knew: the Speaker of the House of Representatives would soon be dead. Diagnosed with stage four colon cancer, the disease had already progressed to his lungs and liver and the Speaker had declined further treatments which would prolong his life. The only people who knew were the Speaker, his wife and Tyler.

A news conference was planned for the next day. The Speaker planned to announce his immediate retirement at the news conference. Following his resignation, the Republicans in the House would meet in caucus to elect a new Speaker and Tyler knew it would be him, with his only competition having committed suicide a few nights earlier. Decades of slapping backs, gathering favors and more than a little dirt on his fellow members of congress, assured him of the votes. By the end of the week, he would be the new Speaker.

Some men waited for Providence to land in their laps. Tyler created his own Providence, with help from the Lord of Light, Satan. A battle would soon arrive, with those who followed the Lord of Light helping him reclaim his rightful place in Heaven.

In his position as leader of the Church of the Light Reclaimed, he directed the battle on Earth. His goal? To create as much chaos in the world as possible. Chaos bred opportunity to turn people away from God. When he became the Speaker of the House of Representatives, he would become the second most powerful man in the country.

But Tyler did not plan to stop there, with another rung of the ladder to climb: to become President of the United States. Gazing out the window, he could see the White House in the distance, the front lit by a host of flood lights. Before long he planned to be the one sitting in the Oval Office, the most powerful man on the planet. And when he was, he would set the world on fire.

CHAPTER SIX

Samantha nibbled on my ear and I struggled to wake up. I felt her hand move down my stomach, and then lower, and I began to respond. I slid my hand slowly down the curve of her back, caressing her with the tips of my fingers. I tried to turn my head and find her lips with mine, but it felt as if the messages from my brain to my body traveled around the world before registering.

I pulled her tight and breathed out, "I love you, Samantha."

"Who is this Samantha?"

My eyes snapped open and staring down at me was not Samantha, but the woman from the bar. It took a moment, but I remembered her name. "Elizabeth?" I said hoarsely.

She sat up on the edge of the bed, naked with only the sheet pulled around her lap. I tried to sit up, but she pushed me down easily and I didn't have the strength to resist.

"Yes," she said. "I will ask again. Who is this Samantha?"

I felt light-headed and found it hard to focus on what she was saying. Then another fact battered its way through the fog in my brain: I was also naked under the sheet.

I tried to roll over but could not, as my left arm was strapped to the side of the bed with my own belt. "Hey. What the hell is going on?"

I reached for her with my free hand, but Elizabeth stood and walked over to a chair, picked up a robe and slipped it on, tying it in the front. I was forced to admit to myself I missed the view and liked her better with it off.

"You move around too much and I needed you to be still for the IV."

I glanced down at my arm and could see several strips of tape holding the IV needle in place. A funnel with a long tube hung above my head, running down to the needle. I could see the tube was coated with something dark and red. I tried to remember where I was, but the last thing I could remember was going to my car outside the bar and then collapsing on the pavement. I tried to undo the belt, my fingers fumbling at the buckle, and I fell back on the bed, weak beyond anything I'd ever felt.

"IV? What have you been giving me? And how did I get here? And where are my clothes?" I could feel panic rising and I tried to shove it aside, to concentrate on what was happening to me.

She put her hands on her hips. "You needed blood. You nearly die and go into shock. You got here because I bring you here. I throw away your clothes. They were soaked with blood. Very bad. Who is Samantha?" she demanded to know.

"Blood? You don't know my blood type. You could have killed me. Why didn't you take me to a hospital?"

She rolled her eyes and spoke slowly, like talking to a child. "You kill two men at the bar. If I had taken you to a hospital, then they would have taken you to jail, no? I brought you to my cabin, but you need the blood. So I get you some. It is O negative, so you are alright. Nothing to worry about. Why won't you tell me who this woman is?"

"She's a friend. What were you doing just now? With me, in bed?"

She flashed a grin so wicked it almost made me blush.
Almost.

"You know what we were doing. You like it."

She flipped around the end of the tie on her robe and moved her hips seductively.

"You like it very much, no?"

"Don't flatter yourself, lady. You caught me at a weak moment." I licked my lips. "Water. Could I please have some water?"

She pouted for a few seconds, but then she left the bedroom and I could hear her in another room, running water. I took the moment to assess my situation. I lifted the sheet and stared at a strip of gauze over the left side of my stomach. I lifted an edge of the gauze and could see the knife wound, now stitched up, ugly and red. Hells, bells.

I let my head sink back into the pillow. I lay on what felt like a feather bed in a small bedroom. The walls were made of logs and through the two windows in the room all I could see were trees. I wondered how she could have gotten me from the parking lot to this bed. It should have taken several good-size men to carry me this far.

She came back into the room, carrying a blue Solo cup. "Drink this. You will feel better."

She put the cup to my lips and I drank deeply. The water tasted off, somehow, but I drank it all, my mouth being so dry. "How long have I been here? And who sewed me up? You?"

"So many questions. Every time with the questions. Yes. I am the one who closed the wound. You bleed very much. But I have some experience with battle dressing wounds. It will be ok. And you have been here...hmm...three days now."

"Three days? Holy crap. Where's my phone. I need to call someone."

She shook her head.

"No good. There is no cell signal here. You cannot make call. And there are no phones in the cabin. We are," she paused, struggling to find the right words. "How do you say? Off the grid?"

I swore under my breath. I tried once again to sit up, but my body felt heavy and weak. I felt like I'd drank a whole gallon of moonshine at once. I looked at the cup in her hand.

"What was in the water? You drugged me?"

She didn't say a word. She just stood there and watched me until my eyes closed and the world went black.

*****

She set the cup on the nightstand next to the bed and watched him for a few more minutes to make sure he was sound asleep.

She pulled the sheet down and removed the gauze covering the wound and made a clucking sound. The wound was red and she worried infection might be setting in. She would have to find some antibiotics.

With the amount of sleeping pills she gave him, he would sleep for many hours. She would have time. But first, she needed a bath.

She went to the bathroom and glanced at the woman hanging above the tub by her ankles, the rope tied off to a hook she'd screwed into the side of one of the cabin logs.

The woman stared at her with pleading eyes and tried talking despite the duct tape placed across her mouth. She ignored her and began to run water for her bath.

They'd met at a different bar, following the fight at The Mason Jar. It took her hours to find a woman with just the right blood type. She claimed to be doing a study on drinking and whether there was a relationship between it and a person's blood type to get people to voluntarily provide their information.

The woman had been sitting at the bar alone and when it was almost closing time, they left together. She pretended to be parked close the woman's car and walked along with her. Luck was on her side with the parking lot nearly empty. She slipped the TASER out of her purse, pressed it to the woman's side as she was unlocking her car, and squeezed the trigger.

As the TASER discharged, the woman began to fall to the ground, confused and immobile. She caught her easily, opened the woman's driver-side door and shoved her onto the seat. Then she moved her over to the passenger side, climbed in, removed the keys from the woman's still clenched hand, started the car and drove off. No one saw her. She knew how to move quickly.

She turned off the water, the bath now nearly three quarters full. She reached out and took hold of the woman's hands, also duct taped at the wrist. In one arm, the end of an IV line hung loose, clamped at the end. She pulled the arms over the tub and then loosened the clamp.

Blood began to flow out in a steady stream, turning the steaming water a burgundy red. The woman began to scream, but they were muffled by the tape. After a moment, she closed the clamp, cutting off the blood flow. Tears flowed from the woman's eyes, dropping and mixing with the blood.

She stirred the water with her foot, mixing the water and blood, and then shrugged out of the robe and sat in the water, sinking down to her neck and closed her eyes.

In the past, she would have killed the woman and been done with her. But she was trying to do things...differently. She would not kill the woman if she could avoid it. She breathed deeply and let the water relax her.

When the time came, if the woman still lived when it was OK to move the Hand of God, then she would let the woman go. It would be up to her to survive the wilderness and find help. It wouldn't be her problem.

She smiled to herself. Things were going even better than she could hope. Before long, the Hand of God would be hers.

CHAPTER SEVEN

"You know that bill will never see the light of day in the Senate, Cyrus. You guys continue to waste the time of the American people."

Tyler wiped his mouth with his napkin and dropped it in his lap. From the terrace of Charlie Palmer Steak House right off the National Mall, Tyler and Senator Hedley Stafford enjoyed the finest cut of steak in the city while enjoying a great view of the Capital.

"And your bill will never see a vote in the House. You need to move those socialists in the far Left of your party more to the center. We can't get anything done until you do."

"Socialists? Is that any way for the new Speaker of the House to talk?"

Hedley Stafford, a black man in his mid-sixties, had been the Senate Majority Leader for almost six years. They'd known each other for the better part of thirty years, with both of them being from Philadelphia.

Stafford's parents had been teachers. Early on, Hedley followed in their footsteps, first teaching at Philadelphia public schools and then a professor of ethics at Temple University.

Driven into politics by what he saw as a failing education system, he ran for Congress, winning a close election in his first race, then serving four more terms in Congress before running for the Senate, and winning.

Adept at party politics, he moved up the political food chain, landing in the top spot when the Democrats regained control of the Senate in a landslide mid-term election.

A quiet man when away from the microphones, Stafford preferred to listen and watch, missing nothing. Stafford bucked the modern political trend and sported a full beard, now mostly gray.

Tyler raised his hands in mock surrender. "Fine. I will tone it down." He sliced off another piece of steak and popped it into his mouth, chewing thoughtfully. "Changing the subject, I was sorry to hear about Dr. Michaels. He was your knee doc, right?"

"He was. Damn shame. Really screws me up. I need to have my knee replaced when the August recess starts next week and he was going to do the surgery. Now I'll have to find a new doctor, which will take time. I'd like to put it off, but it keeps me up at night and I don't want to take meds to help me sleep. You know how it is. Men in our position have to be alert and ready for anything."

Tyler nodded knowingly. "I think I can help you out. You and I go way back and despite you being a card-carrying Communist, I know who you need to talk to. And she's in the same practice."

Stafford raised an eyebrow. "We communists don't carry cards anymore. Just like you fascists don't wear swastikas. Who are we talking about?"

"Dr. Teresa Collins. She operated on my knee a year ago when I tore my meniscus and it's done really well. With her being in the same practice, you won't have to have all your records transferred. And the A.M.A. rates her higher than Michaels, so it will be a step up."

"Most of these specialists stay booked. It might be hard to get in."

Tyler held up a finger, pulled out his phone, searched for a moment, then selected a number and dialed. Tyler placed the call on speaker and after a few rings a woman answered. "Well, hello Cyrus. Having more knee problems?"

"Not me. A friend of mine." Tyler explained the situation. "I was hoping you might be able to work him in. He's right here with me. You're on speaker."

"Senator Stafford, when were you scheduled to have your surgery?"

"A week from this Friday. How soon could you get me in?"

There was a pause while she checked her schedule. "I tell you what. Considering your circumstances, I will move some things around and we can do the surgery as you currently have it scheduled. Dr. Michaels was a good friend of mine and I know he would want you taken care of right away."

"Thank you, doctor. I can't tell you how much I appreciate you doing this for me. Anything I need to do?"

"I will have my assistant contact you. Have you already had your pre-op blood work completed?"

"Scheduled to do the blood work this coming Monday."

"Then come on in as scheduled. I will have some additional paperwork for you to fill out, but I'll make sure the transition is a smooth one. We'll have you up and back on your feet in no time."

"Thanks, doc. I'll see you next week."

They said their goodbyes and Tyler hung up and put the phone away. "See. How's that for bipartisan cooperation?"

Stafford laughed. "Step in the right direction, Cyrus. Step in the right direction."

CHAPTER EIGHT

I awoke in the middle of the night to find myself still in bed, still naked, with Elizabeth snuggled close, her head on my shoulder and her arm draped across my chest. She was sound asleep and also wasn't wearing anything. I loved the feel of her skin against mine.

I took a moment to take stock of how I felt. Physically, the wound in my side had gone from a sharp pain to a dull ache. My left arm was no longer strapped to the bed and attached to an IV. A Band-Aid covered the needle hole in the crook of my elbow. I ran my fingers gingerly over the gauze over my knife wound, and while it was sore, it wasn't more than I could handle.

With the drugs she gave me to sleep having run their course, my brain felt clearer. I'm guessing it had been for my own good, but I'm not sure I liked being drugged up by a stranger.

Then again, the only reason I was alive and not either dead or in jail was evidently because of her. Moonlight streamed through one of the bedroom windows and I watched her for a moment. She was worth the look.

Which lead to the other self-assessment, the mental one. Being in bed with this woman made me wonder about Samantha and the life I dreamed we would share together. Lying in bed with Elizabeth felt like cheating, but was it? If my relationship with Samantha was totally one-sided, was I like a high school boy pining for the prom queen he would never have?

Right here, right now, a beautiful woman who had saved my life, lay next to me. I was torn. I closed my eyes and thought about my life. Screwed up would be a good description. I knew the work I was doing was the right thing. The evil I removed from the world made everyone safer. I also knew it was the only way I could save my own soul.

Yet I spent all the time I wasn't kicking bad guy ass by thinking and obsessing over Samantha. I didn't know how much longer I would be alive on this planet, but, at best, it would likely only be years, not decades. The bar fight proved how quickly my life could be snuffed out. If not for Elizabeth, I might have died bleeding out in a parking lot in some backwater Tennessee town, far from home.

In the time remaining to me, shouldn't I do my best to enjoy the world around me? Experience the few shots at happiness life offered? Introspection was not one of my strong suits. I'm the kind of guy who rips off the rearview mirror and plunges straight ahead, never looking back. Kurt, a computer geek I use in my fight with the Church of the Light Reclaimed, even suggested I see a therapist.

Can you imagine the therapy sessions? "Yes, I kill people for God and love a woman who is the daughter of Satan's pope, who won't talk to me anymore because I shot her to force a demon to leave her body. What do you think my issues are?"

My guess is there would be a phone call to bring in the guys in the white uniforms and straight jacket. I laughed to myself over the weirdness of it all.

I opened my eyes to find Elizabeth staring at me, the moonlight turning her eyes luminous. She shifted and moved on top of me, careful not to put too much weight on my injury.

"So. Dreaming of this Samantha?"

"As far as I can remember, I didn't dream at all." I paused a moment, then continued. "Thanks for saving my life."

She smiled, leaned forward and kissed me, her hair falling around my face. My hands slid down her back and across her bottom. Responding to my touch she lifted and guided me inside her and we spent the next hour making love and not talking.

When we were finished I sank back into the feather bed, exhausted. The Toby Keith song, *As Good As I Once Was* played in my head. Elizabeth put her head back on my shoulder and made small circles with her fingers on my chest while lying next to me.

"Before we go any further, we need to get back to those questions you don't seem to like."

She didn't answer but flipped her hand in a "go ahead" gesture.

"Since they sent you into the bar to get me drunk before they came in to kill me, you have an association with them. What is it?"

"I'm a mercenary. Freelance gun for hire. They brought me on board to do this thing in the bar. But they were pigs. If I know this before, I not have worked with them," she said.

"You double-crossed them. Won't they want revenge?"

She laughed.

"I did what they ask. You were drunk when I went into bar. They could not handle you. That is their problem. It was three on one. Incompetent pigs."

"Yeah, but they almost succeeded. Would have, without you. These guys are not the kind of people to forget what you've done when they find out I'm still alive and kicking."

She raised up and looked at me, one eyebrow arching high in a way which reminded me of Samantha and I felt a pang of guilt deep inside.

"They will not want to mess with me. This I promise you. But there is more you do not know."

"Sister, you could fill the Grand Canyon with what I don't know. Feel free to enlighten me."

"These men, they were excited. Not just because they kill you, but because they have something big in the works. But not them, I think. They are not very important men, these men sent to kill you. The man they worked for, he knows more. For this thing, they needed you dead before something happen in Philadelphia. You must be someone very important."

I grunted in a noncommittal way. "Part of my job description is to screw these guys over any way I can. Philadelphia, huh?"

"Yes. Philadelphia. This means something to you?"

"Oh, yeah, it means something." I thought to myself, "Cyrus Tyler is what it means."

She started kissing my neck, then nibbled my ear. "What will you do?"

"To them, or to you?" I rolled over on top of her, my fingers in her hair.

A wicked smile on her face, she said, "I much rather know about me."

"How about I show you, instead?" And I did.

CHAPTER NINE

The next morning I awoke, famished and feeling ready to rejoin the world. Elizabeth fixed breakfast while I spent time in the bathroom taking a long shower, the hot water working out cramped muscles from spending the last four days in bed.

The face staring back at me from the mirror looked tired despite the days spent recovering. I could see bags under my eyes and my beard and mustache were in need of a serious trim, not to mention my hair, which dove down below my ears. I looked like a wild mountain man.

I stepped out of the bathroom to the smell of bacon, eggs and fresh coffee. It was all I could do to not run to the kitchen. I settled for walking quickly back to the bedroom where Elizabeth put my bag with my clothes. The night she rescued me from the parking lot, she managed to get me into my own car and drove away. Good thing. I would have hated to lose all my gear.

I re-dressed the wound with gauze she left for me on the dresser, then slipped into a black T-shirt, jeans and my steel toed shit kicker boots and made my way to the kitchen where Elizabeth put down a full plate and mug of coffee on a small table in the breakfast nook. A bay window gave a breathtaking view down the mountain, but I spent my time watching Elizabeth, who wore a tight fitting beige top, black leggings and knee high black boots.

I took my seat and she bent to give me a kiss, then I dug in. She poured herself a cup of coffee and took the seat across from me. She sipped from the cup while I devoured my breakfast, both of us quiet while I ate.

When I sopped up the last of the egg yolks with a piece of toast and wolfed it down, I put my fork and knife on my plate and stretched contentedly. "Damn, that was good."

She dipped her head in a nod of thanks. "I have many talents, as you will find out. How do you feel today?"

"All things considered, not too bad. My side is sore and stiff, but I'll manage. Just getting up and moving is helping. And this breakfast? Wow. Thank you. Aren't you going to have any?"

"I ate before you got up. I don't sleep much. Never have. What will you do now?"

I scratched at my beard, thinking. "First thing is to return to civilization. I need to check in with some people who are probably freaking out with me being gone for so long. Then I want you to tell me about this man who hired you. I think he and I need to have a talk. Where's my phone?"

"It is out in your car, in the glove box. You should be able to make calls when we get to the bottom of the mountain. This man will not want to talk to you. You know this."

"He will, whether he wants to or not. Cooperation is not optional. Tell me where I can find this guy."

She shook her head. "No. I will take you to him. I will help you in this."

"Not a chance. Listen, I appreciate what you've done for me. I really do. But I prefer to work alone when it comes to matters like this."

"Too bad," she countered. "Because I will not tell you unless I go with you. You need me. I watch your back."

"I have people to do that for me, if needed. Please, just give me his name and where I can find him. Then I'll be happy to drop you off wherever you want."

She leaned back in her chair, crossed her legs and said, "No." Then smiled at me.

I grounded my teeth for a moment, but then sighed. "Fine. You can come. But you have to let me handle things. Kapeesh?"

"I let you handle. Then I clean up when you screw up. Like last time," and smiled again.

"It ain't happening again. I can promise you that much. You packed?" I was getting ticked off.

"Yes. My things are already in the car. I guessed you would want to leave right away."

I got up, taking my dishes to the sink. I washed them and set them in the rack to dry, then went to get my gear from the bedroom and the two of us walked out to my car. I threw my things in the trunk, next to the flame thrower and then glanced into the front and back seats.

"I don't see any blood. You clean that up, too?"

"I tell you. Many talents. Besides, you have leather seats and floor mats. Make things easy."

We both got in and fired up the car, punched up "home" on the GPS and started down the mountain. The device told me we were in the Great Smokey Mountain National Park. The day was pleasant at this elevation so we rolled the windows down. We were a bit under five hours to Louisville.

"This man I need to talk to, do you know his name?"

"Yes. Of course. Before I tell you, I must have your word I will get to go with you. You make this promise?"

"Do I have a frickin' choice?"

No. You do not have a frickin' choice. Only my choice. You promise?"

I growled out agreement and she patted my cheek in response. "You are smart man. His name is Preston Deveraux. He is also a pig. But he pays well and is very handsome. You know this man?"

I felt my blood freeze over at the mention of the name. The last time I'd seen Preston Deveraux, he held a gun to Samantha's head, promising to shoot her if I so much as twitched a finger. Moments before, he'd shot and killed Dominic Montoya, the previous Hand of God, while I looked on, helpless to stop him.

Deveraux had movie star good looks and an incredibly evil world outlook. Over the past ten months, I'd kept my ears open, hoping to catch wind of where he was hiding out. Seems he'd once again tried to have me bumped off.

I tried to keep from ripping the steering wheel off in my hands. "Yeah. I know this man," I said, trying to contain my growing rage within. "Where can I find him?"

"I know not where he is now, but I can arrange a meeting, between him and me. This is how you find him."

I drove for nearly twenty miles, thinking as the world

passed by barely noticed. If Deveraux was out to punch my ticket, then they must have something really big planned. Considering their last two efforts included infecting children with a genetically altered form of bird flu and releasing the Watchers, badass fallen angels buried for several millennia who were looking for some major payback against mankind, I hated to think what they had planned next.

I had to hand it to the Church of the Light Reclaimed: they went for the home run. And I'd proven to be quite the thorn in their side and knew I was public enemy number one. There was some thought whether it was better to watch me rather than kill me, since with my death a new Hand of God would be tapped to continue the good fight and they wouldn't know who it would be until he (or she) made their presence known.

Bumping me off would give them a short window to pull off something big with a chance a new Hand would not yet be in place. Something to think about.

"Here's what I want to do. Let me get back to Louisville and see if my crew knows anything about what's going on. Then you can call Deveraux and try to set up a meeting. I'm gonna kick his ass from there to Sunday and back before I kill him."

"Sounds like plan. It would be a shame to spoil such good looks, but if we must we must."

I opened the console, picked up my phone, thumbed in the passcode and accessed my contacts list. I found the listing for "Big Honcho" and pressed call.

A few moments later the dulcet tones of Brother Joshua, the minister in charge of the Derby City Mission, picked up.

"Victor?" A man of many words, is Brother J.

"Yeah. It's me. Returned to the land of the living." I gave him a brief description of what transpired both in North Carolina and in Tennessee. "I'll be back at the mission around mid-afternoon and I'll fill you in completely."

"This woman, is she with you now?"

"Yep. She saved my life, J. Without her help, you'd be ringing up another poor soul to run around and whack the bad guys."

"Can you trust her?"

I glanced at Elizabeth as she stared out the window. "Not

a chance." I hung up and slipped the phone into my jeans pocket. She looked my way and I leaned over and we kissed. "My friends can't wait to meet you."

She snorted in a very un-lady like manner. "I listened to what you told him. You did not go into any detail about my being part of the team sent to kill you."

I shrugged. "But you didn't. You did the opposite. Puts you on the side of the righteous."

She wagged a finger at me. "All the same, when we get to Louisville, I prefer you drop me off at a hotel. I would rather we proceed slowly. I do not know your friends or how they would react to me. One must be cautious in my business."

"You said you were a mercenary. You're for hire? Then I would like to hire you. How much?"

She turned in her seat and ran a hand down the inside of my thigh. "For you? I think of discount plan. I think you will like it."

"I'm sure I will. You can go with me to the meeting with Brother Joshua. I can vouch for your safety."

She pulled her hand back and sat in her seat, crossing her hands in her lap. "I say no. I mean no. I not want to meet this man. If you can't do as I ask, then you can pull over and let me out here. Find this Deveraux on your own."

"How do I know you won't bolt on me the moment I drop you off at the hotel?"

"You have my word. That will have to be good enough."

She was right. Forcing her to come with me wasn't my style and I don't think she would have cracked even if I did. I would play things out her way and see what happened.

"Alright. Your way. The Galt House is right downtown. You can stay there while I meet Joshua and see what's what. Good enough?"

"They have room service with cute waiters?"

"Room service, yes. Cute waiters? I have no idea." I shook my head in mock disgust. "Women."

"Ehh, can't live with us, can't shoot us," she responded.

"Don't count on it," I thought.

CHAPTER TEN

After getting Elizabeth squared away at the Galt House, I drove over to the Derby City Mission, parking out front. I carried my gear to my room, a monkish ten by ten space down past the maintenance room. My digs were quite a bit away from the homeless men and women who stayed at the mission. Seems I made most of them nervous. Go figure.

I strolled down the hall to J's office and knocked on the door frame before stepping inside. Brother Joshua, a middle-aged black man, hair cut short with streaks of gray at the temples and black framed reading glasses on his nose, sat behind his desk going through some papers.

I plopped down in one of the two seats facing his desk, and waited. If J was curious about my absence over the last few days, he sure as hell wasn't in a hurry to ask me about it.

He finished perusing the last sheet and set it to the side. Then he pushed his glasses on top of his head and steepled his fingers, resting his elbows on his desk.

We stared at each other for a few minutes, neither of us speaking. I used to play this game in elementary school and usually I won. Today, I lost.

"I met a girl."

He continued to stare at me for a moment longer before joining the conversation. "I'm sure you meet lots of women. Tell me about this one."

And I did. From how she gave me the heads up about the men planning to kill me to how she saved my ass.

"Lift up your shirt. Let me see how she sewed you up."

I stood and pulled up my shirt. J leaned closer, and then evidently satisfied, sat back. "Her work is first rate. There are battlefield doctors who might not have closed you up any better. What do you know about her?"

"Not a damn thing, other than she says she was hired by Deveraux to help the men plant me six feet under. She claims she became a turn coat because the men were pigs."

"And you believe her?"

"Hell no. She's playing her own games. I'll play my part long enough to learn what she's up to. No one who has any brains would double-cross Deveraux and from everything I can tell, she's smarter than your average merc. So she's playing an angle, but I haven't a clue what. What I do know is I'd be trying on wings and picking out a harp if not for her."

"Don't count your harp strings before they're plucked. Why didn't you have Winston with you on this job? Sounds like you could have used him."

Winston Reynolds is a former bounty hunter and now my top warrior in the battle with Satan and his lackeys. Winston was a former All Big East linebacker for the Louisville Cardinals. After a brief stint in the NFL, he went to work for bounty hunter J.B. Booker. That's how he and I met, following J.B.'s murder by the Church of the Light Reclaimed, Winston joined up with me for some sweet payback. Now he was my go-to backup when I needed the help. At six foot two and nearly two-hundred and forty pounds, he packed quite a punch.

"Winston and Kurt are taking care of some loose ends from the crap that went down in Hawaii. I expect them back by the end of the week."

Brother Joshua moved the glasses back into place, picking up another stack of papers. "Do I want to know?"

"I could tell you, but then I'd have to kill you."

He sat the papers down and stared at me. I got up and left. Some people have no sense of humor.

*****

Kurt closed his eyes, squeezing the grip of the gun hard enough he feared it would go off without him even touching the trigger.

He sat in the dark in an off-campus apartment near the

University of Wisconsin, a stone's throw from Camp Randall Stadium. He set the gun on the small coffee table next to his chair and rubbed his hands on his jeans. Despite the latex gloves, it felt like his hands were still sweating.

He thought about the events which brought him to this place to kill a man. Following the big throw down with the Church of the Light Reclaimed, he'd left Vic and Winston to hide out in Hawaii. He worked hard to hide his tracks, but somehow, the Church still found him.

They sent a fallen angel by the name of Kokabiel, to first seduce him, having possessed the body of a beautiful woman, and ultimately to kill him. Kokabiel, or Ruth Anne as he knew her, buried Kurt in a coffin with a pipe coming to the surface. The fallen angel threatened to drop fire ants, scorpions or rattle snakes into the coffin with him unless he gave up where to find the money Vic stole from the Church of the Light Reclaimed.

When they learned it would take both Kurt and Vic to retrieve the money, Kokabiel opted to fill up the coffin with water and leave him to drown. If not for Winston saving the day at the last moment, they would have succeeded.

True, once they kicked Kokabiel out of the body of Ruth Anne Gardner, he and Ruth Anne fell deeply in love, which means he did get a girlfriend out of the deal. But it took him nearly dying for that to happen.

What always bugged him was how they found him in Hawaii. Kurt had been very careful hiding his tracks. He was terrified the Church would one day come after him and went to great lengths to make sure they never did. But never say never, right?

When the Watchers were finally defeated and sent to whatever hell it is they go to when forced out of a body, Kurt began the process of finding how the Church tracked him down.

Kurt belonged to a collection of hackers much in the vain of Anonymous, the famous hackers known for wearing Guy Fawkes masks and taking on corporate and government stooges.

Kurt enlisted the hackers he knew to take on the Church of the Light Reclaimed and they laid siege to every facet of their operation, from the money supply chain to discovering who made up their membership. It was a tip from one of the hackers which led to the rescue of Samantha from captivity down in Naples, Florida.

It took him several months, but in the end he found out one of his own hacking buddies sold him out to the Church. All it took was a grand and a new laptop. Kurt thought he would be worth more money. He was worth two grand if he was worth a dime.

The hacker's online name was the Silver Ghost. His real name was Sarka Buranak, an exchange student from Romania, majoring in computer science at U.W.

Sarka was a Black Hat. They considered themselves the outlaws of the hacking world and at one point he found out the Church put a bounty on Kurt's head and he claimed it. Like the bounty hunters of the Old Wild West, they didn't care who put out the bounty, only getting paid when they claimed it.

Kurt didn't know if Silver Ghost knew it would mean Kurt would die a horrible, excruciating death, but after making his way into Buranak's system, it didn't matter. The Romanian Black Hat now worked for the Church, trying his best to track down and drop polymorphic viruses into any computer Victor or Winston may have access. His goal? Find the money Victor stole from the Church. Nearly thirty million dollars. It is why they travelled to Hawaii to begin with. Follow the money. They offered Buranak a ten percent cut of any money recovered.

And when they had the money, they wanted him to help plan an ambush of anyone associated with the Hand of God. This included another run at Kurt. Seemed Buranak put key logger and logic bombs in the computers at the Derby City Mission. Kurt went in behind Buranak and removed them, despite the fact he doubted the mission possessed any information they would find useful.

After talking it over with Victor and Winston, the decision was made to remove Sarka from the board. Permanently. With Vic out in North Carolina dealing with hellhounds, it fell to Winston and Kurt. They spent a few days following Buranak and formulated their plan to eliminate him.

Winston was happy to be the one to pull the trigger, but Kurt felt it important to be the one to take out Buranak. After all, it was personal. Buranak was in bed with the most evil of evil people. It was up to Kurt to avenge Ruth Anne's mother and brother, killed at the hands of another demented fallen angel. And as far as Kurt was concerned, Buranak was as responsible for him being buried six feet under as the fallen angel hiding out in Ruth Anne's body.

But now the time was here and Kurt found the thought of killing another person unpleasant. Winston and Victor told him they were at war and in a war people die. And they were right. The "new" Kurt wanted to be a part of the war, taking on the bad guys on the frontline.

And here he was, as far forward on the frontline as a man could get. Yet now that he was here, he wasn't sure he deserved the chance. Winston waited in a car down the street and Kurt wondered if there was time to call him and switch places.

Before he could text Winston and ask, the front door opened, and then closed. A person was whistling, and Kurt heard what he assumed were keys dropped into a bowl.

A few moments later, the door to the room where Kurt waited opened and a young man walked in and dropped into a swivel chair in front of a bank of computer screens. He pushed a few buttons and a moment later his fingers began to fly over the keyboard.

Buranak was of average height with wild, spiked blonde hair. Kurt almost busted out laughing when he realized the song Buranak was whistling was the theme to Gilligan's Island. Kurt picked up the gun, stood and walked silently until he was right behind Buranak. He pointed the gun at the man's head. "This is for—"

Before he could get the words out, Buranak whirled around in the chair, knocking Kurt backwards. The gun went off, the bullet striking one of the monitors, punching a small hole in the glass and blowing out a large hole in the back.

Buranak hurled himself out of his chair and onto Kurt, the two of them crashing to the ground, fighting for control of the gun.

Buranak shouted at him in what Kurt assumed was Romanian, but was too busy trying not to die to point out he didn't understand what was being said.

Buranak kneed him hard in the groin and Kurt almost

lost his grip on the gun, but managed to hold on. Barely. The other man held onto his wrist with both hands, trying to turn the gun towards Kurt's face.

The hacker began to grin, as inch by inch, the gun began to point at Kurt's nose, yelling out, "Yes, yes, yes."

"No, no, no," Kurt thought. Kurt tried to think of what Vic would do in a situation like this and it came to him, he knew what Vic would do.

Instead of resisting Buranak's efforts, he used his anger and fear for a burst of strength and pulled the gun up and over his head. Then he rolled slightly to the side and drove his forehead into Buranak's nose.

Pain exploded as it felt like his head would tear apart from the attack and his eyes began to water, but they weren't tears, he told himself. Buranak seemed to be in an equal amount of pain, letting go of the gun and falling onto his back, holding his nose as blood poured between his fingers.

Kurt got to his knees, shaking his head back and forth, trying to clear the cobwebs from his brain. He needed to think, but all he could think about was the pain.

"You broke my nose, you asshole," screamed Buranak in English, and he lunged for the gun, trying to pull it from Kurt's hand.

The gun barked once and a look of surprise crossed Buranak's face, his hands going to his chest, blood welling out between his fingers. "You shot me."

"Well, yeah. That was kind of the point. I'm Kurt Pervis. This is payback for what you did to me."

"Who?"

Before Kurt could explain, Buranak fell back onto the carpeted floor, dead.

Kurt stared for a moment at the blood pooling on the carpet, mesmerized by what he'd done. The largest thing he had ever killed in his entire life was the occasional bug, and even then he usually picked them up with a tissue and then let them loose outside.

He forced himself to get moving, doing everything he could to avoid looking at the dead man on the floor. He gathered up Buranak's three laptops, and dropped the computers into the duffle bag next the chair where he'd waited for the hacker to come home. He felt a surge of excitement about getting the computers home and learning all of Buranak's secrets. Kurt knew he might even learn more about what the Church of the Light Reclaimed planned for future attacks.

When he was sure he had left nothing of importance behind, he again averted his eyes from the dead body and went to the front door. He cracked it open, and not seeing anyone, slipped the gun into his jacket pocket, left and quickly walked down the hallway, leaving the building by a side stairwell.

He forced himself to walk slowly down the block to Winston's car. He admonished himself: next time no monologue. The one doing the monologue always ends up catching the bullet. Kurt was lucky his desire to let Buranak know who was killing him had not ended up with his own death.

He reached the car, opened the door and slid into the passenger seat, pulling the door closed. Winston put the car in drive and they left, ghosts in the night.

Kurt glanced at his hands in his lap, amazed they were not shaking. In truth, he found his breathing to be easy, his pulse rate normal. Surprise, surprise.

"Everything go O.K? I saw the dude go inside and wondered what was taking you so long. I almost came to check on you."

Kurt looked at Winston, and with a slow grin spreading across his face, said, "Just like we planned."

CHAPTER ELEVEN

The next morning I picked up Elizabeth at the Galt House, half-surprised she was actually there, and drove out to Wild Eggs on Dutchman's Lane for breakfast.

I chose the omelet with every known form of protein tossed in with green peppers, onions and tomatoes. She chose strawberry pancakes. We both drank our coffee leaded.

"How did you sleep?" I asked. She sat across from me wearing a yellow sundress and flats to match. Her perfume smelled like an early spring rain.

She forked a generous amount of pancakes into her mouth, chewed for a moment, and then flipped her hand back and forth.

"Yeah. Same here." We avoided the small talk for the next few minutes while we both demolished our breakfast, Elizabeth keeping up with me forkful for forkful.

I took a sip of coffee and spent a moment watching her. The longer I did, the more beautiful she seemed. Her pale blue eyes haunted my dreams the night before. For the first time since meeting Samantha, I couldn't remember a single dream about her, which bothered me.

She paused, her fork half-way to her mouth, and said, "What? Why do you stare?"

I shook myself out of my private thoughts. "You have some strawberry on the corner of your mouth."

She wiped the corner of her mouth with her napkin, but seeing nothing on it, looked dubious, but shrugged and went back to eating.

"When we are finished, I want you to place the call to Deveraux and set up the meeting."

"What, no small talk? Right to business? No 'you look beautiful,' Elizabeth? No, 'the dress is pretty,' Elizabeth?"

Laughing, I shook my head. "You're gorgeous and the dress is lovely. Happy?"

"No. Elizabeth is not happy." She gave me a fake pout, then kicked my shin under the table. "Next time, tell me nice things without me having to ask you. Women like to hear compliments." She shook her head. "Men can be very stupid sometimes." Her accent seemed particularly thick when irritated.

"You won't get any argument from me. I have no doubts the person who wrote *Everything There is to Know about Women* isn't a man."

"This is probably why this Samantha left you. Because you can be a pig, too."

The dig hit me deep down in my soul. I worked to control the anger which blossomed at her comments. In a voice barely above a whisper, I said, "You don't know what you're talking about and I would take care in how you use her name."

She was quiet for a moment, drinking coffee and watching me. She put the cup down. "I am sorry. The comment was meant to be a joke, but it did not come out right. Forgive me. Sometimes I talk before I think. Do you want to talk about this woman?"

"No. Not now. Not ever. Let's call Deveraux and get this train rolling."

She sighed, but reached into her purse and got her phone and made a call. She listened and then mouthed, "Voice mail."

When the message was over she said, "This is Elizabeth. The man is still alive and I know where he is. I tell you where, but I want more for the efforts I make. You send stupid men. Do the right thing this time and pay me and I will bring you his head."

She hung up and smiled at me. "Satisfied?"

I rubbed my neck. "I kind of like my head where it is. You sounded convincing. Almost too convincing."

She stuck her tongue out at me. "If I wanted you dead, I could have let you die in the parking lot. I could have killed you many times while you slept. Instead I sew you up, get you blood, make you better. And still you doubt me?"

"Trust but verify. Why don't you tell me about yourself?"

"I only tell small amount. I am from Hungary, but I move around a lot. I worked with *Terrorelhárítási Központ,* the anti-terrorism force. But they don't use me well and I leave. Now I hire out to those who can afford me. Deveraux asked me to come to America and do work for him. But when I meet men in Tennessee, they spend more time trying to get in my pants than planning to attack you." She shook her head, disgusted, and after a moment continued. "Then I learn they have big plans. They hint it will lead to many deaths, so I make decision to warn you about their plans to kill you, see what you can do. When you take them out even though you were so drunk, I like. When you fall down in parking lot, I make instant decision. Help you, hurt them."

It sounded good. Sounded believable. The question was how to separate the truth from the bull shit, because I knew what she was telling me wasn't the whole truth.

"Is Elizabeth your real name?"

She snorted. "I work intelligence for my home country, and now for others. I have many names. But this one is all you will know. I chose it because I see dancer with this name I like. Now I am Elizabeth."

Before I could respond her phone rang. Looking at the screen, she moved to sit next to me, putting the phone next to her ear, but tilting it so I could hear.

"Hello?"

"What happened in Tennessee? You were supposed to kill Victor McCain for me."

Preston Deveraux even sounded smooth on the phone. If I could jump through the phone and wrap my hands around his throat, I would do it in a heartbeat.

"What happened is you sent idiot boys to do real man's job. But you are wrong. You did not hire me to kill this man, but to be bait. I was bait and he was there for your men to kill. They screw this up, no? This time, I do the job for you. He will be killed. I want five-hundred thousand. You do this?"

"Where is he?"

"He is back in Louisville, but I know where he will be in three days and I will kill him for you. But I must have money before then. Cash."

"I can do that, but if you double-cross me, you will regret it. Do I make myself clear?"

"Do not insult me. I always do what I say I do. Where your men failed, I will not. Do we have a deal?"

"Yes. We do. Where would you like me to wire the money?"

"No good. I just tell you, I work in cash. You tell me where to meet you and I will be there. I want it from you. I not trust anyone else. You do this, and I will kill this man."

"I will be in Columbus, Ohio tomorrow. Meet me at the Dublin Cemetery tomorrow night, eight p.m. Drive through the main entrance and bear to the right when the road forks. There's a huge tree on the left. I will meet you there."

He hung up and Elizabeth put her phone away. I could not help but groan. "A cemetery? Nothing ever good happens in a cemetery. Doesn't he know he is perpetuating the Satanist stereotype?"

"Satanist? This man is a Satanist? There are really such people?" She rested her hand on my leg, casually massaging the inside of my thigh.

I cleared my throat. "Yes he is and yes there are. Do you know anything about me?"

"I know you are supposed to be a man who is hard to kill, who they want to kill very badly. But no, I don't know about you. What is there to know?"

I gave her a brief rundown about being the Hand of God, what the job entails and who the hell Preston Deveraux is and who he worked for.

She laughed long and loud. "You kill people for God? And you believe this? Do you have visions or do you have a phone to call for your assignments?"

"Mind keeping your voice down, please?" I glanced around the restaurant, but no one seemed to be paying us any attention.

I have to admit, her laughter was a blow to my ego. The only people who I ever talked to about my job were Winston, Kurt, Samantha and Brother Joshua. Elizabeth was the first person outside of our group with whom I shared my situation and her disbelief bothered me.

"How I get my jobs is not something we will be talking about. Whether you believe me or not, Preston Deveraux does. If you think I'm some nut, forget it. I will go to Columbus on my own and take this son of a bitch out."

She wrapped her arms around my neck and pulled me to her, and kissed me. I resisted at first, but then gave in. She was a better than average kisser.

Breaking the kiss, she said, "I am sorry." The amusement in her eyes said otherwise. "But I do believe you. More importantly, I know this Preston believes it. I will go with you to meet him. If he do not see me, he may not show."

She had a point. Deveraux was expecting to meet Elizabeth and if he got a whiff of Vic being there then things were likely to go very badly. Deveraux was a smart guy. They would need to get there early and scope things out.

"We will need to get there way ahead of them and take a look around. How about we check you out of the Galt House and hit the road?"

"I am afraid I cannot. I have other business, unrelated to this, and must take care of it first. We can leave at first light in the morning."

"Other business? Like what?"

"Other business which is not your business. I am a mercenary. I must make a living and I have an interview with a prospective client tonight. It cannot be helped. We leave in the morning."

I did not like this development one bit. I didn't trust Elizabeth any further than I could throw her, though I could likely throw her a pretty good distance.

"You are one frustrating woman, you know that?"

"Yes, but lovable. I need to rent a car later today. For now, I would like you to take me back to hotel."

"And what is back at the hotel?"

She slid her hand higher up my inner thigh. "My bed, which you have yet to see. I thought I might show you how firm is the mattress. Does this work for you?"

I snagged the waitress walking by. "Check, please."

CHAPTER TWELVE

Hedley Stafford sat on the edge of the examining room table, his legs hanging off the side. Dr. Collins sat on a rolling stool and explained the process.

"I know Dr. Michaels told you about how the surgery would take place, but I wanted to go over it with you again to make sure you understood what would happen."

"Doctor, being overly prepared when you plan to saw my leg in half is not a problem for me."

"Not your leg, Senator, just the bone. We are doing a total knee replacement, due to extensive arthritis in the joint. I will start by making a ten inch incision from here to here." She ran her finger from a spot above his kneecap to a few inches below it.

"Once I do this, I will have access to the knee. I start by resurfacing your femur and attaching the metal component of your new joint to the end of the bone. I will then do the same thing with the tibia. In between there will be a plastic component for flexibility. Once I am happy the joint is properly sized and bending properly, then I will close the incision. I use staples to keep the skin closed."

Stafford nodded. "How long do you expect me to be laid up?"

"We will put your knee to work following your surgery. Once you are back in your room, you will be attached to a continuous passive motion machine, or CPM. You will use this during the first day. We will have you on your feet the following morning, if you're doing well enough. You will be home in three days. We will have a regiment of pain medication we will want you to adhere to so we can stay ahead of the pain. During the surgery, I will be inserting a pain block which will keep the pain at bay for twenty-four to forty-eight hours. Following surgery, I will want you to take the Hydrocodone at the prescribed intervals. Then we will move you to Tylenol."

"Good enough. How soon before I will be able to return to work?"

"That is up to you and how well you do with your physical therapy. Most people do their physical therapy at home for the first one to two weeks, then they are well enough to continue with physical therapy at a nearby facility. Because of your unique position, I understand Dr. Michaels arranged for you to have your physical therapy at the Capital. I see no reason why you can't still do this, again, based on how well you do the first week you are home."

"Most excellent. I can't thank you enough, doctor, for keeping my surgery on schedule. This will allow me to be fairly full strength when the August recess is over. We have many events leading up to the election and I want to participate as fully as possible."

She stood and Stafford did the same. "We will have a list of do's and don'ts for you. It is almost as important to not do what we tell you not to do, as it is to do what we tell you to do. You are a very healthy man and you have a reputation for being a workaholic. If you feel you must stay very active, there's no shame in using a wheelchair to get around the Capital."

"You can count on me to behave, doctor." He extended his hand and she took it. Stafford was pleased to note her grip was firm and steady. He hoped it would be the same when she held the scalpel.

"Then I will see you next Monday at six a.m."

They said their goodbyes and Collins watched the Senate Majority Leader leave. She then went to her office, closing the door. She sat behind her desk, opened her briefcase and pulled out the burner phone which arrived in the mail. She pushed a button for speed dial. A moment later a man answered.

"Yes?"

"We are on schedule. Stafford just left. The surgery is next Monday. You will need to make sure I get the product this weekend."

"It's all been arranged. I will meet with you Sunday at the hotel. You're sure you can make the switch with no issues?"

"Yes. The entire surgical team are my people, from the anesthesiologist to the nurses. There won't be a problem."

"Good. See you Sunday, doc."

The man ended the call and Collins put the phone back into her briefcase and shut the lid softly. She closed her eyes and took deep, steadying breaths. Soon it would all be over. Until then, she needed to continue to act like she did not have a care in the world. No matter how hard it would be.

*****

Brad Stiles walked to the large oak door, knocking twice before opening it and stepping inside, closing the door behind him. Tyler sat behind his desk, feet propped on the edge, the phone to his ear, gesturing with his hands while he talked.

"Look, Bob, I'm not going to barter with you. I'm the fucking Speaker of the House of Representatives. When I tell you how I want you to vote, that's how you're going to vote. Being the chairman of the Agricultural Committee helps to bring a lot of donations into your campaign coffers. Screw with me over this vote and I promise you when the next session of Congress starts in January you will be lucky to be chairman of your son's Boy Scout troop."

He slammed the phone down, dropped his feet on the floor and broke into a Cheshire Cat grin. "I do love this job. Whatcha got for me?"

"Everything is a go for Monday. I will need to be gone for a day or so, to get things ready."

"No worries. I'll get Randy to do the driving. Let Brenda know when you go back out and she'll take care of it."

Stiles nodded and left. He did as he was asked and informed Brenda, Tyler's scheduling secretary, he would be gone for a few days and to have the other driver, Randy, handle things while he was gone.

He left the Capital, found his car in the security lot and made his way out of the city. He stopped to gas up on the Beltway and punched an address in the GPS. The machine found the proper mapping and he saw it was a bit over thirty minutes.

He stopped briefly in a strip mall, parking in the back long enough to remove a stolen license plate and switched it for his government plate. Once finished, he pulled out and resumed his trip.

He turned on the satellite radio and found the MLB channel. The Nationals were having a hell of a season and he wanted to hear about the previous night's game.

Traffic was heavier than normal, even for D.C., and it took him nearly forty-five minutes to make it to his destination, a non-descript building at the end of a row of warehouses. The sign over the door read Bio-Enhanced Robotics.

Only one other car, a Toyota Prius, was parked out front and he pulled his Navigator in beside the smaller car and got out. He could pick up the Prius and put it in the back of his car.

Glancing around and seeing no one else nearby, he removed a handkerchief from his suit pocket and held it in his hand while he turned the knob and opened the door. He knew from previous reconnaissance trips there were no obvious security cameras to worry about.

Inside, he used the handkerchief to softly close the door. He found himself in a classic corporate waiting area. A receptionist's desk sat in one corner, empty. Several comfortable chairs lined one wall with an end table supporting a lamp and a smattering of different magazines.

Stiles crossed the room to the only door, and once again using the handkerchief, opened it and stepped through, closing it behind him. A hallway ran straight ahead, three doors on the left side, two on the right. He knew the two doors on the right ran to advanced development laboratories.

B.E.R. was involved on the frontlines of creating prosthetics which combined cutting edge technology and the latest in surgical techniques. The company was the brainchild of Isaac Peck. Peck double-majored in engineering and computers at M.I.T.

When a close family friend was injured fighting in Afghanistan, Peck went to work developing new arms and legs which were inching closer and closer to the stuff of science fiction. The latest success was the development of a prosthetic leg which worked exactly like a human leg, even to the point of being controlled by the unconscious thoughts of the recipient.

Peck's office was the last door on the left and Stiles could hear music through the closed door. Holding the handkerchief, Stiles checked the labs and the other two rooms to make sure they were the only two people in the building.

Satisfied they were alone, he turned the knob and opened Peck's door an inch, putting the handkerchief away, then pushed the rest of the way open with the toe of his shoe.

Peck, thin and balding and in his late twenties, sat bent over a drafting table, his left knee pumping up and down in continuous motion. The music came from a computer on his desk, hip-hop turned up to ear splitting levels. A box the size of a bread box sat on the desk next to the computer.

When Stiles kicked the door shut, Peck jumped out of his chair, his hand flying to chest. "Jesus. You scared the crap out of me, man. What the hell?"

Brad sat down in one of two chairs in the room, crossing one leg over the other and resting his hands in his lap and stared at the other man, saying nothing. Peck went to his desk, tapped a few keys and the music stopped. Sitting back down, his knee pumped double time, while Peck gripped the arms of his chair like a man who believed it would rocket into outer space at any moment.

Nodding at the package on the desk, Stiles asked, "Is that for me?"'

"Yeah. Just like you ordered. Man, this was a fun project. Never ever considered using quantum computing this way. Some of my buds at M.I.T. would shit their pants if they knew this kind of technology existed. This is way beyond anything Farhi, Goldstone and Harrow are working on. Any chance I could get a look at the research white papers? This is science fiction-type stuff. Really cool."

"I don't think so. Anyone else here, Isaac?"

"Nah, man, I gave everyone a half-day off, like you asked. They loved it, with it being Friday and all. So this is our little secret. Did all the work myself. What's this going to be used for?"

"You take notes on this, Isaac? I find out you wrote

anything down, took notes, I won't be very happy."

Peck raised his hands. "Hey, man. No. Nothing. When I make a deal, I keep it. Besides, we don't want a paper trail, do we? Am I right?"

Brad stood, pulled a pair of gloves out of his inner suit pocket and slipped on first one, then the other.

"Isaac, when you're right. You're right. We don't want a paper trail. Or a people trail."

Stiles reached under his suit coat, slid the gun out of its holster and shot Peck twice in the chest and once in the head. Putting away the gun, he spent the next ten minutes going through Peck's desk and briefcase, looking for anything related to the job. Finding nothing, he picked up the package and left the way he entered.

Back at his car, he opened the rear hatch and sat the package down carefully and shut the door. Climbing back behind the wheel, he entered another address from memory, this one to a hotel in Philadelphia. With any luck he would be there early enough to catch the last part of the Nationals game with the L.A. Dodgers.

A Nationals win would make it the perfect ending to a good day.

CHAPTER THIRTEEN

After spending the better part of the morning in bed, we made our way to an Avis store, where she picked out a Mercedes. I guess being a mercenary pays better than average. She promised to call me later and then tore out of the parking lot, cutting off two other people in the process, the sound of horns showing their displeasure.

I was still hungry and found my way over to Molly Malone's Irish Pub. I sat in my usual booth where I could watch all three doors. Being a regular helped as my server placed the Guinness in front of me moments after I sat down and let me know my order was already entered.

I thanked her, picked up the glass and drained about half of it in one pull. I couldn't ever remember being this conflicted about anything in my life. Not hearing from Samantha made me want to find someone right this very moment and pound the ever lovin' daylights out of them. And this thing with Elizabeth wasn't helping. The sex was beyond fantastic, but when it was over, I felt like I was cheating on Samantha. But how can you cheat on someone who is not a part of your life?

I polished off the Guinness and motioned for another one. When my meal arrived, that glass was nearly empty as well and I told her I wanted one more. I dug into the shepherd's pie, but ate without really tasting it.

Near the end of my meal, Winston walked up to the booth and sat opposite me. The server asked if he wanted anything and he shook his head no, then stared at me.

I forked the last bite of food into my mouth and finished off the second glass of Guinness, set it to the side and picked up the new one.

"How many have you had?" he asked.

I held up three fingers and he shook his head. "Man, it's only one in the afternoon. Hitting it pretty hard, aren't you?"

"Listen, if you plan on being my mother, you need to put on a dress. Hell, I know my limit and I'm not there yet. I can handle it."

"I'd put on a dress, if it would help. But I'm not shaving my legs for you. And, yeah, you can handle it. Just like you handled North Carolina. Brother Joshua filled me in on how it went. Hear you got sliced and diced. Lucky to be alive. What if they come for you again, when you leave here, with you all liquored up?"

"Then I'll kick their ass, like I always do."

A long belch slipped out and Winston waved a hand in front of his face.

"Dude, you need to ease up. You want to die, that's fine. But do it the right way. All you're doing is making it easy for them. You need to stay sharp. These are bad MoFos you're after."

"Whatever." I didn't appreciate the lecture. Winston and I were now good friends, but he had no clue what I was going through, what I was dealing with. It didn't help I knew he was right. The drinking nearly cost me my life. True, I wasn't expecting an ambush in Tennessee, but I should have considered the possibility.

He was also right I didn't care anymore. It was more than not hearing from Samantha, although her silence played a huge part. I was getting tired of the fight. Even the time spent in bed with Elizabeth, while enjoyable in the moment, did nothing for me when it was over.

I found myself taking more and more chances and sooner or later it would catch up with me. Maybe not today, but soon. I began wondering what the point was. I take out bad guy number one and move on to bad guy number two. Once I wipe his ass off the face of the planet, the next one steps up.

I knew I needed to keep working as the Hand of God, for as long as possible, to win back the soul I lost when I caused the death of Dominic Montoya. But even if I did this another ten years or more, there was still no guarantee I would win back my soul.

I took a deep breath and, for the moment, crushed my personal pity party. "How did things go up in Cheese Land?"

"Well enough. He almost blew it when it came time to pulling the trigger. He didn't know I put a mini-camera in the dude's room and I was watching it all go down from out in the hallway. I thought for a moment I would need to bust in and help, but he got it done. He's back at the mission working on the laptops the guy was using."

"How was he after? Did he seem to be handling it O.K.?" I kept thinking about the Clint Eastwood movie. *Unforgiven.* There's a line in there where Clint's character says, 'It's a hell of a thing, killin' a man. Take away all he's got, and all he's ever gonna have.' Some people can do it and never lose a second of sleep. I worried about how it would affect Kurt.

"Too early to tell. He did talk ninety-miles an hour on the way home, but then again, he talks a lot anyways. Dude never shuts up."

"That's Kurt."

"What's up next for you? You and your new lady friend have big plans?"

I filled him in on the plan to drive to Columbus and meet with Preston Deveraux.

"You know this is a trap, right?" he asked.

I nodded, draining the last of my beer. "Yep. Only question is for whom? Her or me? Deveraux agreed way too quickly for the meeting. No negotiations on price. No pressing for details."

We both got up and I dropped some cash on the table to cover my meal and drinks, plus a healthy tip, and we made our way outside.

"You want me to ride up with you guys? Help back you up?"

"No. I don't. She won't allow it. She says it has to be the two of us because she doesn't trust you guys yet."

"That's bullshit."

Before he could get going on a full rant, I held up my hands. "Hang on, hang on. You're not going up with us because you're going up first. I want you to leave as soon as you can get ready and scout the place. You can bet they picked this meeting place for a reason. Get up there early and find a spot to hang out, watch who comes and goes. Then let me know what I'm walking into."

"Now that's more like it. I can be on the road inside of an hour. If I hit the road by two, I can get in Columbus by six. What time are you guys supposed to meet with him?"

"Eight tomorrow night, just before dark. I've looked at a Google map view of the cemetery and there are a couple of large trees and several large monuments near where they want to meet. I'll need a good threat assessment."

"You got it, man. Late on a Saturday night, I can't imagine there'll be many people in the cemetery so they should be easy enough to pick out. And watch your ass, Vic. They may not wait until tomorrow night to take a shot at you. Which does raise one other question. Why now?"

"No clue. But I plan to find out. Right after I put a bullet between the eyes of Preston. He thinks Satan will send him right back here. Time go give him the chance to find out."

CHAPTER FOURTEEN

I parked my car in the Galt House parking garage and made my way to the lobby. The day started out hotter than Hades and promised to climb even higher before the day was through. In Columbus, the temperature was predicted to hit a high of ninety-eight with a heat index near one-hundred and three.

Carrying my duffle it didn't take long for me to break out in a sweat, even in the short walk to the lobby. I dropped my gear next to the concierge desk, gave the man behind the counter her room number and asked him to let her know I was here.

He picked up a white phone, punched a few numbers and a moment later passed along my message. I thanked him, picked up the duffle and found one of the chairs in the lobby and had a seat.

A half hour later I watched Elizabeth as she rode down the elevator, the back half of which was all glass. She wore a white T-shirt tucked into blue jeans, and black running shoes. The strap of her purse was slung over one shoulder. When she walked from the elevator over to where I sat, the eyes of every man followed her. Including mine. I had to admit, she moved with the kind of grace most of us dream of, but sadly never achieve.

I stood and we embraced and shared a long, slow kiss. If public displays of affection bothered her, she didn't show it. She took my hand and we walked out the front doors. She pulled a slip out of her pocket and handed it to the valet and a few minutes later, her Mercedes stopped in front of us.

She glanced at me, expectantly, and I fished a five out of my wallet and tipped the valet. He smiled a thank you and handed me the keys. I used the fob to unlock all the doors and opened the passenger side for Elizabeth. She got in and I shut the door. I made my way to the driver side, stopping long enough to toss my duffle into the back seat, then got in behind the wheel.

It took me a moment, but I finally figured out the built-in GPS and entered the address for the cemetery in Columbus. It could be an easy drive up I-71 for most of the trip, passing through Cincinnati on the way, with a total drive time of a bit over three hours.

I got an early morning call from Winston and there was both good and bad news. The good news was there was no one already in the cemetery waiting. I figured if we were going to get there early, then the bad guys were likely to do the same. Winston would keep watch on the cemetery to let us know if someone showed up early to set up.

The bad news was there were many houses nearby and if they had access to any of them, then any person in the cemetery would be an easy shot with a rifle. Not much we could do about it, so there was no real point in worrying about it.

"Mind if I roll down my window?" I asked.

"No. I like the breeze."

I hit the buttons and rolled down all the windows, but left the air conditioner on high, getting the best of both worlds. The Mercedes, an E class coupe, purred down the highway. Not exactly the kind of car which blends in, but Elizabeth was anything but normal.

"So what did you do with the rest of the day?"

"I needed time to take care of some business. Then I found a place where I could be pampered. I took a long bath, with a few extra perks. Why? You worry I spend time with another man?"

I laughed.

"No. I really couldn't care less. You're a big girl, you can do what you like."

She shot me the bird and started flipping through the dial on the satellite radio. I thought about what she asked me and wondered if I did care. I wasn't sure one way or the other. To say I was conflicted would be an understatement. What I did know, it made me realize I needed to get past my current rut where Samantha was concerned. There was no way to know how many more days I would have on this planet. How many of them could I spend pining away like a love sick puppy?

Traffic was light with only a minor delay going through Cincy because of a jack-knifed big rig. Dublin Cemetery was on the north-west outskirts of Columbus, so we took I-270 around the city and got off on US 33 East. From there it was less than a mile to the cemetery.

I raised the car windows and we drove past the front entrance and then circled the block, checking out the area from all sides. The Mercedes windows were fully tinted and I wasn't worried about someone seeing me. I'd made sure on the way up we weren't followed and I kept an eye in the rearview mirror to make sure we didn't pick one up while we were here.

I pulled into the parking lot of a middle school across the street from the cemetery where we would have a full view of the entrance and texted Winston to let him know we were on the scene and he could take a break and grab some lunch. When Elizabeth looked at me questioningly, I told her I'd texted my team to let them know I'd arrived on the scene. She seemed satisfied and began to search the radio for a different station.

I got a "thumbs up" picture in text response and Elizabeth and I settled in for our turn keeping watch. I used the power button on the side of the seat to lower the seat until my head was barely above the bottom of the window, trying to keep a low profile. Elizabeth matched me and we let the car run for a bit, keeping the interior nice and cool.

"How do you want to handle this when it comes time for the meet?" I asked.

"I have looked at a map of the area. I will meet them as they have asked. I will drive in with the car. There is a park to the west and I think it best you enter this way, no?"

"Monterey Park. I saw it on the map as well. Good entrance point. There is a tree line I can use to make my approach and get some cover. Looks to be a fair-sized mausoleum near the end of the circle. I will work my way as close as possible using it for extra cover. Are you sure you want to do this?"

"But of course. I am on your side now. I like you. And I don't like them. I will help you with this Preston Deveraux."

"And after? What's next for you?"

She shrugged a shoulder. "I always have offers. I may go back to Europe. Many things happening. Many opportunities for intelligence work. And the pay is good. Very good. Will you miss me?"

I smiled, saying nothing. We spent the next hour sitting and watching, neither of us speaking, until my phone beeped with Winston saying he was back on the job. I raised my seat upright, Elizabeth following suit and I was impressed. I never saw Winston leave or return. I was tempted to ask him where he was holed up, but didn't.

I pulled out of the school parking lot and we drove into downtown Columbus, killing time. Elizabeth wanted to see the Franklin Park Conservatory and Botanical Gardens, saying the gardens reminded her of where she grew up. To me, they were a bunch of flowers and my only thought was how much weeding would need to be done.

When it got closer to dinner time we made our way back to Dublin, hung a right at the Convention Visitors Bureau and pulled into the Dublin Village Tavern. I was hungry and you have to eat when you can.

The tavern, an Irish pub with a Victorian feel, suited the bill just fine. I ordered the Irish Kettle dinner, simmered corned beef, Irish bangers and vegetables, while Elizabeth got the meatloaf. We both ordered Guinness to wash it down.

We made small talk until the waiter brought us our food and we tore into it. The corned beef was excellent and Elizabeth devoured her meatloaf. Lord, I do love a woman who likes to eat. I can't tell you how many times I'd take a girl to dinner and I would finish off half a cow in the time it would take them to eat a small salad. Elizabeth ate like it would be her last meal.

And I did the same. For all I knew it would be. When we finished we got back in the car, crossed the Scioto River and found a park on the other side, pulling up near the river's edge. We got out and wandered down to the river bank and spent the next hour stretched out, watching the sun sink lower in the west. The river wandered slowly by, the current in no hurry to get to where ever the ultimate journey would be.

The day was hot, the woman next to me hotter and for a

bit it was easy to forget why we were there: to kill a man, perhaps several, depending on who Deveraux brought with him.

My phone beeped, a new text from Winston. The only activity in the cemetery during the afternoon was a backhoe digging a new grave in the area where they wanted us to meet. He added several people came in and out to pay respects at one grave site or another, but no one stayed overly long.

An hour before the meeting time, we left the location next to the river and drove to Monterey Park. I snagged the duffle from the back seat and she got out, moving behind the wheel. She pulled out, planning on driving a few blocks down, waiting for the appointed time. I watched her go and I felt a pang of worry. I tried hard not to be a chauvinist pig, but the last two times Samantha went with me on a job, she ended up in the hands of Satan's minions—the last time with a demon buried so deep in her brain, the only way to get him out was to shoot her.

I knew Elizabeth was different, having been trained to be on the front lines. Hell, she was paid to be on the front lines. But my track record with women wasn't great. Lord's will be done, right?

I crossed the tennis courts and waited behind a stand of trees where I could see, barely, the place where she was to meet with Deveraux. I wondered if he would really show. I wondered if he would be surprised to see me. I hoped so.

The next fifty minutes went by slowly and I could feel my adrenaline ramp up. These are the moments I live for: brief moments of intense violence. Me against them, with the ultimate prize on the line: my life.

I knew Winston could be counted on to back me up. We'd seen enough action together and the man worked well under pressure. Nothing seemed to faze him. Elizabeth was the wild card. We knew nothing about her, how she would hold up if and when the bullets started flying. She talked a good game and she exuded the kind of confidence you can't fake, but I couldn't be sure until the moment came. I only hoped it wouldn't be her last.

I also needed to keep in mind she could be leading me into a trap. True, she could have killed me several times over, as she herself pointed out. It would make no sense to keep me alive only to bring me here to die. But I'd seen many strange things over the last nine months.

Time would tell. And it would tell soon. Through the leaves I watched as the Mercedes eased down the cemetery's main drag, pulled into the circle and came to a stop. She parked so the driver's side window faced me, rolling down both windows and turning off the car waiting. But not for long. A Lincoln Town Car made its way into the cemetery and into the circle, coming around the opposite way from the Mercedes, parking so the cars were nose to nose.

Elizabeth pushed her door open and stepped out, leaving the door open and standing behind it, keeping her hands low and out of sight. I could see the butt of a hand gun tucked into the jeans in the small of her back. A moment later, the doors of the town car opened and four men got out. One of them was Preston Deveraux.

Show time.

CHAPTER FIFTEEN

The sun dropped nearly to the horizon and it was behind me as I crossed the street into the tree line bordering the cemetery. Other than the two cars and the five people near them, the place was empty. Well, of live people. It was full of dead people. And one way or the other, the total of dead would be going up.

I unzipped the duffle and pulled out my Heckler and Koch UMP, the gun of choice for shooting a lot of rounds quickly and accurately. It was a change from my usual H and K MP5, but the UMP used larger cartridges and sometimes I have to shoot very large things which don't always want to stay down. I slipped an extra magazine into the back pocket of my jeans.

I needed to be careful. A residential area surrounded the cemetery and I didn't want a stray round to miss and find its way into someone's home. Collateral damage was not an option.

I took out one of my coms, hung it around my ear and switched it on. I texted Winston to do the same. A moment later I heard a quick series of three clicks in my ear to let me know he was plugged in and ready to go.

I stashed the duffle behind a large oak and slowly eased my way up to the mausoleum which would put me about forty yards from the two cars and with only the newly dug grave between us. The backhoe remained parked a few feet away, ready to push the dirt pile back into place.

I passed several headstones, some with kind words for the dead. "Loving Husband, Father and Son" and so on. It made me wonder about what would be on my tombstone when I died. If I even got a tombstone. I could end up dying in some backwoods place and buried where no one would ever find me.

Even if I got the full funeral, American flag and all, what would go on mine? My mother dreamed of grandkids, but the dream became less likely the day I became the Hand of God. With Mikey dead, my mother was likely to die with no grandchildren.

I shook off the thoughts and tried to get my head back into the game. I could hear Deveraux and Elizabeth talking, but not quite what was being said. I reached the mausoleum without issue, got onto my stomach and belly-crawled my way around the corner, keeping low behind a hedge row which lined both sides of the mausoleum.

A flower pot capped off the end of the hedge, a bronze colored pot holding some type of blue lily. The pot and hedge left enough room for me to see what was going on and I was now close enough to hear the conversation, but it wasn't going well.

Deveraux's men spread out, one starting to walk down the other side of the Mercedes, the other two took up positions on both sides of Deveraux's car, trying to see the whole cemetery at once. No one had guns out. Yet. Deveraux stayed behind his own door, much like Elizabeth, his hands crossed and resting on the door frame.

Elizabeth motioned with her head in the direction of the man moving to flank her and said, "If your man moves another foot, I will kill him."

The man froze and looked to Deveraux, who motioned for him to stop. The man did so, but squared up, with the car between him and Elizabeth.

Deveraux held his hands out to his sides, a smile on his face, but not in his eyes. "I thought we were all friends here, Elizabeth," he replied.

"What was it one of your presidents say? Trust but verify? Me? I trust no one. Especially a man who says he will bring me money for information but who gets out of his car empty-handed. Where is the money?"

Deveraux shrugged and slipped his hands into the pants pockets of what I assumed was an Italian tailor-made suit. "About that. I don't think I'll be paying you anything. Will I, Elizabeth?"

I saw Elizabeth stiffen and could tell she expected trouble.

"If you think you can cheat me, then you know nothing," she hissed.

"Thanks to the Lord of Light, I know everything there is to know about you. You've been a very naughty girl and he is very upset with you. You have not been doing what you promised him you would do. He sent me here to ask you why not?"

Holy crap. The Lord of Light meant Satan to these dumb asses. I knew making promises to Satan usually came with some pretty stiff eternal strings attached. Ask my brother how it turned out for him. Eternal damnation was his normal choice of payment. Was Elizabeth another lost soul? Or had she made him a different promise. Like to deliver my head on a platter?

Elizabeth relaxed visibly, the tension in her stance melting away. "Why not? Because I chose not. You should have brought my money. Time for you to leave now."

Deveraux lost the smile. "You're right. It is time for me to leave. And you're coming with me. Now. You can ride with me. One of my men will follow in your car."

"I think not." And then things happened very fast.

When I was a kid, I was fascinated with who history thought was the fastest gunman in the Wild, Wild, West. Many thought it was Wild Bill Hickok. Others claimed it was Johnny Ringo, who took on Wyatt Earp and died under mysterious circumstances.

I would practice facing my bedroom mirror, over and over, wearing a huge white Stetson hat my dad got me for my birthday one year, along with pearl-handled fake six shooters. I would draw, fire and then blow the pretend smoke from the end of the gun. I got to where I was fast. It has paid off many times over my career.

She was faster than I ever could have been. Her hand flew to the gun tucked into the back of her jeans, then her arm straightened, pointed through the car window and she pulled the trigger, shooting Deveraux's thug in the stomach before he could so much as take a breath. Her hand was a blur I could barely follow. Damn.

The gun's sound was large in the quiet of the night. I could almost picture the entire neighborhood stopping whatever they were doing and trying to decide if what they heard was a gun shot or a car backfire.

In a moment they would have no doubts. I rose to a shooting position, watching as Deveraux's two men pulled guns from shoulder holsters, and started to draw a bead on Elizabeth.

Using the car door for cover, she crouched and headed to the back of the car, while Deveraux dove inside his, pulling the door closed behind him. I squeezed off a quick three shot burst from the UMP, taking one of the men down. From somewhere off to my right, I heard another shot and the second man was down for the count, neither having fired a shot. Score one for Winston.

I moved from my covered position and closed in on the Town car, with plans to air out the backseat where Deveraux was hiding. The car's driver must have dropped the car into reverse as the rear wheels spun gravel, dragging the car backwards and away.

I pushed the switch on my UMP to full auto and squeezed the trigger. Bullets hammered the front windshield, six-hundred rounds a minute, but all they did was spider the glass. Bullet proof glass. To stop the kind of rounds I was firing, I knew the windows must be made from two inches of a polycarbonate and lead glass layers.

Elizabeth moved into view, firing her own shots at Deveraux, but doing no more damage than I did. The car did a swerving three point turn, tires churning up the grass and knocking down a tombstone, and floored it down the cemetery drive.

I emptied the thirty round clip, dropped the magazine and pulled the spare from my back pocket, then slapped it in and got off a few more rounds before the Town car made it to the street. The tires squealed as it swerved into traffic and disappeared from view. The body of the car was punctured with dozens of bullet holes, but my guess is the people inside were protected by bullet proof plating.

I dropped my gun to my side, frustrated and pissed. I turned to Elizabeth, my mind flooding with questions, when her eyes went wide, and she grabbed me by the front of my shirt, lifted me off my feet and threw me into the newly dug grave as easily as I would push a small child to the ground.

A fraction of a second later, a bullet passed through the space she tossed me out of, and struck her in the chest, causing her to stagger. A clean shot, center mass. Laying on my back in the grave, I could see her face travel from shock, to anger. Yet she did not fall to the ground dead.

Winston's voice shouted in my ear, "Mausoleum to your right."

I stood, my head barely clearing the top of the hole, facing the mausoleum, and let loose, with Winston doing the same. The gunman who had snuck up behind me, followed the same path I had moments before. He danced in place as each bullet struck him, then fell to the ground dead.

I quickly scanned the area for another shooter, but found none and turned to face to Elizabeth. She stood there for a moment, then raised her shirt and looked at the wound. A black hole showed where the bullet entered, slightly below and between her breasts. She let the shirt fall back into place and then she sprinted past me to the dead shooter and began kicking and stomping him, over and over.

I was stunned. She should be dead. In my ear, Winston asked, "How is she still alive? Man, she was shot. I saw her take the bullet for you. How's she still breathing?"

I pulled myself out of my would-be grave, walked over to her, my gun raised and pointed at her head, my blood frozen in my veins. I knew how. The strength to throw me around like a rag doll, the incredible speed drawing her gun, taking a rifle shot and living to talk about it? A deal made with Satan?

She was a vampire.

CHAPTER SIXTEEN

A vampire.

I'd been sleeping, eating and driving around with a vampire. Elizabeth stopped stomping the man on the ground, took a step back, her breathing still hard. The man's body was barely recognizable, with every bone from the neck up crushed flat, blood and gore spreading on the ground where his head used to be and spattered over her black shoes.

She watched me for a moment, her face expressionless. Then she slowly tucked her gun back into her jeans at the small of her back, her movements exaggerated, my guess in hopes of keeping me calm.

Satan allowed twelve people, twelve truly evil people, to have a second chance at life on earth. His versions of the twelve disciples. When they died the second time, they were stuck in Hell forever. But while back on earth, they were directed to do Satan's bidding and cause as much chaos as humanly possible.

I'd fought one once before by the name of Eamon. A demented little prick who died the first time during the potato famine in Ireland back in the 1800's. He'd nearly beaten me to a pulp before Samantha took his head off with a sword. Samantha told me they'd been the inspiration for the vampire legends from centuries ago.

There are several ways to kill them. You can burn them, grind them up, or cut off their heads. I did have a short sword, but it was in my duffle behind the oak tree.

"A frickin' vampire? Really?"

She shot me a dirty look. "We hate the name vampire. We are not vampires. Can we help it if humans can't understand us, so they make up things?"

"But you don't deny it?" I'd pressed the button on my com so Winston could hear the conversation. I could only imagine what he thought.

"No, I don't deny it. I am one of the *Infernus Domini*. But I wish to no longer be so. I wish to…change."

"Change? You wish to change? A vampire wants to change. Sure. And I want to be a jockey in the Kentucky Derby, but that ain't happenin' either."

She tilted her head, like a dog does when it hears a dog whistle. "We must go. The police are on the way. I can hear the sirens."

I could not, but then again I didn't have super human hearing. "We need to go? Sister, I'm not going anywhere else with you."

"If you wish to stop what this Deveraux has planned, then you and I must work together to stop him. It is the only way."

I could now faintly hear the sirens. She moved by me, walking to the Mercedes. "What will it be, Hand of God? Without me and my contacts, you will have rough time stopping this man."

I stood still for a moment, then made my decision. "Wait one second."

I jogged back to the oak, grabbed my duffle, ran to the Mercedes and threw my gear in the back. The vamp got in behind the wheel and I hopped into the passenger seat.

"What are you doing," Winston practically yelled in my ear.

"Following my instincts. Get away from here. I will call you later."

I turned off the com-link, reached behind me and tossed it into my duffle bag.

The vamp floored the Mercedes and it jumped forward, her natural reflexes matching the response of the car effortlessly. We came out of the cemetery, turned left and hit the ramp for I-270. Looking over my shoulder I could see the cops coming around the corner and then heading into the cemetery. Won't they have fun?

She eased the car into traffic and punched the cruise button. She reached over and turned on the radio, and I quickly turned it back off.

"What, we talk now?" she asked.

"Hell yes, we talk now. Why are you really doing this? What's you game plan?"

She didn't answer at first. Then in a quiet voice said, "You have never been to Hell. If you had, you would know why."

She was right. I'd never been to Hell. But Satan gave me a taste of what Hell would be like for my brother, the day he visited me in my office. The vision lasted less than a minute. The memory would haunt my nightmares for as long as I lived.

"But why now? How old are you?" It was weird. When Satan gave the people he chose a second time at bat, they came returned in the same condition they were when they died. Elizabeth must have died young. She was nearly flawless.

"I am sorry. But I am not permitted to discuss such things. I am older than you, which is all you need know."

"What did you do to deserve another chance among the living?" There were only twelve of them at any one time. Satan did not send back low level evil people. Only the crème de la crème of the most wicked people to have ever lived got the call.

"Many bad things. More bad things than we have time to discuss. What does it matter? I am one of the damned. I would like not to be."

"*Infernus Domini.* My Latin is a bit rusty. Inferno Master?"

"Inferno Lords. Lords of the Inferno. I wish to no longer be such." She paused for a few beats. "You know what I am. Yet you come with me. I am surprised at this."

"Like you said earlier, you could have killed me any one of a number of times, but didn't. I still don't trust you, but I am curious. I am trying to understand what you want from me."

"The final battle for who will sit in Heaven is drawing closer. From all I see, I am on the losing team. When we lose the last battle, then I will be back in Hell. Maybe it is not possible to be redeemed. But I think so. So I will do what I can to help you."

There is no doubt not going back to Hell would be incentive enough for anyone. It wasn't exactly Club Med, even for those who were high in the good graces of the Lord of Evil.

On the other hand, I don't think a tiger can change its

stripes even if she wanted to do so. Mikey sold his soul to Satan and it was clear he could not be saved. True, he wasn't trying to be saved, so I guess he didn't work as a blueprint.

If I was a betting man, switching sides because you wanted to live in a better home in the end was not reason enough to be saved. Not like I was the man to make the decision. One thing I did know, it was my job to kill the person sitting in the driver's seat.

"And if you can't be saved? What then?"

"There is no way to know if I can or can't. I can only do what I can. I must. But I am afraid. For maybe the first time in my life, I am afraid."

Good call on that one. "I'm not sure how I'm even supposed to respond to what you're saying."

"Will you help me? To find redemption?"

"I can't help you find what doesn't exist. I can talk to some people. See what they think. But this is a longshot, you know this, right?"

"What else can I do, Victor? You tell me?"

A single tear tracked down her cheek. It did make her appear more human. Yet for all I knew, this was part of her shtick. She claimed she was good at intelligence work and playing different rolls would come easy to someone in her line of work. Was she playing me? Certainly. Was the tear genuine? Perhaps.

All I could do was run out the string and see what happened. And be ready for anything. At least I now knew what I was dealing with. Hells bells, riding with one of Satan's top killers. It felt like riding down the highway with a sleeping cobra. When it woke up, what would happen next? If nothing else, it did give me a chance to learn a few things.

"A few other questions. When you got shot, did it hurt?"

"Not like it would have before my rebirth." She raised her T-shirt and I could see the bullet wound was no longer there, the blackened hole now a slight smudge on her skin. "It is more like discomfort. But I heal again, quickly."

"Can Satan track where you are? Does he have like a spiritual connection?"

"No. We are independent. Once we are sent back, we have free will. But rebellion against the Lord of Light by one of the Inferno Lords has never happened. I am the first. It means when I die, if I go back to Hell, then my punishment will be worse than you or I can ever imagine. I have risked all for a chance to be redeemed."

"Do you keep in touch with the other eleven Inferno Lords? Do you guys have like a clubhouse? Membership dues?"

"You are a silly man. There are no dues. Once a year we must meet, all in the same place, with the Lord of Light. If we cannot make it, we must get word to Lord of Light."

"Let me make a suggestion. If you do wish to ever get to Heaven, then I suggest you stop calling Lucy the Lord of Light. Just sayin'. When is the next group meeting?" Lucy was the pet name Dominic Montoya had for Lucifer. I kept up the tradition.

"It is always the same night. The last night of October."

"You can't be serious? Halloween?" These guys were trying hard to meet every stereotype.

"Once again, people take what they don't understand, and create something they can deal with. It was not uncommon for the Lords to leave the meeting and terrorize whatever country we were in for the rest of the night."

"Where will the next meeting take place?"

"We never know. The month before I will have a dream which will tell me where to be. It is up to me to show. I will not be there this year, no matter what happens. Refusing to join this Deveraux to meet with the Lord of—my former master, declares my rebellion. I am now on a path with no return."

Sucks to be you, I thought. But if I could find out where they were meeting and the exact time, perhaps I could find a way to wipe out all twelve at one time.

But as soon as I started to think "what if" in my head, I just as quickly thought "why bother?" Even if I managed to kill all of them, Lucifer would tap twelve more on the shoulder and send them back to torture and torment all over again.

Lord, I needed a drink. I remembered my uncle used to carry a flask around of "tea." The only thing the contents of the flask and tea, however, had in common was the color, as it was normally filled with cheap Irish whiskey. Right now? I would have given anything to have a flask in my duffle. My North Carolina flask sat on the end table in my room at the mission.

My phone beeped and I pulled it out, expecting to find a text from Winston berating me for losing my mind. Instead, it was Kurt. He found something in the hacker's computers and needed to talk to me right away. I texted him indicating I would call him in a minute.

"Is that the person you had at the cemetery? I asked you not to bring anyone else with us."

"What was it you said before? Trust but verify? I wanted to make sure I had someone there watching my back. If you were on my side, he was watching yours, too."

She pouted for a moment, then put her hand on my thigh, running it to my crotch. "I forgive you."

I took her hand in mine and moved it over to her side of the car. "I think under the circumstances, I would like to keep the hand of an Inferno Lord away from Mr. Happy. Nothin' personal."

She once again stuck her tongue out at me. "Your loss," she replied.

Losing a part of me was exactly what I wanted to avoid.

CHAPTER SEVENTEEN

Kurt answered my call on the first ring.

"Hey, big guy. How did things go up in Columbus? Did you get him?"

"No. I don't think so." I filled him in on what happened, leaving out the part about the woman next to me being a vampire.

"Well, that sucks. We'll get him. Just a matter of time. And I may have a clue to what they have planned. You said they wanted you dead now because they have something in the works and I think you're right. I've been making headway into cracking the files on Benedict Arnold's computer. I've gotten into his emails and one thing they asked him to do was to keep track of what this dude is doing in Alexandria, Virginia. They told him it's a high priority that he must keep a cyber-watch on the guy's computers."

"Alexandria, Virginia? Any idea what he's doing for them? What's his name?"

A fraction of a second passed before both Kurt and the vamp said the name at the same time, "Isaac Peck."

I stared for a moment at the vamp, while Kurt said, "Not sure exactly what he's doing for them. I'll try to hack into Peck's system later tonight. Ruth Anne and I are going to see *The Rocky Horror Picture Show*. I'll hit it hard when we return from the movie. Well, once Ruth Anne goes to bed. Sometimes she wants to, well, you know," he stammered.

"No. She sometimes wants to...what?" I liked yanking Kurt's chain. He may now be the "new" Kurt, but there was still a lot of the "old" Kurt left in him. I could practically see the blush coming through the phone.

"Dude, I'm not telling you details. I don't tell war stories.

That's between us. Sheesh." He hung up on me and I put the phone away.

"How did you know who my friend was going to name?"

She drove for another mile, the darkness crowding around us, before she answered. I watched her closely in the glow of the dashboard lights.

"Because that is the name of a man they pay me to get close to in Alexandria. I was the first contact. This could not be coincidence."

"Did they tell you why?"

"No. They did not share the why. But they want him for a project they were working on."

"Why you? What did they tell you?"

"They want me to get him to fall in love with me. To get him to do what I ask. I do this. He is very needy. I don't think he spend much time with a woman. It was easy."

"So you slept with him. Is this why you slept with me? To get me to do what you wanted?"

"Of course I slept with him. He is what is called…a genius. But he think more with what is in his pants than his brain when it comes to beautiful women," she stated in serious tone. "And no, I do not sleep with you to get you to do what I want. I sleep with you because it is what I want."

I'm not sure I believed her when it came to her motives for sleeping with me, but I didn't make an issue of it. "What type of genius? What does he do?"

"Again. Not sure. He make robots or something. When I had him wrapped around my finger, I asked him to work with this one guy. Told him it would make me happy. He agreed. Then later they pulled me away from him to come meet you."

"You were supposed to get me to fall in love with you, too?"

"Yes. They bring me to Louisville, but then you showed up in North Carolina killing one of their men, and they had me change plans to meet them in Tennessee. But they were pigs and I not like them. Then I meet you, and I made a decision to help you instead and here we are."

Once again, I'm sure there was a grain of truth in what she was telling me, but how much? "You said you introduced

Peck to a man. What's the guy's name?"

She shook her head. "I don't know. But I do have his picture. I take it the night I introduce him to Isaac. I not tell him I do this."

She slipped her phone out of her front pocket, thumbed to her photos app and pulled up the picture, showing it to me. "You know this man?"

I took a long look at the picture and searched my memory. "Yeah. I know him." The name came to me. "Brad. His name is Brad. Does that sound familiar?"

"I never know his name. He met Isaac and me one night out at dinner. He sat down and I left. I told Isaac he must do what this man say, if he and I were to stay lovers. Isaac would have killed his own mother, if I'd asked him to do so. Who is this man?"

"The last time I saw him, he was driving for Congressman Cyrus Tyler." In Elizabeth's photo he was still sporting his flat top haircut. I remember he mentioned he was ex-Marine. "My guess is he does a lot more than drive. If this is the man who was meeting with your Isaac, then you can bet Tyler is mixed up in this. You know about Tyler, right?"

"We have never met. But yes, I know of this man. He is one of the main followers of my former master. I understand he is also big in your government. I spend most of my time in Europe. They brought me to this country for Isaac. Then you."

"Gee, thanks. Let me see what I can find out about Isaac Peck."

I tapped my screen until I found the Google app, typed in Peck's name and hit the search button. A second later, several entries popped up, including the top heading under news. The headline? "**Young Entrepreneur Murdered at Work**."

I pulled up the article from the *Washington Post*, dated this morning indicating he was shot three times. There was no forced entry and nothing stolen, as far as anyone could tell. He was the owner of a company called Bio-Enhanced Robotics. The cops had yet to develop any leads. They found it curious he had given the staff Friday afternoon off, having never done so in the past, fueling speculation he was meeting with someone.

The rest of the article was dedicated to his background

and his philanthropic endeavors. I closed the app and turned off my phone.

"Seems your former boyfriend is dead. Someone shot him yesterday." I gave her the run down on the newspaper article.

"This cannot be coincidence. We must go there."

"We are not going anywhere. If I decide to check it out, I will go on my own. I haven't decided what to do about you yet."

"You will take me with you. This I know." She smiled and I didn't like it.

"Look, Elizabeth. You saved my life and I thank you. You say you want to redeem your soul. I wish you luck. But when I say you won't be going with me, I mean it. I can't trust you as far as I can throw you." I didn't add in the thought I would also likely kill her, sooner rather than later.

"You will take me because I know something else you don't know," she paused and looked at me. "About Isaac."

"And what, pray tell, would that be?"

"Isaac was scared of this Brad, and who he worked for. They tell him not to keep any records of what he do for them. But he did. He called it his CYA file. You know what this mean?"

"Yeah. Cover Your Ass. Where did he keep it? Surely the cops have already found it."

She shook her head no. "They will not have. He hid the file where only he would find it. And one night he told me. I know where this file is and how to get it."

"O.K...Where and how?"

She wagged a finger at me. "I will not tell you. I will show you. You must take me with you."

"And if I refuse?"

"Then you will need much luck. If they kill Isaac, and try and kill you, then they are close to putting into action what they have planned. Perhaps you can find out what and stop them without the file. Perhaps not. Are you willing to run the risk?"

She had me over a barrel and she knew it. I needed to get a look at that file. No matter what Cy Tyler and his crew planned, I knew it was something horrific. I needed every edge possible and the things Peck hid in this file might give me one. But if it meant working with an Inferno Lord, was it worth it?

Would the ends justify the means? While I couldn't be

sure, I was fairly certain working with one of Satan's twelve super villains would not be something Joshua would want me to do. But if I didn't, and this was another plan to murder thousands of innocent children? Or release another plague on the world like the Watchers? Or worse?

When I was nothing more than a bounty hunter, I often worked with people who were only shades better than the ones I was hunting. Was this situation any different? Well. Yeah. Elizabeth was more than your average scum ball.

I would have to think carefully about what I did next. Another thought occurred to me. What if the goal had not been to kill me, but to keep me occupied chasing phantoms which had nothing to do with the real objective? If so, Elizabeth could be leading me around by the nose, keeping me busy until it was too late.

We drove on through the night, neither of us talking, both lost in our own thoughts. When we got close to Louisville, I said, "Fine. You can go with me. I will need to make some plans and talk to my crew. If you do go, you will do what I tell you to do, when I tell you to do it. Understood?"

She blew me a kiss. "Of course, Victor. I will be an angel for you."

Wrong choice of words, lady, I thought. Your chance of being an angel ended a long time ago.

CHAPTER EIGHTEEN

It was after 1 a.m. when she pulled up to the Galt House drop off area. I was worn out, the adrenaline of the fight had worn off a long time ago. I started to get out of the car, but she put her hand over mine, stopping me.

She opened the car's console, took out a pen and then turned my hand over, writing a phone number on my palm. "This is my new cell number. The phone will be off, with the battery removed, until eight tomorrow morning. I will turn it on so you can call me. I give you fifteen minutes. After that, the battery is back out. I will not stay here tonight. You call me in the morning and let me know what you plan to do."

I glanced at the number, then back into her ice blue eyes. "What, you don't trust me?"

"No further than I can throw you. Though, I throw you a long way," she replied.

Thinking about how easily she threw me into the open grave, I knew she wasn't bragging, but stating the cold hard truth. "Suit yourself."

I climbed out of the car, opened the rear door, snagging my duffle. I walked around to the driver side window, and she rolled it down.

"If you run on me, I will dedicate my life to tracking you down and breaking that pretty little neck."

"I will not run. I promise you I will help. And I will."

She rolled the window up and drove off, leaving me standing there, thinking hard. I'd threatened her, trying to push her buttons, to get a reaction. She claimed she wanted to change, to find a way to redeem her soul. But how in the hell could I know if she really meant it?

She hadn't jumped at the bait, threatened me back, or seemed pissed. She'd answered in a matter-of-fact way, and left. If I'd hoped to learn something, I didn't.

I dragged my ass to my car parked in the hotel garage and returned to the mission. I took the long way, changing directions and moving slowly through downtown, watching for tails. Nada.

I pulled into the parking lot, grabbed my stuff and locked the car. I pushed through the front door and could see Brother Joshua's light in his office down the hallway. I wondered whether he ever slept.

I thought about heading to his office and hashing out what happened tonight, what I'd learned about Elizabeth, but decided to hell with it. I was tired and all I wanted right then was to go to bed. And that's what I did. I went to my room, kicked off my boots and fell into bed, still dressed. I drifted off to thoughts of Elizabeth and how both of us wanted the same thing: redemption. And that both of us might not get it.

If I dreamed, I didn't remember them the next morning. I woke up around seven, stiff and sore. I wrote her number down on a notepad, then ambled to the shower, cranked up the hot water, and worked out the kinks. By the time I got dressed and headed to J's office, I felt almost human. Almost.

His door was open, so I knocked on the door jam and stuck my head in the door. J was sitting behind his desk, as usual, calm and composed. Good thing because, occasionally, he found himself hosting the essence of the archangel, Uriel. I could generally tell when Uriel was with us because the man oozed power when the angel made an appearance. When the Watchers claimed possession of someone's body against their will, Joshua allowed Uriel to take control. Freaky.

Today, J was his normal self. The woman sitting in the chair opposite him, however, was anything but normal. She was tall, her long blonde hair tied back in a ponytail. Dressed in a white shirt, brown leather vest and pants, with what I thought of as elf boots, she looked like a Tolkien wet dream. The sword laying across her lap didn't hurt the look.

She turned to face me, her features hard and unforgiving. She had high cheek bones, a prominent chin and hazel eyes which held as much warmth as an Icelandic glacier. She looked me over like she was trying to decide if I needed to be welcomed or dispatched. I thought her sword hand may have twitched, but that might have been my imagination. She would not be the first woman to react that way around me.

The sword was some type of katana, the handle worked in silver with what looked like a family crest on the pommel.

"Nice toothpick you're carrying around. Bet it drives all the boys crazy."

Her eyes narrowed. "You might want to watch your tongue before I cut it out."

I laughed and looked to J. "Who's this Xena warrior princess wannabe?"

She stood, the sword held tight against her thigh. "I will not warn you again to watch your tongue. I would choose your next words carefully."

"Whoa, slow down, princess. I'm guessing when you were born, you missed the line where God handed out a sense of humor."

Joshua stood. "Mirsada, please. Victor, show our guest more respect. She is, after all, a fellow Hand of God."

The statement hit me like a thunderbolt. "Hand of God? I'm the Hand of God. You mean, there's more than one?"

She pointed at me with the sword, as incredulous as I was about the revelation. "This is the man you were telling me about? This...this..." She was at a loss for words.

"Yes," Joshua said to the woman. "Victor is the Hand of God we were talking about." Then to me he continued, "And, Victor, surely you must have guessed there was more than one Hand of God. This is a very large planet, after all. Victor McCain, meet Mirsada Vesela."

"To be honest, J., I've been too busy trying to kill things that were usually trying to kill me to stop and give it much thought."

Lowering her sword, Mirsada relaxed, but only by a smidgen. "I am sorry. I expected something different."

"Yeah, most women tell me that." I glanced between the two of them. "Where do you call home?"

She sat back down and I took the chair next to hers. "I

am from Bosnia, but was educated here in the States. I am tracking a woman I have reason to believe is here. And when I find her, I will then remove her head."

Bloody hell, I thought. Removing heads? Needing a sword? I knew the answer to my next question, but I asked it anyway. "This woman, does she have a name?"

"Yes. Elizabeth Bathory. The Countess of Blood. And a member of Satan's twelve demons let loose on Earth."

Hells bells, did I have to be right? Now I knew Elizabeth's last name, which tickled the back of my mind. I remembered reading about her when I was younger.

"Countess of Blood? I think I've heard of her. She's from your neck of the woods, right?"

Mirsada nodded. "Yes. She died the first time in the year 1614. She earned her name because of her torture and murder of nearly six-hundred and fifty young girls. She believed their blood could keep her young, taking baths filled with the blood of virgins. Following her death, she struck a deal with Satan to stay young forever, but this time instead of bathing in blood of young girls, she agreed to spill the blood of as many innocents as she can, no matter the age."

"Sounds like a real witch. I hope you catch up to her." I was stalling. I didn't want to tip my hand to what I knew until I got the chance to talk it over with J. But his next question torpedoed my delay tactics.

He asked, "This woman you have met, you said she sounded like she was from Europe and claimed to have worked for Hungarian intelligence. This cannot be a coincidence. Do you think this woman is Bathory?"

"I would like the chance to talk to you about what I think, in private." I looked at Mirsada. "No offense."

She practically seethed. "Of course you mean offense. If you know where this woman is, tell me. Now."

"Hold your horses, sister. This isn't your home base, it's mine. You have no right to come here and make demands."

"Enough," Joshua said. "Victor, we don't keep secrets from other Hands. If the woman you have met is Elizabeth Bathory, then share what you know."

"Starting with where she is," said Mirsada.

"I don't know where she is. And that's the truth." Only barely, as I had not called her yet this morning. I needed to be careful. I wanted time to think things through, but lying to Joshua would not be good for my eternal soul. "I suspect this woman is who you claim. Yet she saved my life and has information about the plans of Cyrus Tyler. They targeted me because they have something major in the works. She has offered to help me. As hard as it is to believe, she claims she wants to redeem her soul."

Mirsada laughed. "She is playing you. Like so many others in the past. Let me guess. She took you to bed? Am I right?"

It was all I could do to not blush. I didn't answer.

"This is what she does. She seduces men to get what she wants. Then she kills them."

"If she wanted me dead, then she could have killed me several times by now."

"Which means," Mirsada continued, "she has yet to get from you what she wants. The knife in the back is coming. You are too stupid to realize it."

"Stupid? Why do I get the feeling you don't play well with others. But what if you're wrong, and what she wants from me is to help her soul to go to Heaven? What then?" I looked to Brother Joshua. "Is such a thing possible?"

He steepled his fingers under his chin, thinking. "I don't know. It would be unprecedented. None of the Twelve has ever sought redemption before."

"But it's possible?"

"Yes," he replied. "I would think it possible."

"No, it is not," said Mirsada. "She cannot change. Will not. She is working for Satan and it will mean your death to trust her."

"And if I have no choice? If she holds the only key to stop Tyler? What then? What if killing her now means the death of thousands? Millions? The first time I ran into these wackos they planned to kill thousands of children. I stopped them, but barely. Until we know more, killing her is a risk."

For a long moment, Mirsada was silent. "She cannot be trusted." And that's all she would say.

"Hell, lady. I don't trust her. It's as much my job to kill her as it is yours. But I've seen what these guys are capable of doing. No matter what Tyler has planned, he needs to be stopped. She might be the key to bringing him down."

"And if it means your death?" she asked.

"Lord's will be done. What do you think, J?"

"It is not for me to tell you what to do. You are both the Hand of God. You must make your own choices and live with the consequences."

"You know, J, there are times you frustrate the hell out of me, you know that? You could tell me, but you won't."

"It comes down to—"

"Yeah, yeah, yeah. Free will. I know. But you have a direct pipeline to the Big Guy upstairs and could make this really simple for me." He started to say something, but I waved him off. "Never mind."

I stood and started for the door. Mirsada also stood and began to follow me. "Where do you think you're going?" I asked.

"You say she wants to help you. Which means she will contact you again. When she does I will be there as well. Where you go, I will also go."

"And if I tell you to kiss my ass? What then?"

"I have tracked her here. Do you really think you can lose me? I will be with you, no matter what you wish."

I appealed to Brother Joshua. "Dude. Really?"

He said, "One Hand of God has always extended cooperation to another Hand of God. In her own way, Mirsada is asking for your help. But again, the choice is yours."

"Great. Thanks a lot." I turned to face Mirsada. "If I allow you to come with me, you do as I say. My house, my rules. If you can't agree, then you're on your own. And I *will* lose you if you say no. Want to risk it? This isn't exactly my first rodeo. And I've already killed a vamp. How about you?"

She shot a look at Joshua. "This is true?" He nodded it was and her attitude softened. The way a mountain loses a few pebbles when a hard rain hits it.

"Your house, your rules. Unless the game changes. Then I use my rules."

"And no killing Elizabeth until I say so. I want your

word as the Hand of God you won't make her a head shorter until I say so. This is a deal breaker."

She walked to the door and picked up a small pack next to it, along with a sheath for her sword. She slid the katana home, the pommel still visible. "For now, I give you my word. I hope you will not be the death of both of us."

"That makes two of us," I thought.

CHAPTER NINETEEN

We stepped out into the steamy morning, the temperature already soaring. I glanced at Mirsada's outfit. "Doesn't the leather get a bit hot?"

"I am used to the feeling. I wear leather because it is stronger than regular cloth, better protection during a fight. The heat is but a minor inconvenience."

"Whatever floats your boat. Does Elizabeth know you are after her?"

"Yes. She does. It's one of the reasons she left Europe. I got close to finding her on two occasions. I made sure to burn her bridges behind her, trying to force her into the open. Her old contacts were no longer willing to protect her."

"Great. This should be a real joy." It was now eight a.m. straight up. I took out my phone, along with the note with Elizabeth's number and called her.

She answered, "You are punctual. Rare for most men."

"Yeah, right. Whatever. Everyone's a comedian. Are you ready to hit the road?"

"Yes. I will drive."

"Not this time. I get to drive. And we will have someone with us."

"Your friend who was at the cemetery?" she asked.

"Not exactly. An old friend of yours from back home. Woman who dresses in all leather, looks like an elf? Ring any bells?"

Mirsada narrowed her eyes and tightened the grip on her sword, but otherwise remained quiet.

I could hear Elizabeth hiss. "Mirsada. She is there? With you?"

"Yes. She is. And she is coming with us to Alexandria."

"I cannot allow this. I will not travel with this woman. She wants me dead."

"Then I guess you didn't mean it, when you said you wanted to find redemption. She's going with me to Alexandria and she has given me her word she will not try and kill you, without my O.K. When a Hand of God gives their word, they are bound to keep it. Time to prove you meant what you told me, Elizabeth."

For the longest time, she did not say anything. I raised my face to the sky, letting the sun bake my skin, but it did little to warm the cold I felt deep inside.

"This woman. She will kill me. No matter what she promises. She will kill me. You know this, right?"

"Elizabeth, she won't. You have to trust me. As long as you play it straight, she won't lay a hand on you. She will have to go through me first. But understand, you betray us, all bets are off and we both come for you. Time to decide if you want that chance at redemption. You have to trust me."

"You ask much, Victor McCain. She has told you who I really am? My past?"

"Yes. She told me who you are. You are Elizabeth Bathory, the Countess of Blood."

"And yet you say you will protect me? Why?"

Good question. Was I trying to save my brother all over again? Did I not learn anything from what happened with Mikey? The last time I trusted one of the damned, it lead to Dominic Montoya being murdered, setting me on the path I now traveled. This time it could be me taking a bullet, moving over to the ever-after. Yet Brother Joshua didn't say she couldn't be saved. Only that it had never happened.

"Elizabeth, you say you want to help me. I believe you. I'm not sure why, but I do. I will protect you, as long as you keep you word. In return you have my word, as the Hand of God. The decision is yours."

"Then I will trust you, Victor McCain. With my immortal soul. Bring this woman. My life is now in your hands."

"Where do you want us to pick you up?"

"I am here." The phone disconnected and Elizabeth

stepped out of the doorway of the building across the street. She stood on the sidewalk, waiting. She once again wore jeans, a white T-shirt and boots, a small travel bag slung over one shoulder.

Mirsada saw her and drew her sword faster than I could have pulled my gun, the bright sunlight glinting off the slender blade. She took a step in Elizabeth's direction, but pulled up short when I moved in front of her.

"Out of my way, Hand. It is time for me to end this."

"You gave me your word, Mirsada. Put the sword away or I will take it from you. To kill her, you will have to kill me first."

Mirsada flicked the sword up, the point digging into the skin under my chin. She moved in close, her face inches from mine. "She is a monster. She will kill us both, given the chance. Join me, Hand of God, and together we can take her before she can leave."

"No. By all that's holy, no. Your word, Mirsada. Does it mean nothing?"

Her lips pulled back from her teeth, a look both feral and fearsome at the same time, and for a moment I thought she would ram the tip of her sword straight up through my chin and out the top of my head. But instead, she dropped it and re-sheathed the blade.

I ran my finger to where the sword had been and came away with a drop of blood. Close. I glanced over at Elizabeth, but she had not moved. With her improved hearing, I knew she'd heard every word. She had a brief chance to escape, to run for it, but she never moved. Trust in me? Maybe.

I unlocked the car and stowed my gear in the rear of the Ford. I held out my hand for Mirsada's bag. She gave it to me and I tossed it in with mine. She held on to the sword.

I got behind the wheel while Mirsada got into the back seat. I looked into the rearview mirror. "No backseat stabbing, O.K.?"

I got no response other than her hard stare. I started the car and pulled up to the curb in front of Elizabeth. She stared for a moment at Mirsada in the back seat holding her sword, then got into the front passenger seat. She did her best to ignore the woman sitting behind her with the deadly weapon.

I asked Elizabeth if she had an address in Alexandria.

"Yes. We go to the Jones Point Lighthouse. It is on the Potomac River, in Alexandria."

She gave me an address and I programmed the GPS for the trip. It did its calculations and told me the trip would take about nine and a half hours to reach our destination, putting us there late in the evening. Nine and a half hours in a car with two pissed off women: one carrying a sword, the other imbued with hellish abilities sitting just inches from me.

The road trip from Hell. Almost literally. Heaven must love me.

CHAPTER TWENTY

Brad Stiles turned into the parking garage of the Double Tree by Hilton on South Broad Street in Philadelphia and made his way to the back corner of the first level. He pulled into a spot next to a black BMW 3 series and turned off his car.

An attractive woman in her late fifties got out of the Beamer, pushed a button on her key fob, and popped open her trunk. Stiles got out of his car, doing the same thing. Walking around to the back, he picked up the wrapped box and carried it over to her vehicle and placed the box carefully into her trunk. Closing the door gently, he faced Dr. Teresa Collins.

"You're almost home, Doc. Perform the surgery tomorrow, as scheduled, and your part is finished."

She glanced around nervously, wringing her hands. "My daughter. When will I get my daughter?"

"For obvious reasons, we will need to hold on to her for a few weeks."

"I promise, I won't tell a soul what I did. I swear it. Please bring my baby home to me."

Dr. Collins' baby, Stiles knew, was thirty years old and a meth head. After getting hooked on prescription drugs, her daughter, Misty, started turning tricks to help support her habit, transitioning from crack to meth. She found her way onto the radar of the Church of the Light Reclaimed and Stiles arranged to have her picked up and admitted into a rehabilitation clinic. After several months, she came out the other side, clean and sober.

The Church found her a good paying job working as an admin for a local law firm, the owner of which was a long time member of the Church.

Dr. Collins at first, was over-joyed at her daughter's transformation. Then came the day they approached the good doctor with their plans and she had balked. Pressure needed to be applied.

Misty went on a business trip with the law firm, but never returned. The Church let Dr. Collins know they had her daughter and the only way she would return, alive and in one piece, was if she did what they wanted. Misty was Collins' only child and they knew she would come around. Eventually she relented and the plan moved forward.

Stiles said, "I tell you what, Doc, when the surgery is over, why don't you take some time off? Use whatever excuse you want. When you get the time off, I will take you to your daughter and you two can hang out until this all blows over."

A single tear tracked down her cheek. "You plan to kill us both, don't you?"

"Doc, that's not how we work. We make you a deal, you take it and we keep our end of the bargain. We already have the money we promised you in the numbered account in the bank in the Caymans. You and your daughter can live out your lives wealthy and well. By this time tomorrow, your part will be done. The surgery is scheduled for seven tomorrow morning, right?"

She nodded. "Yes. We asked him to arrive at 5:45 a.m. for registration. Surgery takes about an hour and a half." She hugged herself. "This means my career is over. All I've worked for will be gone."

"Look, Doc, we've gone to great lengths to see to it that you're not implicated. When the investigation into what happened cranks up, we've created a paper trail that will lead them to a white supremacist group in Georgia. They've been calling for someone to kill the Senator for years. Everything will point to them, not you. You will be completely in the clear. You have my word."

She walked back to her car and opened the door. Before getting in she said, "Your word? I only want my daughter. I do have some time coming to me. I can clear my schedule by Friday. I would greatly love to see my daughter."

She got in, closed the door and started the car. Backing out of the spot, Stiles watched her drive away. When she was gone, he pulled out a burner phone and dialed a number from memory.

A man answered and Stiles told him what he wanted and when.

"The charge will be twice the cost of the first doctor. There are two of them, after all," the man said.

"Not a problem. I will have the timing lined out by the end of the week. Go ahead and move into position."

The man hung up without saying another word and Stiles did the same. He got back into his car and a few moments later was pulling out of the garage and heading to D.C. The Nats lost the night before and he hoped they could turn things around today. He looked at his watch. If the traffic was good, he could even make it to the park and watch the game live.

Whistling *Take Me Out to the Ball Game* he decided a dog and beer at the park would make the day complete.

*****

I remember one long distance trip my family took to Gulf Shores, Alabama. I must have been around ten years old and the entire trip, Mikey and I fought in the back seat of dad's Oldsmobile. Even dad's threats of a major belt whipping couldn't stop us. Both of us were even afraid to fall asleep for fear of what the other brother might do to them. My mother still calls that vacation the "trip from hell."

Well mom, you ain't seen nothing until you take a long distance trip with a vamp and a Hand of God who want to kill each other. For long stretches of highway, the two would sit quietly, Elizabeth looking out the window, Mirsada staring at the back of her head. Then the same argument would begin again. Like the one which had been going on for the last few miles.

"Why don't you admit your plans to betray us, witch," Mirsada said to Elizabeth. "If you do, I promise your death will be quick. You have my word."

Elizabeth snorted. "Quick death? That can be arranged for you, too, bitch."

I did my best to listen to the music on the radio, pretending I was on my way to Disney World and this would all be over soon, but the problem was I wasn't traveling with Mickey and Goofy.

Mirsada opened her mouth to say something else, but before she could say a word, Elizabeth's hand came out of her bag, holding a Beretta Nano 9 mm, and she pointed it at Mirsada's nose.

"We must come to an agreement, you and I. You do not like me? I understand why. You want to kill me? I understand why. For what I did, in my past, perhaps I even deserve to die. But I make promise to Victor, to help him in any way I can to stop this Tyler. But I grow tired of your constant yapping, like some little dog. Yes, you have big sword, can take off my head. You are good, yes? But I can also kill you. Even easier than you can kill me, I think. Until such time as we find out if you really can be faster with the sword than I with my gun, may we please stop this fight? Let's help Victor. I may even let you kill me, when this is done. I grow tired of this life."

She pulled the gun back and slipped into her purse, and I let out the breath I'd been holding. For her part, Mirsada, who'd pulled her katana partially out, slipped it into the sheath.

I looked out my window at the car passing next to us and a woman stared at me, her mouth hanging open and her eyes wide. I smiled weakly and shrugged. Elizabeth leaned forward, locked eyes with the woman and mimicked shooting her with her finger. The other car sped off in front of us.

I glanced up and watched Mirsada in the rearview mirror and I could see her fighting for control of her anger, the battle playing out across her face. I could understand such anger. It filled me more often than it should or was even good for me. Towering anger, wanting to strike out at anyone or anything.

I didn't doubt she thought less of me for working with a vamp. Hell, I couldn't blame her either. When you become a Hand of God, there are things that go bump in the night and it's our job to slam them back into the deep dark pits they crawled out of and into oblivion.

Working with one, no matter what Elizabeth claimed, was a risky business. Often I went with my gut when it came to decisions and I was not often wrong. And my gut told me Elizabeth was sincere in trying to find her way to heaven. That didn't mean she wouldn't revert to her previous ways when things got tough. Mirsada's anger was understandable.

Mirsada didn't respond to Elizabeth's pistol-backed plea, but she did stop the haranguing, choosing to continue to watch the back of the vamp's head. One didn't need to be a mind reader to tell what she was thinking. Kill.

I wondered at her story. I'd become the Hand of God because of my vanity in thinking I could save my brother's soul proved incorrect, one time my gut had been wrong. I'd allowed Dominic Montoya to be murdered while trying to protect Mikey, even though I knew him to be evil personified. Montoya became the Hand trying to atone for years serving as a hit man for a Mexican drug cartel. One does not come to the job as the Hand of God from being a gentle keeper of souls. The job called for someone to be able to perform incredible acts of violence and to punish those chosen with extreme prejudice.

Mirsada brushed back a stray lock of hair behind one ear, and I could see her hand was scarred and rough, nails at the end of long fingers, cut short and devoid of nail polish. Fighter's hands.

She wore no makeup. Hell, it would be like putting makeup on a wildcat. If you were to stand her in a lineup with other women, you would take one look at her and say "warrior."

The contrast between her and Elizabeth was stark. Now that I knew Elizabeth's past, you could see the regal bearing in her movements, even after all these centuries. She was used to giving orders and confident in every fiber of her hellish being they would be obeyed. I had to guess being given near super human powers only made her feel even more the noble compared to the rest of us.

Mirsada, on the other hand, seemed to be wound tight, her intensity switched on, unable to ever turn it off. I wondered if she was comfortable in her own skin. Hour after hour, she never relaxed, her gaze staying almost strictly on Elizabeth, like two heat-seeking missiles.

Now that no one died in the exchange, I was very happy Elizabeth took steps to end the bickering. If she hadn't, I might have pulled my own gun out and used it on myself.

We stopped for a quick lunch at Wendy's and I learned

something else I didn't know about Infernal Lords. While they don't have to eat, some of them still enjoy eating food. In Elizabeth's case, she loved greasy cheeseburgers. Between the sex and her culinary tastes, she could almost be the perfect girl. Other than the whole "most evil woman who ever lived" thing.

Mirsada chose to eat a salad and drink water. I bet she also ran ten miles a day, did five-hundred sit ups without breaking a sweat, and saved puppies in her spare time.

I gave myself a mental slap. I needed to cut Mirsada some slack. She was here to kill a woman who, by her own admission, was evil. Or had been. And is there really a difference? Sure, Mirsada was incredibly intense. But I would bet that's what kept her alive. I'd nearly died several times over since taking the job and I was twice her size. Though size wasn't everything. She managed to get the point of her katana under my chin faster than I could blink.

After lunch, we returned to the highway and this time the tension seemed to have been cranked down a few notches. Perhaps breaking bread helped the two women come to some unspoken agreement.

Mile after mile drifted into the rearview mirror as we cruised down I-64 through the mountains of West Virginia, then headed north on I-81 through Virginia. It gave me time to think, especially about Samantha and what the future might hold.

And I didn't think it held much. Deep down inside, I knew a final confrontation was coming with her father and it likely would end with one or the other of us dead. Cyrus was the only family Samantha had left in the world, with her mother dying when she was very young.

What would it mean for the two of us if I ended up putting a bullet between his eyes? Most men, when they worried about a potential father-in-law, wondered how things would go at family gatherings or how protective they would be over their little girls. Here I was worried we might be taking each other out, with the victor burying the body in an unmarked grave. The irony made me laugh out loud, with both women in the car shooting me strange looks.

Samantha knew her father was rotten to the core, yet she loved him, much as I had my brother. While in her heart she might appreciate why I needed to whack her dad, forgiving me for doing so would be another matter.

I could picture the family Christmas parties, all of us standing in front of the fireplace for the family photo, with both Cy Tyler and I pointing guns at each other behind the backs of the rest of the family.

It was hard to imagine. Yet here I was in a car with a vamp on my way to try and ruin yet another one of the congressman's plans. I was willing to bet a vamp and Hand of God, let alone two Hands of God, had never worked together. Strange times.

Night had descended on Alexandria when we came to a stop not far from the Jones Point Lighthouse park front gate. I rolled down the windows and turned off the car, listening to the sounds of the world calling it quits for the day.

The lighthouse surprised me. I pictured a tall lighthouse like I'd seen on the coast of Massachusetts, stretching up into the night sky, but the Jones Point Lighthouse was not. This lighthouse was a two story clapboard building perched on the edge of the shore. The lighthouse tower sat in the middle of the roof, flanked on either end by a chimney. It looked like there was a smaller outbuilding off to one side.

During lunch I'd looked up the history of the lighthouse and park. The Jones Point Lighthouse was the only surviving lighthouse left on the Potomac. Built in 1855, it continued to be used until 1926. Its main use was to keep boats from slamming into the Washington Navy Yard. It switched hands several times in the decades since and the main building was now boarded up to keep out looters and vandals.

The lighthouse was part of a federal park and a large sign said the park would be open until ten p.m. It was now twenty after ten and a large gate closed off the parking lot from traffic, so this was as close as we were going to get by car. I turned slightly in my seat and looked at Elizabeth. "O.K. We're here. What next?"

"I'll show you." She opened her door and got out. I reached up, turned off the interior lights and then Mirsada and I both joined her. I told Elizabeth to wait a second, walked to the back of the Ford, lifted the hatch and accessed my hidden weapons locker. I opened a side flap and got Mirsada a Glock like mine and another clip.

I handed them to her. "I noticed you weren't carrying. Figured you might want one." She took the gun and clip and slipped them inside her leather vest, sliding neatly into a hidden pocket.

"My thanks. Your TSA does not take kindly to foreigners bringing in guns. Getting in my sword was hard enough."

I nodded my sympathy. I tucked mine into the back of my jeans, pulling my shirt down over the gun to cover it, then I got a Maglite flashlight and offered it to Elizabeth.

"I do not need it. I see fine in the dark." I would have sworn she sounded smug, but it could have been my imagination.

"Of course you do. How silly of me." I motioned for her to lead the way. She walked near the front gate, turning right and followed it around and into the woods nearby, I followed her and Mirsada followed me. The heat, barely reduced despite the hour, caused my shirt to stick to my chest. I slapped occasionally at mosquitoes who seemed to view every bare section of skin as their personal banquet. Damn bugs.

Walking deeper into the darkness, it became harder to see and I brought out the Maglite, turning it on for Mirsada and myself. Through gaps in the trees we could see the bay and lights shining on the other side of the Potomac River and hear the traffic from behind us on the Capital Beltway. A bit further down the river, I could see fog rolling in, devouring lights as it drifted in our direction.

Elizabeth stopped between two large oaks while her eyes scanned the brush nearby. Finding what she was looking for, she strode up to a large hedge of wild blueberries and reached deeply into the bush. When her hand re-emerged, she held a small satchel.

"Isaac loved to come to the park to relax and think. He always carried his backpack with him," Elizabeth said. "A couple of days before he was murdered, he called me to say if something happened to him, to come to our favorite spot, and reach past the dessert. That was code, in case someone was listening. We found this spot during one our visits. Isaac loved the blueberries and would eat a couple of handfuls every time we came here. This was the first spot where we..."

She trailed off. Mirsada finished the thought. "Where you had sex with him. Little did he know he was sleeping with the enemy."

Elizabeth bristled. "I was *not* his enemy. Despite what you may think, I actually liked Isaac. You know not of what you speak, bitch. Keep it up and I may forget my promise to Victor."

Before things could get out of hand, I stepped between them, both hands up. "Ladies, ladies. Instead of fighting each other, how 'bout we open up the bag and see what he left for us to find."

They stood and glared at one another in the glow of my Maglite, but Elizabeth broke eye contact first and practically ripped open the satchel. I shined my light into the bag, showing its contents.

The first thing I pulled out of it was a label. I tipped it towards the light so I could read the writing. It was from Dabney Industrial Tech and it listed a serial number. Nothing else. I knew from my time in the military that Dabney was a weapons manufacturer, but they also owned many other companies. I showed it to both women and they both shrugged. I tucked the label into my pocket. I would have Kurt track down what Dabney made which used this type of label.

Next out was a small pamphlet. In the glow of the Maglite I could tell I was holding a copy of the U.S. Constitution. I flipped quickly through the pamphlet, but there were no notes or markings inside. I shook my head in frustration.

The last thing in the bag was a single folded sheet of paper. I opened it all the way, and began reading what to me was gobbledygook. There was a diagram of what appeared to be an electric circuit, but beyond that I had no clue what the rest entailed.

The two women crowded in, one on each side, and they had no more clue about the paper than I did. "What the hell?" I asked. "I was a history major, not electrical engineering."

"Isaac was very smart. It is what made him attractive to the Church. That and his cocaine habit. They kept him supplied and on their leash."

"I'll have to check with a few people, see if they can

figure out what this is all about." I refolded the paper and shoved it into my pocket with the label. "If he was so smart, why didn't he leave something more useful? You know, like a taped video of what the hell they were up to instead of all this Da Vinci Code crap?"

Elizabeth was about to answer when she stiffened, her eyes darting around. She hissed, "Turn off your light, now."

I did so and strained to hear what might have spooked her, but I couldn't hear anything. The fog began to ease between the trees, causing our path to the car to disappear with the lights in the parking lot.

"What's going—" I didn't get anything else out as she covered my mouth with her hand. I could hear Mirsada behind me draw her sword from its sheath, the blade whispering as it cleared the leather. I yanked my gun from my jeans and held it down by the side of my leg.

Then I heard it. Laughter. But not "ha-ha, funny" kind of laughter, but crazy as a loon kind of laughter. And it was getting closer.

"Muramasa. It's Muramasa," whispered Elizabeth, the closest thing resembling fear I'd ever heard in her voice.

"And that would be?" Mirsada asked.

"Muramasa Sengo. Former swordsmith to generations of samurai warriors. One of the greatest swordsmiths to have ever lived. He went mad before he died and it is believed all of his blades possess some of that madness. And now, he is an Infernal Lord."

A sword wielding samurai madman vampire, in a fog, at night. What could go wrong?

CHAPTER TWENTY-ONE

The laughter was coming from the direction of the lighthouse. "Can you guys see through fog?" I asked Elizabeth, my voice pitched softly enough for only her and Mirsada to hear. So I thought.

"No. But we don't have to. Our improved hearing will guide him in our direction. There is no need to whisper. Speak normally or not at all."

I turned my light back on. "Then there is no need for us to go around in the dark." I flicked the light around, but there was not much to see as the fog engulfed us. "Can you take him?"

She glanced around looking for the best way out. "On an open field, with clear vision, we would be nearly even. But I cannot say. Now that I've made my intentions clear, I think he is here for me, not you. There is little which frightens an Infernal Lord more than a sword in the hands of a Master."

"Then let him come," Mirsada said. "I've trained my whole life in the use of the sword. He will find me no coward."

"Then you are an idiot. You will not be facing any average swordsman. But one of the greatest the world has ever known. He has spent the last few centuries getting even better. You will be like a child to him. But please, why do you not see if you are better, while Victor and I try and return to the car?"

"Damn it, will you two give it a rest? Elizabeth, try and lead us back to the car and let us know if you think he is close. I have something in the car which might slow his ass down."

Elizabeth started out, Mirsada right behind her and I brought up the rear. We could only see about five feet in any direction. Trees seemed to spring out of nothing to block our way, and branches slapped against my face and arms.

By my guess we were about half-way to the car when Elizabeth first froze, then dove to the ground, doing a quick somersault and landing in a crouch as Muramasa stepped forward, his sword whistling through the air where she had stood only seconds before. Without the dive, Elizabeth would be a head shorter.

I raised my gun to take a few shots but stopped short as Mirsada slid forward, her sword snaking out to take the ancient Samurai in the side.

He pivoted with ease, his own sword sweeping sideways, deflecting her strike while never taking his eyes off of Elizabeth. A man of average height, he wore a black silk kimono, tied at the waist with a red sash. A blood red sword sheath was tucked into the sash. His katana gleamed when my flashlight beam struck it. The handle, also blood red, was covered in several symbols I assumed was Japanese, but hell, it could have been Greek for all I knew. The disturbing thing was his Kabuki mask. It was designed from some type of metal, with a large grin showing pointed teeth and two devil horns adorning the top. Unlike most Kabuki masks, this one covered the back of his head as well.

He backed up a step and bowed slightly to Elizabeth. "I did not believe it possible, but it is true. You work with our enemy." He wagged a finger at her. "The Lord of Light will see you suffer for your treason, once I kill you."

Mirsada circled one direction and I the other, as we tried to make him fight multiple fronts.

He gestured in our direction. "Run now. You get head start. I kill her quick. Then come for you. Kill you quick, too. Run now."

Elizabeth picked up a large log about six feet long that I would have struggled to lift, let alone wield as a club. She didn't even break a sweat. "I don't think even your sword can slice through this much wood, Muramasa. Come near me and I will flatten you with this toothpick."

"To hell with this," I thought. I took aim and fired several rounds, popping him in the side of the head. The bullets ricocheted off the mask, and other than rocking his head back and forth, appeared to do no damage. Now I understood why he wore the mask. Protection. I knew shooting him anywhere else would have little to no affect. He would heal quickly, like Elizabeth did in the cemetery. Punching holes in his body wouldn't stop him.

He turned his head slowly in my direction. The only thing not covered by his mask was his eyes, and they were the eyes of a full-fledged nut-bag. "I change my mind. I kill you slowly now."

I glanced at both Elizabeth and Mirsada. "Well, just remember what ol'Vic McCain says at a time like this. Ol'Vic always says...WHAT THE HELL!" And I attacked.

Even knowing it wouldn't hurt him, I shot him in the head twice more, while I rushed towards him. Ringing his bell might not hurt him, but perhaps it would disorient him for a few seconds. Mirsada shot in behind him, forcing Muramasa to spin her direction, while Elizabeth swung her improvised club in an overhead arc, trying her best to drive the swordsmith into the ground like a tent peg.

But Muramasa was fast. Incredibly fast. Elizabeth missed him by inches, her log splintering in half as it crashed into the ground.

Mirsada and Muramasa traded a flurry of blows and I pulled up short, worried I would hit Mirsada instead of the samurai. Elizabeth did the same, watching for an opening.

Mirsada's sword blurred, her movements flowing from one form to another with a skill I'd never seen before. Her footwork made it seem as if she floated above the ground, effortless. I'd seen Samantha wield a sword and had been impressed, but Mirsada was on a whole other level. She was good. Damn good. But he was better.

Muramasa barely seemed to move, a statue in the midst of the storm. His blade countered all her attacks, his wrist unbending. Then he went on the attack and one of his thrusts got past her guard and nicked her shoulder, causing a grunt of pain. But to her credit, it didn't slow her down. Her life depended on it.

She pressed another attack and their two swords slid down together, until they caught on each other's hilt guard. He laughed again and shouted, "It is time to end this dance."

"I agree," I said. His head might be protected by a large metal helmet, but his hands weren't. I stepped forward, putting myself inside his sword's reach and prayed I calculated correctly. I pulled the trigger and half his right hand exploded, taking his thumb with it. I don't care if you are an Infernal Lord, or vampire, or whatever you wanted to call him, you can't hold a sword with half a hand and no thumb.

The next two seconds saw more action than most battles do in an hour. Muramasa howled in fury and shot a foot out in a side kick which sent me flying backwards onto the ground. I kept the flashlight on him and watched him drop the sword with his right hand and snatch it in mid-air with his left. But the fraction of a second cost him.

Mirsada spun in a tight circle and her sword flashed in a feint towards his head, only to alter the arch when he raised his own sword in defense. Her sword met dead flesh and passed through his shoulder with his right arm hacked off at the joint.

She ducked and rolled past the infuriated sword master when he counter attacked. She started to stand when Elizabeth shouted, "Duck, child." Mirsada did as commanded and crouched low, while Elizabeth swung her club sideways, whistling inches above Mirsada's head, but catching Muramasa high in the chest with a large thump. He flew backwards into the fog, howling once again, crashing through trees and underbrush, disappearing from view. It was a swing to make Babe Ruth proud.

She said, "We run now." She took off into the night, with Mirsada and I right behind her, the light from my flashlight trying to cut the fog, but having little affect. I bounced off several trees in our flight to freedom, my face scratched from limbs that slapped me in the face.

I heard several accompanying grunts from Mirsada taking her own punishment from the trees. We broke out of the tree line and the fog thinned a bit. I could make out the Ford in the haze and we hit an all-out sprint.

Only a few seconds behind us our silver helmeted foe emerged in pursuit. I glanced over my shoulder and felt a moment of Deja Vu, reliving the chase by the hellhound.

I shouted to the two women, "Try and keep him busy for as long as you can. I need about sixty seconds."

I didn't even watch what they did, but pulled the key fob

out my pocket and hit the unlock button, ran to the trunk of my car and lifted the hatch. I threw the blanket off the flame thrower, and quickly unscrewed the propane canister from the back of the rig, and replaced it with one of two spares I kept in the car. Another example of how far I'd slipped. I should have replaced it while in North Carolina, a blunder I hoped didn't cost me or either woman their lives.

I didn't bother to put the damn thing on, but carried it tucked under my arm, the nozzle extended in my other hand. And just in time. Mirsada was only barely able to keep Muramasa off her, with Elizabeth swinging but missing the other vamp with her log, while he countered with blows in her direction. He may have been fighting one handed, but the man remained incredibly dangerous. Her shirt showed several spots where the sword ripped through to her torso, but seemingly doing little damage. If he managed to connect with her neck, that would be a different story.

"To me," I yelled. Both of them retreated in my direction and they gained a moment when Elizabeth scored another hit with the log, staggering the samurai backwards. Mirsada sprinted behind me and then, for a second, both vamps were in my sight. I could have ended two Infernal Lords at once. Mirsada screamed at me to pull the trigger.

But I hesitated. I'd given Elizabeth my word. The Hand of God was put on Earth to destroy people like her. She, by her own admission, had tortured and killed hundreds, if not thousands, of people. A death by fire was what she deserved. I knew that to be true. But I'd also given my word. I told myself I still needed her, to see this through. But now that I had Isaac's stash, did I really?

I might find out, to my eternal ruin that Elizabeth was beyond redemption. Like my brother, she had chosen a path of evil and the only end for her would be suffering in the fires of Hell. But if it were true, then what would that mean? How evil was too evil to right the ship and sail in the other direction?

My finger tightened on the trigger, but still, I did not pull it all the way. "What are you waiting for? End them. Now!" Mirsada shouted as she grabbed my arm.

And then the moment was lost. Elizabeth tossed her log

at Muramasa's feet, forcing him to dance in the air, while she ran behind me. With her now safe, I let loose with a steady stream of fire, advancing on the samurai. He both screamed and laughed, almost at the same time. His body engulfed in flames, he staggered towards me, waving his sword as if trying to slice the flames in half.

I back-peddled a few steps keeping my finger on the trigger and the flames roared, but then he closed the gap with a rush and with a final lunge, he stabbed with his sword, trying to spill my guts across the ground. I was shocked he could move at all, let alone attack. Thankfully, he was slowed by the damage from the flames and I parried the thrust with the backpack. Just. I dropped the nozzle and swung the flamethrower backpack with everything I had and caught him across the side of the head, staggering him.

He fell to his knees and the sword slipped from blackened fingers onto the ground. I guess even Infernal Lords have their breaking point. I kicked him in the chest, sending him onto his back, steam rising from the eye holes of his mask. I snatched his dropped sword from the ground, singeing my fingers in the process, and with a quick strike, severed his head from the rest of his body. I may not be as graceful as Mirsada, but I make up for it with brute strength.

A moment later, his body turned to brimstone, black in color with red streaks running across his entire body. I kicked him hard and the whole thing disintegrated into dust, with the mask the only thing left. A small sulfur cloud hovered in the air and I stepped away.

Anger contorted Mirsada's face, her fury barely kept in check. I am sure if there was a way to remove me as the Hand of God, short of killing me, she would have found a way to do it.

Elizabeth watched me, her face expressionless, impassive. She knew I could have taken her out as well, but didn't. If she was grateful, she didn't show it. Perhaps the former Countess in her took it for granted people would do what she wanted. Hell if I knew.

I walked past both of them and tossed what was left of the flamethrower back in the car, covering it and laid Muramasa's katana behind our bags. "There will be people who heard the shots I fired back in the woods. We better get out of here, even if there isn't a body to be found."

I drove several miles from the lighthouse and turned into a school parking lot, made my way into the darker shadows under a line of trees, parked and turned off the engine.

"Everyone out."

I didn't wait on them and got out and went to the rear of my car, once again accessing my weapons locker. The two women exited the car and watched while I walked around the car holding a small electronic device.

"What are you doing," asked Mirsada.

"Checking for bugs. I once had one planted under my car and that's how the bad guys kept track of me. We were the only ones who knew we were going to Alexandria. So how did Muramasa find us?"

Mirsada turned a thumb in Elizabeth's direction, causing Elizabeth to sigh heavily.

"No, she didn't. The man was there for her, not us. He made that clear." I finished my sweep of the car, but found nothing. I opened the rear hatch and checked out the bags, but they were also clear.

I walked over to both women. Mirsada stood still while I ran the device up and around her body. Nada. Then I started on Elizabeth and the thing went nuts: right where she'd been shot during the shootout with Deveraux. She took hold of a rip in her shirt from one of Muramasa's sword cuts and widened it. The signal finder redlined at the spot.

"Bloody hell. I thought the bullet made a funny sound when it hit you, but lying in the bottom of that grave I thought it was my imagination."

"What do you mean? What are you talking about?" Elizabeth asked.

"Tracking bullet. Cops use them to shoot the back of cars so they can fall back and track criminals instead of engaging in high speed chases. The guy who shot you had to know a regular bullet would have no real effect on you. I mean, why bother? But shooting you with a tracking bullet would allow them to follow your movements."

Elizabeth said some things in Hungarian which I

assumed to be swear words. She then turned to Mirsada. "Cut me open. Right here, please."

Mirsada drew her katana, her knuckles white on the handle. Elizabeth held her hands out to her sides and waited. With a low growl, Mirsada thrust the tip of her katana at the spot indicated and gave her wrist a twist, opening up a good sized wound. She yanked the sword out, pulled a small towel from an inside vest pocket and wiped the blade clean.

Elizabeth reached into her own chest, her fingers searching around, until she found the bullet. She pulled it out and held it up, examining it. She held it out to me and I ran the scanner over the bullet and the little machine lit up like a Christmas tree.

Elizabeth turned and threw the bullet into the darkness. She then went to the car, got out her bag and changed shirts.

I tossed the bug sweeper back into my locker and removed a first aid kit. I walked over to Mirsada and examined the cut she'd received from Muramasa. It wasn't very deep and I didn't think it would need stiches. I put some hydrogen peroxide on a cloth and cleaned the wound, then applied a pressure bandage.

"You are an idiot and it will get you killed," she said.

"I have no doubt you're right. But I keep my word. Remember that."

I finished and Mirsada stalked to her side of the car and got back inside. Newly clothed, Elizabeth did the same. I breathed easier with the mystery of how they found us resolved.

In Alexandria, we found what we'd come for, not that I knew much more than I did before the trip. At least we now had clues.

And the world was down an Infernal Lord. Rumble, rumble, scratch one bad guy.

CHAPTER TWENTY-TWO

Senator Stafford watched on as the attending nurse swabbed his elbow with antiseptic and inserted the I.V. needle. Wearing the backless gown all patients hate and covered with a blanket to the waist, he rested his head back onto a pillow and tried to relax.

Giving up control to anyone, even an operating team, was hard for Stafford. Truth be told, he felt a sense of foreboding about the surgery. His mother, following surgery to remove a gallbladder, found it difficult to come out of anesthesia, and spent nearly a day on a respirator. While he never experienced the same thing, he always worried the next time would be when it would happen to him.

His thoughts were interrupted when Dr. Collins pulled back the curtain surrounding his bed and moved to stand next to him, pulling the curtain closed behind her.

"Good morning, Senator. How did you sleep last night?" she asked.

"I didn't. I stayed up most of the night taking care of last minute Senate business. We may be on our August break, but that doesn't mean things stop. Besides, the more tired I am, the easier this will be. When you give me the Valium I will be out long before you give me the gas."

Dr. Collins laughed, but to Stafford it sounded forced. She pulled down the blanket, took a marker out of her pocket and wrote on the left knee THIS ONE. On the right knee she wrote NOT THIS ONE.

"We wouldn't want to take out your good one, would we?" Again she smiled, but briefly.

Stafford rose to power by being able to read people and

watching the body language of Dr. Collins, she seemed tense. "Everything O.K, doc? How did you sleep last night?"

She pulled the blanket back up to his waist, avoiding eye contact. "I slept like a baby. You're in good hands, Senator." She watched the nurse put a needle in the I.V. and push down on the plunger, administering the Valium. Finally, she looked him in the eyes and he wasn't sure what he saw there. Apprehension? Worry? Maybe his own feelings were coloring his perceptions.

He would have asked more questions, but the Valium hit him quickly and with the lack of sleep he started to drift off. While he did, in his mind's eye, the doctor's face grew larger, her eyes huge. Then her face contorted and changed, becoming the head of a dragon. Her mouth opened wide and fire erupted from her throat. He tried to raise his hands, to protect himself, but his body would not respond, and he screamed.

When he awoke hours later, following the surgery, he would not remember the dream.

*****

Stafford opened his eyes slowly, blinked several times and woke up to find his wife Delores sitting in a chair reading a book. When she noticed he was no longer asleep, she put her book aside, stood next to his bed and kissed him.

"Could you give me some water, please," his voice just above a whisper.

She picked up a Styrofoam cup with a straw and let him take a sip. He swished the water around his mouth for a moment, then swallowed. He thanked his wife and then let his head fall back onto the pillow.

A nurse came in a few minutes later and greeted him, then went about checking his temperature and blood pressure. Shortly afterwards, they brought in a Continuous Passive Motion Machine. They removed his knee brace, gently lifted his knee into the device and it began to slowly work it back and forth.

Near the end of his first CPM session, House Speaker Cyrus Tyler knocked on the door and came into the room carrying flowers and a gift wrapped box. He waited until the nurse left the room and said, "The flowers are for your lovely wife for putting up with you. As for you, I brought Kentucky bourbon. I know the kind that will bring you more enjoyment."

Tyler kissed Delores on the cheek and handed her the flowers. She sat them on the windowsill and he set the bourbon on a table near his bed. He glanced at the knee moving back and forth with a steady hum of the CPM. "Things go well?" he asked.

"I guess so. I don't really feel anything at the moment, thanks to the pain block and meds. They want to get me up and walking around later this afternoon. Let's see how it does then."

"I'll let you boys have a few minutes. I need to call some more family members and let them know how you're doing." Delores grabbed her purse and left the room.

Tyler watched her go, then pulled up a chair next to the bed. "How long will you be here?"

"Three days. Once I get home, I'll hit the therapy hard. I have a good friend who went through a knee replacement and he's never been able to bend it all the way. That's not going to happen to me."

"Nor would I expect it. Hard work has never been your issue. Taking this country into the crapper because of your liberal politics is the issue."

Both men laughed. "You know what, Cyrus? You coming in here and giving me shit lets me know everything is going to be just fine". He turned serious. "Thanks for arranging for Dr. Collins to get this done during the break. I appreciate it. I can't tell you how much."

"Don't say that where people can hear you. There were some in my party who were saddened by the death of your doctor, but were hoping you would have to have the surgery during the fall, taking you off the fundraiser trail."

"True, that. We have several big events planned and I likely would have had to miss some of them. Now things can keep on schedule. And that includes our legislative slate. There have to be things you, me and the President can find common ground on and move some bills forward. Cyrus, the country needs to see we can work together."

"Don't worry, Hedley. There will be a lot getting done this fall."

"Too bad you won't be around to see it," thought Tyler.

CHAPTER TWENTY-THREE

Elizabeth, Mirsada and I spent the night at a Comfort Suites off the Capital Beltway. I made sure both women were in their rooms before I went to mine. Elizabeth offered to join me in my room, but I politely said, "No." Not only did Mirsada not offer to join me, but she hadn't said a word to me since we left the school parking lot and slammed her door closed.

Once I got to my room, I used my phone to take a picture of the Dabney Industrial Tech label and the circuit schematic. I texted them to Kurt and asked for details on both as soon as possible.

I then stripped out of my clothes, headed to the bathroom and took a long, hot shower. I let the water wash over my head, deep in thought about the label, the schematic and the U.S. Constitution, hoping to have an epiphany. Sadly, I didn't.

I toweled off and made my way to my bed, exhausted beyond measure. The aftermath of the fight with Muramasa had been exhausting enough. But dealing with Elizabeth and Mirsada wore me down mentally.

I checked out the mini bar in my room, found a couple of small bottles of Jack Daniels, opened them and poured their contents into a hotel room plastic cup. I sat on the edge of the bed and started to sip the whiskey, but changed my mind and tossed it down in one shot. I felt the burn in my throat and wanted more, but all that was left in the mini bar was vodka and gin, so I passed.

I did wonder if I had a drinking problem, with Winston's admonition bouncing around in my head. I came from a long line of professional drinkers, but it was never an issue for me in the past. I could go down to Molly's and tie one on with the best of them and then not have another drink for months. Recently, however, you were more likely than not to find a drink in my hand. Something to consider. I only wished I could consider it with another belt of bourbon.

I turned off the lights and crashed onto my bed, my arms out to my sides, and tried to will sleep to overtake me. I thought I would be asleep in minutes. Unfortunately, my body failed to cooperate and the rest I desperately needed alluded me.

An hour later, I was still awake. An hour after that, no change. I'd hoped the whiskey would help turn my brain off, but it didn't. I found it hard to keep my thoughts in one place, racing from one thought to the next. I thought about what we'd learned, trying to put the pieces of the puzzle together, but no dice. Then my mind switched to thoughts of Samantha, with feelings of anger, sadness and shame tagging along for the ride.

And as quickly as thoughts of Samantha would come, they were replaced by thoughts of Elizabeth and what I was going to do about her. Had our nights in the sack tainted my judgment as Mirsada claimed? I didn't believe that was true, but hell, how could I be sure?

I started humming an old country song I'd heard years ago, about a preacher who held sermons while handling snakes, only to be bitten by one and dying. Is that what could happen to me with Elizabeth? Was I trying to prove if she could regain her soul and redemption that I could do the same thing, only to die because my hope turned around and bit me in the ass?

Then I spent a few minutes thinking about my brother. Was he proof positive Elizabeth was damned beyond saving? Elizabeth, at least, claimed she wanted salvation. Mikey didn't. He embraced his role being the point man for chaos and mayhem for Satan. Not only did Mikey not want to be saved, he believed Satan would be the one holding all the cards during the final showdown with God and he would be made a king among men. He now had the rest of eternity to find out how wrong he turned out to be.

My random thoughts were finally interrupted when my cell phone dinged indicating the arrival of a text message. I sighed, picked up the phone to find a text from Kurt asking me to call him when I got up. I thumbed to his number and hit dial.

He answered with a hushed request for me to hang on. A moment later he said, "Dude, I didn't expect you to call me back in the middle of the night. You almost woke up Ruth Anne. What are you doing up?"

I explained my inability to find some shut eye and he commiserated. "I know what you mean. Ruth Anne likes to keep at it until late. I didn't get to do your research until after midnight. Best time for hacking anyways."

"What'd you find out?"

"I got good news and bad news. The good news is I found out what the label belongs to, but you aren't going to like it."

"Do I ever? Let me have it."

"Looks like Dabney Industrial Tech has invented a new form of plastic explosive. Do you know how C-4 works?"

"Yeah. We used it all the time when I was Special Forces. It uses RDX mixed with a bunch of other crap. Very stable. You have to have heat and a shockwave to detonate. You telling me this is a C-4 label?"

"Kind of. They've developed a newer nastier version. They worked out a new type of nitroamine, whatever the hell that is, and you only need a quarter of a brick of their version to get the same explosive power as a full brick of C-4. It also takes less heat and a smaller shockwave. That makes it a bit more unstable, but, man, what a blast."

Dabney Industrial seemed to always be on the cutting edge of the technology used to kill people. Good thing they were on our side, though some claimed a lot of their weapons seemed to end up on battlefields far from any American soldier.

"How about the schematic? What'd you find out about it?"

"That's the bad news. What I can tell you is it's some kind of switch. But, dude, there is a ton of quantum mechanics shit and I don't have a clue what it does or how it works. You don't happen to know any quantum physicists do you?"

"Turns out, I do. Thanks, Kurt. I will let you know what I find out."

"Any clue what's going on, Big Guy?"

"Only that they plan on blowing something up. What that is, I don't know yet. But I will. Thanks again."

I hung up and lay back in bed, this time more relaxed

than I'd been before. The puzzle was becoming clearer and I knew I was close to figuring it all out. And when I did? I would be the one lowering the boom.

*****

The next morning I met Elizabeth and Mirsada down in the hotel dining room for breakfast about 8 a.m. The eggs were likely instant, the sausages greasy and the juice glasses incredibly small, but I ate like a man who won the lottery. While we had yet to uncover what Tyler and his underlings were up to, we were closing in and I could feel the itch. I got it when the back of my brain began figuring things out and I knew it wouldn't be long before we knew it all and we could take steps to stop things.

Both women avoided talking to each other and only barely spoke to me. At 8:30 I took out my phone, scrolled through my contacts and made a call.

On the second ring, a woman answered. "Well I'll be damned, if it's not the soldier of fortune himself."

I laughed. "Hello Bethany. How's life? Keeping busy down at the U?"

Bethany Dezaro was born in California and educated at Cal Berkeley, majoring in molecular biology. Now she taught the same subject at Temple University in Philadelphia. It's where she met Joseph Dezaro, a good friend of mine back from my army days and the reason I called her.

"Classes pick back up in a couple of weeks so right now I've got some free time." She paused briefly before continuing. "If you're looking for Joey, he's not here. Sorry, Vic."

"Let me guess, he's out throwing around grown men for money."

Joseph Dezaro, known to the wrestling public as Joey Image, served with me in Afghanistan and Iraq. Joey was one of the more interesting people I'd ever met. He got his degree in physics from Harvard, his doctorate in quantum mechanics from M.I.T. and then decided to join the Army for shits and giggles.

Reaching the rank of Staff Sergeant, Joey was the top noncom in my unit. He kept the enlisted men in line and could kill the enemy in about three dozen different ways. Five-nine and built like a bull dog, the man could go all day and all night and seem to never tire. Despite being almost a foot taller, even I found it hard to take him off his feet when we would wrestle for the hell of it during our down times.

When we got back to the states, he took a series of jobs with start-up companies looking to cash in on the exploding frontier of quantum physics. With several patents under his belt and a large increase in his bank account, he'd jumped off the corporate gravy train to accept a research fellowship at Temple, met Bethany and settled down.

In his spare time, Joey got involved with independent wrestling outfits in the Northeast and developed a following under the name Joey Image. Most weekends you could find him pinning people to the mat.

"He's at a fundraiser in Houston, Texas. He's helping raise money for an autism group down there."

"And let me guess? Still no cell phone?"

Joey worried what the cell phones were doing to his brain. At the quantum level, of course.

"Like he ever will," she laughed. "He'll be back later in the week. I can have him call you when he gets back, if you like."

"It can't wait that long, Bethany. What's the name of the event? I'll fly down there and talk to him."

"*Bustin' for Autism.* It's being held downtown. Is everything O.K., Vic?"

"Yeah, things are fine. I've run across something in an investigation I'm involved in and it involves me needing to talk to Dr. Dezaro not Joey Image."

I thanked her and hung up, then filled in the girls.

"Looks like I need to fly down to Houston for a day or two. Why don't the two of you hang out here until I get back? I bet whatever's going on is happening somewhere near here. Can you two manage not to kill each other while I'm gone?"

"They have a very nice pool here. I can manage," Elizabeth said.

"I make no promises on not killing people. It depends on her," Mirsada said, pointing a thumb at Elizabeth.

"Great. What more could a guy ask for?"

CHAPTER TWENTY-FOUR

I caught a flight out of Reagan National late in the morning, transferred through Atlanta and arrived at Hobby Airport around 5:30 p.m. I rented a convertible Mercedes because...why the hell not? The Church of the Light Reclaimed paid the bill.

I dropped by Joey's hotel only to find out the whole group had gone to Longhorn Steakhouse for dinner. *Bustin' for Autism* raised money to send special needs children to camp. They brought in celebrities, mainly pro wrestlers, as well as cos players (the ones who dress up like super hero characters) along with writers and other local celebrities.

I made the short drive to Longhorn Steakhouse, parked and walked in the door. At the far end of the dining room they had shoved several tables together for the large dinner party. And when I say large, I mean large. Wrestling royalty sat around the table. Sgt. Slaughter, Hacksaw Jim Duggan, Honkey Tonk Man, the Real Rikishi and Gene Snitsky. It's not often I go out and find men my size, but hell, the whole table came close.

Joey sat near the end of the table with a beer in one hand, laughing and trading tales with Snitsky. He was decked out in a black t-shirt which matched his dark hair and beard, and had a bandana wrapped around his head. The man remained just as ripped as his younger days.

I walked to his end of the table and punched him hard in the shoulder. Joey, showing the kind of reflexes you normally see on big cats, went from drinking and laughing to having me thrown to my stomach with my arm cranked behind my back.

"Good to see you, too, Joey," I said through gritted teeth.

"Victor McCain? Jesus man, hitting me from behind is a

good way to earn a trip to the hospital."

He helped me to my feet and hugged me in a fierce bear hug, while I rubbed my arm, trying to make the pain go away. "I had to see if you still had it. Seems like playing around in the ring hasn't hurt you any."

He introduced me to the guys and gals at the table who raised their glasses in ceremonial greeting, then he grabbed his beer and the two of us found a booth in a corner away from everyone else.

"How ya been, Joey?"

"Life as an independent wrestler is tough, but I love it. I was injured a few weeks ago, but feel great now and will be back in the ring soon."

We spent some time catching up, talking about women, fighting and Fireball Whiskey.

After the waitress brought me another beer, he said, "I'm guessing you didn't fly down here from Louisville to share a few beers. Am I right, or am I right?"

"Flew here from Virginia. But you're right. I need you to take off the bandana for a moment and put your doctorate hat on for a bit." I took out a folded copy of the schematic I'd printed at the hotel and slid it across the table to him.

He took another drink of Coors Light while he looked over the paper. His brows furrowed and he sat the beer down, bending closer for a better look. I watched his eyes read the paper from top to bottom, then do it again.

Finally he met my eyes. Very quietly he asked, "Where did you get this?"

"From a dead man. Ever heard of Isaac Peck?"

"Yeah, man. Most in the field have. Died in a bad drug deal last week, right?"

"Dead, yes. Bad drug deal?" I shook my head no. "He left this to be found in case he turned up dead. So what is it?"

"Armageddon, Vic. Armageddon."

*****

We said our goodnights to the *Bustin' for Autism* crowd and went back to his room at the hotel, with the two of us now in chairs staring at the screen of one seriously large laptop computer. Joey spent a few minutes checking some of the computations listed on the print out.

"Vic, tell me what you know about quantum entanglement."

"Not much. From what I gather when two particles are entangled, whatever happens to one particle happens to the other."

He nodded agreement. "Simplistic, but that's basically it. Entangled particles have no set state until they are measured. But when you do measure one the observed state will be the same in the other entangled members, but opposite."

I must have shown my confusion because he stopped talking like a doctor and more like a sergeant. "Look, if one particle is spinning to the right, the other spins to the left. If you change the spin of the first particle to spin to the left, then the other will start spinning to the right. And the change is instantaneous. Faster than the speed of light. But the measurement always adds up to zero."

"O.K. So?"

"So, the big advantage is, the distance is irrelevant. The big goal for a lot of researchers is using this property to create a quantum computer or a new form of encryption." Holding up the paper he said, "What you have here is the creation of a quantum switch. It appears someone managed to do what others have dreamed about doing."

"A switch? You mean like a light switch?"

"Sure. Or a computer switch. With this switch you can be sitting in a room on Mars, press the switch and the light comes on in a room on Venus. Instantaneously, without the signal having to travel the traditional route between the two places."

"You said this was Armageddon. Isn't this type of technology a great thing?"

"Sure. But think about it, Vic. There are a lot of things you can turn on with a switch. And not all of them good."

And then I got it. What Tyler and his goons planned. "You mean like a bomb? Holy crap." I told Joey about the other items I found in the bag. "One of the problems with setting off a bomb is the trigger. You can set a timer, but you may not know when the target will be there. You can use a cell phone, but if the target can turn off the cell phone towers in the area then your bomb is a paper weight. And you can use an RF transmitter, but there is an issue with the range. You're telling me with one of these you can set off a bomb in New York and be sitting in a bunker in North Korea, right?"

"You got it. Design the switch so that when the particle spins to the left, the device is off and when it spins to the right, it turns on. This switch is designed to do just that."

"How do you stop it? There has to be a way."

"There are only two. Find the bomb and remove the detonator. Or find the person who has the switch and take it away from them. Those are your only options. You can't jam this type of signal, Vic. Once the bomb is in place, there would be no way to stop it from being detonated. None."

We sat there in silence for a few moments then Joey asked, "Let me guess, from the way you look, the guys who have this aren't the good guys."

"Joey, they are as evil as it gets."

I thought about telling him about what was going on, about me being the Hand of God, but decided I was better off leaving him in the dark. I didn't like the thought of Joey thinking I was a nut bag if he didn't believe me.

"Well, one thing I can tell you is I doubt Isaac did this all on his own. The type of testing this would require would be really expensive. We're talking large company or world power."

"Do you think Dabney Industrial Tech could pull it off?"

Joey stared at the ceiling, his hands behind his head. "Yeah. I do. They are involved in all kinds of stuff involving new technology. They are into a lot of nanotechnology stuff, too. Anything to get an edge. So yeah, I can see them involved in this."

"Sounds like I need to get deeper into those guys. I think I have a bigger problem on my hands than I expected."

"How do you think the Constitution fits in to all of this?"

"Hell, I'm not sure. Perhaps they plan to target government institutions. Look, Joey, thanks. But at this point, the less you know about what is going on, is probably a good thing. Plausible deniability."

We both stood and hugged each other again. "Listen, Vic, you need me, you call. I don't mind getting my hands dirty."

"Thanks, Joey. I mean it, thanks. Hug Bethany for me."

I made my way back into the cool night air and to my car. I sat behind the wheel for a few minutes before I started the engine and headed to the airport.

The sons of bitches were going to blow up something or someone and I didn't have a clue how to stop them. Dealing with the supernatural is a hard enough proposition. But when the bad guys start using quantum physics and cutting edge military tech, it had a way of sucking all the fun out of my job.

One on one, I believe I can handle any single opponent and come out on top. But spooky bombs?

Yowza.

CHAPTER TWENTY-FIVE

I spent the night at a Holiday Inn near the airport, sleeping like the dead for once, turned in my car the next morning, and hopped the first return flight to Alexandria.

I got back to the Comfort Suites around mid-afternoon and true to her word, I found Elizabeth doing laps in the pool, while Mirsada sat under an umbrella watching her. Mirsada still wore the leather outfit, but traded the white shirt for a tan one. Such a fashion diva.

I asked them to meet me in the dining room in a half hour and went to my room to do some research on Dabney Industrial Tech.

Behind only Lockheed Martin and Boeing when it comes to defense contractors, the past year saw nearly thirty billion in total arms sales bringing in a profit of almost three billion, with a B, dollars. Owned and run by Alex Dabney, the grandson of the company founder, Levi Dabney, their reach now extended to dozens of complimentary companies around the globe. They invested heavy in Russia, China and Brazil.

Their R & D department made up a large portion of the company. If a new technology needed to be created, then D.I.T. got it done. They also contributed heavily to political campaigns on both sides of the aisle, but the person they contributed the most to, for the last five years running? The newly minted Speaker of the House Cyrus Tyler.

That in and of itself, meant nothing. But knowing Tyler like I did, it couldn't be a good thing. I closed my laptop and went down to the hotel restaurant to meet with Elizabeth and Mirsada.

The women were already there, sitting at a corner table

near the end of the bar, well away from the other patrons eating a late lunch. The TV over the bar, tuned to Fox News, showed talking heads speaking about Majority Leader Hedley Stafford.

I filled them in on what I'd learned down in Houston, about the new type of C-4, the quantum switch and my thought Dabney Industrial Technologies somehow figured into a plot to blow something up.

"There is no doubt Isaac could have helped to design such a thing," said Elizabeth. "I know money was not an issue. He asked and they would provide. That is how it worked."

I started to say something else when Elizabeth pointed up to the TV. "Isn't that your House Speaker?"

I turned around in my seat and glanced at the screen and sure enough, Senator Stafford was at a podium talking with Tyler and a few other senators and congressmen standing behind him.

"Hey, barkeep. Mind turning it up a bit?" I asked.

The bartender picked up a remote and jacked the volume up enough for us to hear Stafford speak.

"I want everyone to know my recovery is going very well. I want to thank Dr. Collins and her team for taking such good care of me. She might even have a future in politics, since she's operated on both myself and Speaker Tyler. The Speaker went to great lengths to make sure she could step in once my doctor suffered his unfortunate accident. Now we have some common ground where we can both agree. Do we not, Mr. Speaker?"

Tyler laughed and nodded an enthusiastic yes. Stafford started talking again, but I was no longer listening. A cold chill ran down my spine and I turned back to Elizabeth. "Isaac worked on creating new and improved joints, legs and arms for people who suffered crippling injuries, right?"

"Yes. He make men walk again. Women who lost arms to hold their babies again. Very talented."

"Knee replacements?"

"Of course, knee—" She stopped, and with wide eyes, stared at the TV screen. "Oh, no. Isaac, what did you do?"

Mirsada scowled. "Please, would you two explain?"

"Holy hell. I know where they put the bomb. The bottom of a knee replacement is plastic. If you used the C-4, especially the new stuff, there would be enough explosives to take out a good sized house."

The three of us watched the end of the press conference but learned nothing more. "What did he say his doctor's name was?" I asked.

"Collins, I think," said Mirsada. Elizabeth nodded in agreement. "But surely, there would be no way this Senator would agree to have his knee replaced with such a bomb."

I agreed. "He wouldn't. But what if he didn't know? We need to talk to that doctor. I can't see a way this could happen without her being in on the plans. If nothing else, we can try and find out where they get their knee joints. If they ordered them from Isaac's company that would almost be like a real clue."

I got out my iPhone and did a search on Dr. Collins and Senator Stafford. I found quite a few news articles about the good doctor and the surgery she performed on Senator Stafford at the Hospital of the University of Pennsylvania. I found her office phone number and dialed.

I got the office receptionist and told her I was a reporter with a paper in Harrisburg and wanted to know if Dr. Collins could answer a few questions, only to find out she was out of the office for the next week, taking some overdue vacation time with her daughter. Citing HIPAA regulations, they also wouldn't tell me where they buy their artificial knees.

I thanked her, hung up and called Kurt.

"Yo, dude. What's up?"

"Dr. Teresa Collins, I need you to track her down. She performed the operation on Senator Stafford. I need you to see if you can get a cell number for me. Can you do that?"

He made a very inappropriate sound and hung up. About ten minutes later, he texted me her number. I sent back a "You da man" text and dialed her number, but it went straight to voice mail. I hung up without leaving a message and called Kurt back.

"Listen, she didn't answer. Any chance you can use the GPS in her phone and get me a current location?"

"Any reason you keep insulting me? Geez, man."

Once again he hung up and the three of us ate our lunch while occasionally discussing Stafford. I stuffed the last bite of my dessert in my mouth, a better than expected piece of carrot cake, when Kurt called me back.

"Hey, dude. Her phone is currently at an address near Seaside Heights, New Jersey. There's a couple of beach houses south of town. That's where she is. I'll text you her address. She also drives a black BMW. I'll shoot you the license plate as well."

"Thanks, man. One last thing. Can you research her practice and see where they order their artificial joints? I have a theory and want to see if it pans out."

"Dude, the only thing you may need replaced is your head. Winston told me you were on a road trip with a demon and a Hand of God babe. Well, that they were both babes, but one was evil, one not, that you had sex with one of them but might want to—"

I hung up the phone when I saw Elizabeth look at me, eyes narrowed, knowing she likely could hear the whole conversation. My phone beeping bailed me out.

"Time to check out, ladies. We have a lead. Time to head to the beach." I pulled up Google Maps and checked the drive time, finding out we could be there in about 4 hours, less with good traffic.

We checked out of the hotel and hit the road. This time, I felt much better than the last time the three of us went on a long trip. For one thing, they fought less than before. It seems they finally found a way to work together until this whole thing was over—not that Mirsada looked any happier, but the constant nagging at Elizabeth had stopped.

For her part, Elizabeth continued to ignore Mirsada, while carrying on about her love of the beach, young men and good food. When I pointed out virtually every man on the planet was younger than her, she very sweetly offered to turn me into a eunuch.

Seaside Heights sat on the Barnegat Peninsula and was a popular resort destination during the summer months. Their latest claim to fame was the reality TV series *Jersey Shore* was filmed there. Maybe I would get to meet Snooky while we were tracking bad guys. My luck, I'd get *The Situation* instead.

This time of year, the traffic was packed in the main part of town and it added a good forty minutes to our trip. Finally, free of the strip, we headed south down Shore Road. The houses became less common and further apart.

I finally found our address near the south end of the peninsula. We drove by at a slow but steady pace. The house looked to be a small villa nestled in the trees, with a view of the beach. A black Beamer took up one of the two spots in front of the house, the other a Jeep Cherokee. A petite woman with long black hair tied back in a ponytail, got out of the Jeep carrying a Krispy Kreme donut box and headed towards the front door.

She glanced our way but we were soon out of sight. Not far up the road, I nosed my Ford into a parking lot for those who were headed to the beach. A dozen or so cars filled the parking lot and I could see people scattered up and down the beach.

I parked the car and cranked up the air conditioning with the sun beating down through a cloudless sky. I turned in my seat so I could talk to both women at once without breaking my neck.

"I'm sure both of you noticed two cars in the driveway and the young woman carrying the donuts. Must be her daughter."

Mirsada snorted. "How can you be so sure they were donuts?"

"Sister, I'd recognize a Krispy Kreme donut box from almost a mile away. My favorites are the chocolate ice with cream filling. Love 'em."

They stared back, not saying anything verbally but saying it all with their looks. "Anyways. Here's what I think we should do. I will go to the door pretending to be a federal investigator. I have a fake badge I can flash. I will put the screws to her and see what I can shake loose."

"And what will the other Hand of God and I be doing while you play cop? I can go with you. We make a good team, you and I. We can do, what you call it? Good cop, bad cop. I would love to be bad cop."

"Hold your horses, Natasha Fatale. I'm not playing Boris. I'm not playing anything. You two can wait in the car until I find out what's what."

"I do not like this idea. What if something happens?"

"An orthopedic doc and her daughter? What's the worst that can happen?"

*****

I went to the back of the Ford and got my fake badge out of my supply locker and tucked it into my pocket. I got a belt holster and secured my gun on my hip, then got back into the car and returned to the villa.

The tires crunched on the gravel driveway and I parked in such a way as to block both cars from being able to leave until I moved my car, parked and got out, leaving the car running so the gals would have some cool air, with the temperature already above the ninety degree mark.

The license plate matched the info Kurt sent me. It amazed me how easy modern technology made tracking down someone who didn't want to be found.

I walked to the door and both rang the doorbell and knocked hard on the front door. Listening, I couldn't hear anything inside, no TV, no sound or movement. I waited a few heartbeats and then repeated the process, knocking loud enough to wake up Rip Van Winkle himself, but still no response.

I glanced through the window closest to the door, but nothing. I stepped off the small porch and started around the house. Elizabeth and Mirsada opened the car door and got out.

"Watch the front door. With the cars blocked in, it ain't like they're going anywhere," I said.

They nodded their agreement and I circled around to the back of the house, where I found a back door and a fantastic view of the Atlantic Ocean. This particular villa came with a small dock which extended out a ways into the ocean. Tied up to the docks I could see a speedboat with a man behind the wheel. The girl I'd seen carrying the donut box was on the dock tossing down some luggage and then the donuts.

I made my way down the docks and they saw me coming. The man, dressed in a sleeveless T, cargo shorts and hiking sandals, smiled and offered a short wave. His olive complexion made me think South America, but I couldn't be sure. I would put him somewhere in his thirties.

The girl, gorgeous in a petite baby doll kind of way, wore a bikini top and shorts with no shoes. She gave me a million dollar smile when I stopped next to her, looking down a short ladder to the man below.

I removed the badge. "Hi. I'm Charles Winstead, U.S.

Marshall's office. I wonder if I could ask you two a few questions about Dr. Teresa Collins."

I used the name Charles Winstead, the man credited with shooting and killing John Dillinger. Another man who removed the bad guys from the land of the living.

The man glanced up at the woman, a confused expression on his face. "I don't know any Teresa Collins. Do you pumpkin?"

She picked up one of the last two bags on the docks and tossed it down to him, which he snagged out of the air.

"Can't say that I do. I'm sorry Marshall, but I think you've made a mistake."

"That's funny. That's her car parked back in the driveway. May I ask who you are, please?"

The man started to answer when the girl, picking up the last bag, swung it around hard, catching me behind the knees, causing them to buckle and for me to fall backwards onto the dock.

Crashing down, I went for the gun on my hip when I felt a stinging sensation in my neck, like being stung by a hornet. I reached up in time to catch the girl's wrist and twisted upwards, making her drop the syringe she'd used to stab me. I noticed the plunger was pressed all the way down.

She twisted back and did a flip over me, wrenching free of my grasp and then scuttled down the ladder to the boat. I stood up, finally getting my gun free of the holster and yelled down to the two of them.

"Make another move and so help me God, I will blow your asses out of that boat."

The two of them stood still, watching me, smiling. I started to ask them what the hell they thought was so funny, when the world started to spin.

I could hear them talking, but it seemed like from a long ways away.

"Do you think he'll fall into the boat or back on the dock," he asked.

"I'm betting the boat. Loser drives next?"

"You're on."

My tongue grew thick and this time, my knees buckled

all on their own and I felt a falling sensation.

The last thing I heard, just before my face hit the floor of the boat was the man saying, "Looks like you win."

CHAPTER TWENTY-SIX

Damn my head hurt. It felt like someone had been using it to drive fence posts into the ground and not being gentle about the process. I tried to grab my face in my hands, but they stopped a good two feet short on either side. I finally managed to open my eyes and what I saw didn't give me the warm and fuzzies.

Both wrists were shackled, each connected to a long chain made of huge steel links, threaded over a large pipe above my head. I stood in the middle of a long tunnel, lit every ten feet or so with a weak lightbulb, giving off the effect of rings of light alternating with rings of darkness. I tried to find a life metaphor in the image, but gave it up. My wrists were sore from taking the weight of holding me upright while I was out.

Dirt and grime covered every inch of the tunnel, including the floor, suggesting little, if any, use. It was about ten feet wide and about the same in height. To my left, the tunnel ended about a hundred yards away in a large door. To my right, it sloped up and out of view. The air smelled of mold and decay.

A bulb to my left gave me enough light to see by and I glanced at the wall behind me, seeing several dark stains and what seemed to be spatter patterns. My imagination told me the stains were blood. My brain said "good call."

Oh, goody.

Physically, other than the head, I felt relatively okay. I could also feel a pain in my neck and the last few minutes of consciousness came back to me. For the second time in as many weeks, I'd underestimated an opponent. Most of my focus had been on the man instead of the woman. I didn't anticipate the attack and never saw a syringe. This time, the lesson could end up being permanent. At least it seemed tracking down Dr. Collins had been the right call. But it did make me wonder about the good doctor's health.

I no longer wore a shirt or my bullet proof vest and my skin prickled in the cool air. I could see no vents anywhere near me, which made me think I was somewhere underground considering how hot the day turned out to be. Which brought up another question: how long were my eyes closed? No clue. It could be the same day or several, and I had no way to tell from my surroundings.

I tested the chains and manacles from here to Sunday, but found no weakness or give. I gave it up and tried to relax and conserve my energy for whatever came next. A few moments later I heard a sound and saw a rat inching his way down the tunnel in my direction. He got within about three feet of me when I gave a loud shout, causing the rat to scamper away.

I've always considered myself to be high on the bravery scale, but if someone were to turn out the lights, leaving me in the dark with a tunnel full of rats? I'm not sure how long my sanity would hang around.

In what could have been minutes, but seemed like hours, the doors at the far end of the tunnel opened and a man walked in my direction and a few minutes later stood in front of me, staying near the far wall, and trying hard not to smirk. He did it anyway.

"I'll be damned. If it isn't the Jarhead. Brad Stiles, right? Congressman Tyler's lackey."

"Good memory, asshole. But that would be Speaker of the House Cyrus Tyler. He's been promoted. You need to get with the times."

"And the world is far worse off for the change. Funny, I ran off one rat only to have him replaced by a bigger one."

"Yeah. Keep on cracking the jokes, McCain. See how that works out for you." He took out a piece of gum and popped it in his mouth. He offered me a piece, but I declined.

"Suit yourself. You're lucky you're still alive. The hired help wanted to head about ten miles out into the Atlantic and drop you overboard. Not to mention the shot they gave you would have killed most men, but I reckon you're leading a charmed life."

"If you're an example of how charmed my life is, then I need to try something new. Maybe it's time to try Feng Shui. What was in the shot?"

"A derivative of propofol. The stuff that offed Michael Jackson. My operatives said they didn't have time to measure it and gave you the whole load. I bet you have a whale of a headache."

"I've had worse, but some Tylenol would be nice."

"Sorry. Left the bottle in my other pants pocket. How about you and I get down to business? How much do you know? You're going to tell me, one way or another. I'd as soon not have to get all bloody. And I'm sure you would rather be all in one piece when your body turns up."

"Torture? Really? And you think that will work with me?"

He smiled. "I was rather hoping it wouldn't. I'm not a pain-inducing kind of guy, but I have people for that type stuff. And they love it."

I'd hoped the guy would get closer and within range of my legs, but he didn't. Smart. I can do a lot of damage with my feet, but he wasn't taking any chances.

"Sure. Why not. What I know is you used Dr. Collins to plant a bomb in the knee of Senator Hedley Stafford. How am I doing so far?"

"Not bad. But I don't think you know much else."

"I know about the quantum switch and how you plan on using it to detonate the bomb."

He tried hard to hide the surprise and the expression on his face was brief, but it told me I'd hit home. "That's what you needed Isaac Peck to do, work the quantum switch into the knee replacement. Who has the detonator? You or Tyler?" It was a shot in the dark, but turned out to be a good guess on my part.

Stiles slipped a hand into his suit coat pocket and pulled out something which looked like a calculator and held it up. "Power it up, put in the code and BOOM. I've never seen anything like it."

"What about Dr. Collins, did she know what she was doing?"

"She did. At least some of it. We had her daughter and it was either help us or her daughter died. She chose her daughter over Stafford."

Not like I could blame the lady. I would have made the same choice when it came to Mikey. And there could be little doubt she would pay some type of terrible price, like I had.

"What else," he asked. He stood with his hands in his pockets, rocking back and forth on his heels, blowing and popping bubbles. Not a care in the world.

"That's about it. When do you plan on setting off the bomb?"

"Sorry. Need to know. And you don't need to know."

"You Satanists need to learn to share. It's like all you guys have trust issues." I shook my chains. "Where am I going anyway? You can tell me. It will be our little secret."

"I'm not a Satanist. I'm more of a raging agnostic. What I am, though, is a merc who likes to get paid. Tyler pays me well and I get things done in return. Like taking care of you."

"You know he's planned to kill women and children, and will do so again. You know this, right?"

He started to leave, but said over his shoulder. "We all die, McCain. Women, children. Men. And especially the Hand of God. It's what we do with that life while we're here that's important." He turned around, walking backwards for a few steps, so he could see me. "I plan on making as much money and having as much fun as I can before I go over the rainbow to see Dorothy and Toto."

When he got back to the doors, he opened them and waved to someone. A moment later, a man wearing a leather apron and carrying a large toolbox walked passed him and started my way. I could feel my breathing pick up and a queasy feeling explode in my gut.

I shouted, "I thought you didn't want this to get bloody?"

"I lied," he shouted back, and left, closing the door behind him.

I watched my torturer make his way towards me. He walked very slowly, no doubt trying to give me as much time as he could to agonize over what was coming. When I served in Special Forces, we trained for these type of situations, but no amount of training can prepare you for the moment torture begins.

The man stopped in front of me, but also out of kicking range. He opened the toolbox, took out a plastic faceguard and slipped it onto his head. Next were a pair of rubber gloves.

"Worried I might have something contagious? Don't worry, I've had all my shots."

"One can't be too careful these days. Why take the risk? Besides, the facemask is as much to make sure you don't spit in my face. I hate it when they spit in my face. It really pisses me off."

He reached back into his bag and came out with a Taser. "Now, I've been warned about you. I think I need to make sure you will be nice and behave for me. It's nothing personal."

"Oh. This is very personal. When this is over, I *will* kill you. You know that, right?"

"I kind of doubt it." He pointed the Taser at me and pulled the trigger. The darts flew across the tunnel and embedded in my chest while fifty-thousand volts of electricity shot through my body.

The last thing I thought of before darkness crashed into my brain was that I doubted it, too.

CHAPTER TWENTY-SEVEN

When I could once again move, I found myself spread-eagled, my ankles tied by rope to bolts in the floor on either side of me, keeping me from being able to attack with my feet. He'd also covered my mouth with duct tape. I worked hard to get my breathing under control, forcing myself to relax.

Leather Apron leaned against the far wall drinking from a bottle of Jim Beam, waiting for me to get back up to full speed. When he saw me staring back at him, he put the cap on the bottle, set it down next to his toolbox, and lowered his faceguard into place.

He walked right up to me, inches from my face. "Welcome back. I guess you've been having a bad day. Well, it's going to get worse."

I could smell the whiskey on his breath despite the facemask and decided it was time for him to know this would not be a one-way street if I had anything to say about it.

I turned my head away, crinkling my nose at the smell, then accelerated forward. I used my forehead as a battering ram and slammed it into his faceguard, right above the bridge of his nose, flattening the plastic and smashing it into his face.

It knocked him backwards and he yanked the faceguard off, both hands trying to stem the flow of blood from his nose. He cursed a blue streak for a few minutes while I laughed at him.

He used some paper towel from his toolbox and held it up to his nose while he glared at me. When I winked at him I thought he would kill me on the spot, which, all things considered, would be a good thing for me.

But he stood there, one hand holding the paper towel to his nose, the other hand at his side, his fist clenching and unclenching. When the blood stopped flowing, he tossed the towel down into his box, exchanging it for what my grandmother called a pruning knife. The blade was short with a wicked hook on the end. She used hers around the garden. A quick glance up and down the tunnel showed no plants needing a trim, so I figured it was meant for me.

"They told me to keep you alive for a few days and I said I would. But now I'm really going to enjoy making you scream. I may keep you alive for a few weeks. If you move so much as an inch this next time, then I'll start on the lower half of your body first."

He put his facemask back on, then carefully used the hook on the end of the blade to cut a horizontal line about two inches long below my left shoulder blade, then two vertical lines on each side, blood welling up from the cuts. He peeled back the skin, leaving a small flap. Next he reached into a pocket to get a pair of plyers and used them to slowly yank the piece of skin down.

I stifled the scream I felt rising from my throat, my body on fire from the wound. Leather Apron got great enjoyment from his work, an expression of almost ecstasy on his face. I tried to stand still, knowing his threat to turn me into a eunuch would come to pass if I didn't.

"See, they want me to flay you alive. I was going to do your chest and arms today. Then your back tomorrow. Then your legs the next night, leaving your face and neck for last. Now, I think I may do only a little each day, make this last four or five days. Every day when you see me coming down the tunnel, you will beg me to kill you. But I won't. I'll even take a few pictures on my smartphone so you can see what you look like. And don't even think about closing your eyes, or I'll cut your eyelids off.

"The real trick will be to keep you from dying due to shock. I've gotten pretty good at keeping people from bleeding to death, but shock is the tricky part. You never know when the body will decide to quit and shut down. But you're supposed to be a real bad ass. Guess my nose proves that, eh? So I have high hopes for you."

He went back to the bottle of Jim Beam for a couple of more swigs while he let what he said sink in. I knew what a flayed body looked like. One of the guys in my unit disappeared while on patrol in Iraq. His body showed up in the middle of the town square two days later, all the skin flayed from his body. I could feel the bile rise up my throat, but forced it back down.

Leather Apron once again capped his whiskey and started back in my direction when the far doors opened and a woman stepped into view. Leather Apron froze, his knife paused in midair, but only for a moment. He quickly went back to his toolbox and got a Glock, switching the knife to his other hand. My Glock. Son of a bitch.

When the woman got closer, I nearly cried. Elizabeth. She wore a white T-shirt, jeans and boots, her hips swaying while she sang a song, sauntering our way. I could swear she was singing *I Feel Pretty* from *Westside Story.*

I watched Leather Apron and he licked his lips, watching her move, his eyes following the movement of her hips. When she got about twenty feet away, he said, "Stop right there. Who are you?"

"I'm your bonus. Didn't they tell you?" It would be impossible for a woman to be more smoking hot than she looked at that very moment. I made a mental note to ask her later if being an Infernal Lord gave you some type of sway over a man's libido. She bit her bottom lip and smiled in a way that would make gay men switch teams.

I watched Leather Apron swallow hard a couple of times, before he managed to find his voice. "Nah. They didn't tell me nothing about a bonus. You got a name?"

"Uh-huh. I do. Death. Mirsada?"

And the lights went out. Leather Apron fired his gun and in the muzzle flash I saw Elizabeth standing beside Leather Apron, having closed the distance insanely fast. In the darkness, I heard a slight gurgling sound, then Elizabeth shouted out to Mirsada once again.

When the lights came back on, Leather Apron stood facing me, a long red slash under his neck, running from ear to ear, where Elizabeth used his pruning knife to slit his throat. He dropped to his knees, then onto his face, landing at my feet.

"Miss me?" she asked. She used the knife to cut my ropes free, then rummaged in the toolbox until she found the keys to the manacles, unlocking them. I nearly dropped to my knees from exhaustion, but she caught me and held me steady.

I hugged her fiercely, holding her tight against my body. She laughed and it sounded like angels singing. Mirsada came through the doors and jogged down to join us. She took in the scene, the wound on my chest and the dead body at my feet.

"Good to see you still in one piece. Mostly."

I thanked her and broke off the hug with Elizabeth, feeling a bit self-conscious after Mirsada's claims I could not be trusted because of the time I'd spent in bed with Elizabeth. I hugged her, too, to prove I am an equal opportunity hugger. To my surprise, she actually hugged me back.

I bent over and removed my gun from the dead man's hand, slipping it into the back of my jeans, then tried to shake the fatigue out of my arms. I walked over and grabbed the bottle of whisky, removed the cap and, after wiping the top of the bottle with my arm, took a long pull, the whiskey's burn a comfort.

"Thank you, both of you, for bailing my ass out. How did you find me?"

"When you didn't come back around the house, we went looking for you and saw the boat leaving the dock," Mirsada said. "A woman was doing her best to rearrange something in the bottom of the boat, and we saw her lift your arm. There was no way for us to follow the boat, so I called Brother Joshua. He, in turn, had a man, Winston Reynolds, call me. He said they had a way of tracking you and with his help, we got close. After that, it was a matter of searching 'til we found you."

"Thankfully this man," Elizabeth said, kicking the dead body of Leather Apron, "talks loudly. I could hear him from the other side of the wall. We found the breaker box next to the door and Mirsada and I worked out a plan to save your bacon."

"And none too soon, it would appear," said Mirsada, pointing to the wound on my chest. "Flaying is very painful. You are a lucky man we came when we did. How did Reynolds track you?"

"I have a tracking device in my belt, it allows the person with the right software to find me."

In truth, I'd had a chip inserted below the skin at the base of my skull. Only Winston and Kurt knew the right website,

ID and password to find me. The three of us decided to take the plunge after Kurt got buried alive in Hawaii. All three of us carried one in the same place. I hated lying to them, especially after they saved my life, but I was only willing to trust them so far.

"When it comes to this guy, I had him right where I wanted him."

Both women snorted at the same time, then looked at one another, almost ashamed to have shared even a snort.

"Dr. Collins and her daughter, were they at the house?" I asked.

Mirsada nodded. "Yes. Unfortunately, both dead. They made it look like a murder suicide. They set it up to look like the daughter shot her mother, then overdosed on heroine. There was a suicide note on the table. How did they take you?"

I spent time bringing them up to speed on my humiliating take down and my conversation with Stiles. "Now we know we are on the right track. The question is, what to do next. First things first, I need get some Neosporin or something on this and a shirt," I said pointing to the spot on my chest where the skin had been removed. "Where are we?"

"This is a tunnel off the Spring Garden train station in Philadelphia. The station has been closed for decades, but there are several maintenance tunnels here and there and this is one of them. Seems over the years the area around it went downhill, drug dealers, high crime and, at one point, the city walled off the station," Mirsada said. "There are many openings which go who knows where. I get a very bad vibe down here. I think we should go."

"You get a bad vibe," Elizabeth said, "because you are children of the light. As a child of the darkness, this feels more like home." She said this while her fingers brushed lightly against the wall. "I wish it not to be so any longer. I wish to be a child of the light. Let us go."

Mirsada reached behind her back and slid out Muramasa's katana, balanced the blade on her palms, and offered it to me. "You need to keep this with you. If they sent one Infernal Lord after Elizabeth, they may send others. Be prepared, Hand of God."

I tossed the whiskey down and accepted the blade with a small bow, the hilt feeling good in my hand. She then handed me a leather sheath with a shoulder strap and I gently slid the katana home, then slung the strap around my neck, positioning the sword on my back where I could get to it quickly. "Thanks. Better safe than sorry."

The three of us walked down to the door at the end of the tunnel. It opened onto a set of railroad tracks with a small sidewalk on either side and a couple of feet higher than the tracks. There were lights out here as well, set further apart, but they still illuminated the tunnel enough for Mirsada and I to walk without tripping. Elizabeth turned to her right, leading the way. "We have about a mile to reach the access tunnel we used to get down here," she said.

The three of us remained silent while we walked, lost in our own thoughts. I'd once again come close to finding out what my fate would be once I died. Winston warned me at Molly's I'd started to slip, drinking too much and not worrying enough about what could happen if I didn't stay sharp. The woman who took me down on the pier once again proved his point valid. If my time as the Hand of God taught me anything, it was danger came in all kinds of packages, sizes and genders.

Another point to his credit was how bad I wanted to bring the whiskey with us and polish off the bottle. I felt a tremor in my hand and I couldn't tell if it was the rush of adrenaline from being rescued or the shakes from wanting another drink. Too often I turned to the bottle to deal with the stress of my life and I worried it now controlled me more than I controlled it.

Hell, next thing you know my troubles would be dramatized as a Lifetime movie of the week. I was in a rut and the sides were too high for me to see a way out. But if I didn't find a way to change this around, I would get myself, and perhaps others, killed.

Maybe I needed a therapist, but the thought only made me laugh out loud, causing Elizabeth to look over her shoulder to make sure I was OK.

I started to say something but never got the chance. We'd come even with two dark openings on either side of the tracks, likely other long lost maintenance access points. From the one on our left I heard the unmistakable sound of a shotgun being pumped, a round being chambered.

The sound would likely make most people freeze, standing in place. The three of us, being far from normal, reacted instantly. Elizabeth and Mirsada, dove down next to the tracks, both women pulling guns in the same motion. I hit the sidewalk and rolled into the opening to my right, my own gun finding its way into my hand, only a slight fraction behind the women. The shotgun blast followed a fraction of a second later, the blast passing over where we'd just been standing. The sound of the blast seemed to fill the whole tunnel.

I let loose a few shots in the direction of the shot and then moved further down the side tunnel I was in, trying to disappear into the darkness. The women also returned fire, then spread out, so they could cover the opening from different angles.

I could hear nothing from the other opening, but then, in the distance, I heard something: a train. Mirsada and Elizabeth looked to the right and then jumped back onto the sidewalk, their backs to the wall on either side of where their attacker had waited.

"Victor, were you hit?" Elizabeth shouted the question.

"No. I'm good. Can you hear anything?"

I knew her hearing put to shame anything Mirsada or I could hear, but she shouted a no. I watched her say something to Mirsada and the other woman nod back. A second later Elizabeth, gun extended, flew into the other opening, Mirsada right behind her. I started to follow them when the train, sounding like an enraged dragon, barreled by me, blocking my path.

I could see people through the train windows, reading, listening to iPods, or staring into space, unaware of the battle taking place outside their windows, ordinary people leading ordinary lives.

I took a few steps back, forced to wait until I could move, when I sensed something behind me. I turned quickly, my gun held out in front of me, all my senses on high alert. I about chalked it up to my imagination, when I saw a soft glow coming towards me.

I moved in the glow's direction, slowly, turning all my senses up to high alert. After a few feet, the glow got stronger and I saw a man standing in the middle of the passageway. The glow got stronger still and I could see the man's face.

I froze and I felt my world turned upside down, my gun nearly slipping from my fingers. It couldn't be. Can't be. Not possible. But there he stood, his arms out wide, beckoning me.

Son.

Bloody hell. It was my father.

CHAPTER TWENTY-EIGHT

Vincent Donal McCain died at the age of sixty-two from a heart attack, following nearly forty years working the line for Ford Motor Company, building pickup trucks. He'd been dead almost six years now, so all things considered, he looked pretty good.

My father topped my six foot six by two inches and weighed nearly three hundred pounds at death. The men picked to be his pallbearers were all strapping young men, not a lightweight among them.

He looked much like he did the last day I'd seen him alive: a full mane of grey hair which looked in need of a brushing, topped a face which showed the results of decades of consuming Irish whiskey and smoking unfiltered cigarettes. His nose was large, red and covered in drinker's veins.

Dressed in dark blue coveralls he wore every day to work, he looked as I remembered him. I felt my heart stop and break. I loved my dad and we were incredibly close. When he died, I refused to believe he was really gone. There could be no way this mountain of a man could ever die. And now that he stood in front of me, there could be no way he was alive.

I steadied the grip on my gun, keeping it pointed center mass of the man standing in front of me. "I don't know who or what you are, but you're NOT my father. My dad's dead."

My father shook his head in agreement.

I've been granted a few minutes to talk to you, son. Allowances have been made for me to do this. You are in grave danger and you will be dead before nightfall if you don't listen to what I have to say.

Could this be true? I'd seen a lot of weird things since

taking over as the Hand of God. I've battled hellhounds, fallen angels, Infernal Lords. Hell, I almost bought the farm when I stopped to gaze at a frickin' cursed painting. I stood next to Uriel, an archangel, when he banished one of the Watchers back to oblivion, wielding the kind of power only surpassed by God.

"Fine. What do you have? Let's hear it."

He walked closer to me and I caught a whiff of Old Spice Aftershave, the kind he used to buy by the gallon. I almost burst into tears and I lowered my gun. He reached out, one big paw sliding around the back of my neck, and pulled me close, hugging me.

A sob escaped my chest and I hugged him back, experiencing something I thought lost forever. I wasn't home the day he died. I'd been halfway around the world in the mountains of Afghanistan, hunkered down behind some boulders waiting for a target to pass by on the trail below my unit. We were under radio silence and I didn't find out about his death until several days after the funeral. The last time I saw my dad alive was Christmas the previous year and I never got to say goodbye.

I have missed, you my son, and am very proud of you.

His words came to me in my mind, without him having to speak. Somewhere back in the deepest part of my brain, warning bells were trying to go off, but they were faint.

You have been fighting for too long, my son. It is time for you to rest. You are weary and you need your strength for what is to come.

His grip on me tightened and I felt a cold settle into my bones, and he was right. I was very tired. Tired of life, tired of the stress of never knowing when my time would come. Tired of worrying about my soul and what would happen when I did die. If I could only shut my eyes for a little while, I would be stronger, ready to face what came next. With my father watching over me, I would be safe.

Safe. Safe. Safe.

The word repeated over and over in my mind. I became distantly aware I was no longer holding my gun, it had fallen from my hand to the ground.

Safe. Safe. Safe.

And then I smelled it. Not the cologne my father always

wore, but something else. Something rotten, a smell of decay and death. The smell wasn't strong, but it was there and the warning bells began to ring loudly, drowning out the feeling of peace and comfort that the words my father brought. The cold in my joints made it feel like each limb weighed more than I could lift.

When I tried to break the embrace, my father squeezed tighter and it became hard to breath. I fought for each breath like a man having run back-to-back marathons, my lungs burning from lack of oxygen.

Stop fighting me, son. I bring you the peace you need. Let me stop the pain of your existence.

And that's when the truth hit home like a hammer. Hell, my father never talked like this. Pain of your existence? My father came from Irish immigrants and cursed in ways that would make a sailor blush. My father would be more likely to say "stop your belly achin' and sit your ass down and kick back for a bit."

When I raised my head to look into the eyes of my father, the thing which held me knew the jig was up. The eyes turned from green to a bright red and his form changed. My father's face melted into one of nightmare, a walking corpse with most of its face rotted to nothing. It wore some type of cloak, black, dirty and torn in several places.

I felt fingernails dig deeply into my back and the coldness intensified. I knew if I didn't do something soon, I'd be a dead man. The thing gripped me so tightly I could barely move my arms. I tried breaking free, but no dice. Fine. Instead of trying to break free, I squeezed the thing with all the strength I had left and lifted it off its feet. While large, it didn't weigh as much as expected and I bent forward and ran the thing into the closest wall.

It screamed in my mind when I smashed it into the wall and I felt a jolt of intense pain when the creature retaliated and bit savagely into my shoulder. I screamed my own shout of defiance, turned and then drove the thing into the other wall, hearing bones crunch.

Its grip loosened and I shoved myself away, gaining a few feet of space.

You will die, human, and your soul will be mine.

Drawing Muramasa's katana, I said, "I think you're

going to find out it sucks to be you." And I attacked.

I may lack the skill of an ancient samurai, or the grace of a well-trained swordsman like Mirsada, but I make up for it by being large and pissed off.

Tears streamed down my face, the thought of losing my father once again, fueling my rage. For a brief moment, I was able to hold my father and thought I would be given the chance to finally say goodbye, but instead I found something wicked this way comes and another slice of evil that wanted me dead.

I swung the sword with abandon, not trying for precision or skill, but to hack off as much of the thing in the quickest amount of time. Only later, when I relived the moment, did I realize I'd been yelling to my father while doing so.

The creature fought back, long finger nails scratching me across the chest and arms, but I paid the wounds no attention. Muramasa's blade, sharp beyond measure, passed through skin and bone, and with one last, mighty swing, I severed the creature at the waist, killing it and plunging the passageway back into darkness.

I dropped to my knees, breathing hard, my body covered in sweat and blood, and I spent the next several minutes, crying and praying to my father. I promised him I would make Cyrus Tyler, Preston Deveraux and any other follower of the prince of darkness I could find, pay for sullying his memory.

I searched in the darkness, found my gun and started back down towards the tracks. The train had long since disappeared into the night and I approached cautiously, listening.

From the other passageway, on the other side of the tracks, I heard someone sobbing and wailing. I practically hurdled the tracks to the other passageway. In the distance I could see the same kind of glow I noticed before my attack.

I picked up my pace and when I got close, I saw another creature like the one I'd encountered, holding Mirsada, her body stretched out in its arms at waist level.

"I tried to save you, I swear, I tried. Heaven help me, but I tried. Radomir, I'm sorry, but I tried."

Her skin, pale normally, seemed to be almost translucent, and I knew the thing was slowly killing her. When I got close enough I tucked the gun back into my jeans and moving quietly, got behind it before making my presence known.

"Hey, asshole. That's a friend of mine."

Flaming eyes turned my way, but too late. This time I aimed my strike, and I'll be damned if I didn't separate the creatures head from its body on the first try. The glow instantly vanished and I heard both bodies hit the concrete floor. I sheathed the sword, careful not to cut off a few of my own fingers in the process, searched until I found Mirsada, picked her up and headed back to the train tunnel and what light it provided.

I sat on the edge of the walkway, holding Mirsada. Her eyes were closed and her breathing ragged. I held her, rocking her like a child, and talked to her softly, telling her to come back.

I'm not sure how long we were there before her eyes opened, but finally, they did and when they met mine, they welled up with tears. She sat up shakily, looking around.

"Where is Radomir? He was here. I don't know how, but he was here."

"I'm sorry, Mirsada, but he wasn't."

I told her about my own battle and how the creature came to me in the form of my father. "Who is Radomir?" I asked.

She buried her face in her hands and cried more, before answering. "I grew up in Bosnia. My parents were Serbian and my father played a role during the ethnic cleansing which ravaged my country. Radomir and I were friends. Close friends. He and his family were Muslims and one night my father and a group of his friends were rounding up any Muslims they could find in our neighborhood. Radomir and his family went into hiding, but he told me where they would be so I would not worry," She choked down a few sobs, then continued.

"My father knew we were friends and when they could not find him and his family, my father came to me and asked me if I knew where they were hiding. I didn't want to tell him, but my father appealed to my nationalism. He told me it was my duty to tell him where they were hiding and I had to make a choice: my Muslim friends or my own family. I told him where Radomir's family were and they sent a mob over to the house, found them hiding in a hidden room in the basement, and drug the whole family into the street. They made Radomir rape his own sister, then shot them. I know all this because my father made me watch." Her whole body shook at the memory. "I begged him, to spare his life, to let him go. He ignored me and, in the end, I did nothing. Radomir *pleaded* to me to make them stop, and I did…nothing." Her voice trailed off, and a tear tracked down her cheek.

A minute passed, then she said, "When the peace came and the widespread ethnic cleansing stopped, my father and his friends? They continued to carry out attacks against Muslims and other non-Serbians, anyone not of pure Serbian bloodlines. I helped them." She shook her head in disgust. "I learned to fight and I was good. I felt numb to the suffering of others."

She stopped crying and held her hands in her lap. "For a time I no longer cared if I lived or died. But every night, Radomir came to me in my dreams, pleading for me to save him. And every night, I let him die. Finally, I met a woman who introduced me to the Faith and in time, I became the Hand of God. I work now, to atone for what happened to Radomir and his family, and all the other innocents we killed."

"The sins of the father are not the sins of the daughter. And, hell, you were only a kid. You did what you did because you didn't know any better."

"That's not true. I knew better. I could have lied and said I didn't know where they were and perhaps, if I'd done so, they would be alive today. But I have no regrets, Victor. I fight those who create such evil."

I nodded. My own story was not much different. I knew trying to save Mikey was wrong, but I did it anyways. I wondered if every Hand of God had a similar story. If we were all wayward people, adrift and trying to find our way back to shore.

I glanced around and then another wave of concern hit me. "Where's Elizabeth?"

Mirsada turned and looked down the passageway. "She was in front of me when we started trying to find the shooter. She told me to hang back a bit because a gunshot would likely do little damage to her, compared to me. I did, and then a glow appeared between us and I saw Radomir. Or, what I thought was Radomir. What do you think those things were?"

"I don't know, but I bet Brother Joshua will." I stood,

went to the passageway and shouted for Elizabeth. Nothing. "You don't happen to have a flashlight, do you?"

Mirsada reached into an inner pocket of her vest and came out with a keychain with a small flashlight on the end. We searched the passageway until it ended in a supply closet, long since abandoned and a ladder leading up. Two bodies lay next to the ladder. I think they were both men, but one was stomped beyond recognition, so I couldn't be sure. The other must have been the shotgun shooter. I figured this to be the case as he had a shotgun sticking out of his chest, having been rammed through his body from behind. There could be little doubt Elizabeth came this way.

I climbed the ladder and lifted the door. It groaned, rusty hinges protesting, but with a last shove, it flopped open.

The warm night air greeted us and we both climbed out into an alley between what looked to be two warehouses. I lifted the door and dropped it shut. We could see a main thoroughfare at one end of the alley and we walked that way.

When we got to the end of it, we got our bearings and Mirsada lead the way back to my car. We got there with no problems and Mirsada handed me the keys and I opened the trunk, got a new shirt and more ammo for the Glock.

She took out the medical kit and our roles were reversed, with her now taking care of my wounds. There were scratches on my body I didn't even know about until she gently rubbed antiseptic covering each one. She did the same for the torture wound and then covered it with gauze, taping it into place.

"Do you ever wonder what the hell we're really doing? If we're making a difference?" I asked as she worked.

She let out a small sigh. "Only every day. Every time we eliminate a threat, two more show up. It's one reason I've been on edge since arriving here in the States. I'd hoped it might be different here and it's not."

I smiled. "Suggesting I need to do better?"

"No. Suggesting no matter how good we are, we won't ever be good enough."

She tore off the last piece of tape, secured the gauze, and then put the kit away. I put my shirt on carefully, trying not to rub the wounds, but did it anyway.

"But there's one thing I know for sure," she said.

"And what's that?"

She stared off at the city lights. "That if you, I and the other Hand of God around the planet weren't doing what we do, things would be even worse. Every time we kill something evil, that's one more thing which can't hurt anyone."

I breathed in deeply and let it out slow. I knew she was right. That was always the argument, it could be worse. Without myself, Winston, Kurt, and others there would be hundreds, if not thousands of dead people from the foiled bird flu attack. And the Watchers would have laid waste to the entire planet, if set free. There could be no doubt we were making a difference. Only it was hard to tell if we were making a real difference or trying to empty the ocean one spoonful at a time.

"Do you think that's enough?"

It took a while, but she nodded slowly. "It has to be."

We got into the car and waited for two hours before we left, neither of us talking about the obvious. Elizabeth was gone and we didn't know why.

CHAPTER TWENTY-NINE

"Do you think she brought those creatures to kill us?" Mirsada finally asked.

"I've been wondering the same thing, but I doubt it. I mean, if she wanted me dead she could have let the guy flay me alive and then try to take you out. For all we know they were sent after her and we were collateral damage. She could have killed me several times over and hasn't. I will cut her some slack until we find out what happened. After all, another couple of minutes and people would be wondering the same about you and me."

We were holed up at a Waffle House in downtown Philly. I ordered the largest omelet on the menu, added hash browns, four slices of toast, butter milk gravy, and a side order of bacon, washed down with a gallon of coffee. Mirsada sat eating a bowl of oatmeal with chocolate milk. Wimp.

I could not ever remember being more tired than right at that very moment. Yet at the same time, I could not be more ready for a fight. I called J when we pulled into the parking lot with a backup burner phone I kept for emergencies and he told me we likely came up against a couple of wraiths and were lucky to be alive. Their main claim to fame came from their ability to, literally, suck the life out of you. They read your surface thoughts and then pretend to be someone you know, to draw you close. Then they drain your life force, thereby extending theirs.

J believed Lucifer and Tyler kept them in the area to act like spiders, capturing anyone who came too close to finding their kill spot in the abandoned train station. I didn't really give a damn one way or the other. They tried to use the memory of my father to kill me and it royally pissed me off. Fine. They want to play hardball, then fuck'em.

My resolve, which left a lot to be desired over the last few months, needed a good ass kicking to get it on track and the last twenty-four hours did the trick. And now they had not one, but two ticked off Hand of Gods to rain down fire and brimstone on their ass. Like me, she was angered to the core with the wraith using Radomir to try and kill her. Sons-a-bitches must pay.

"I'm surprised to hear myself say this, but I think you're right. It goes against every fiber of my body to believe her, but I do. I now think she does want to be redeemed. Do you think she died down there?"

"Anything is possible. But it's been my experience when you kill an Infernal Lord, they turn to brimstone and we didn't find her body or smell any sulfur. Maybe they've captured her, but it would take a small army to put that woman down."

She drank her chocolate milk and took another bite of her oatmeal, with half a bowl left, while my plate was two pieces of bacon short of being clean. "What do we do next?"

I wolfed down the bacon, set my plate to the side, took my laptop out of the carrying case and fired it up. "We know there's a bomb in Stafford's knee and they can set it off any time they want, so the question is when? Let's take a look at his upcoming schedule and see what he has planned."

I spent the next ten minutes checking out his calendar, that of the Senate and found several things which might be the target, but nothing jumped out at me. Then I found it.

I clicked over to the Google Machine and typed in Senator Stafford and schedule and hit enter. Three lines down, under the news tab, I found a short blurb about a fundraiser to be held here in Philadelphia, hosted by Stafford at his home. The guest list? No less than the President and Vice-President of the United States. Every big money donor and bundler would be there as well, not to mention anybody who was anybody.

"Holy hell." I flipped the laptop around so she could read the same blurb.

Her eyes widened. "The Constitution. The one Isaac put in his duffel. The order of succession here in the States. If both the President and Vice-President are killed, then—"

"Tyler becomes the next President of the United States.

The last presidential election was last year, meaning, he would be president for three years before there's another election. Think of the chaos the man could cause between now and then."

"Hold on. If the President and Vice-President are both there, then security will be jacked up for their visit. They will have bomb sniffing dogs and electronic devices. Won't they find the bomb?"

"I doubt it. Stafford will already be there. Besides, the Majority Leader of the U.S. Senate won't be going through the same security checks anyone else will be that night. I'm guessing they won't. I'm sure Tyler will have someone on the inside, and the moment the three men are together, they will set the bomb off and this country will have its second President Tyler. Ironic. The first President Tyler also became president with the death of his predecessor, William Henry Harrison."

"How do we stop them? Is there someone we can call?"

"That's the problem with things like this. We ran into the same problem with the Church's plans to infect thousands of kids with a virus delivered by computers. It sounds like you've been sniffing glue when you say it out loud."

"Still, with the President and Vice-President on hand, they have to take any threat seriously. How could they ignore it?"

"I would normally agree with you. But again, say it out loud. 'Dear Mr. Secret Service agent, the President is in danger because the Speaker of the House arranged for a bomb to be planted into the knee joint of the Majority Leader of the Senate.' See the problem? We would get the same reaction going straight to Stafford. They'd lock us up on a seventy-two hour psych hold."

"Then we need to attack it from the other end. You said this man, Stiles, showed you the detonator, right? So we find him and take it away from him."

"Now you're talking. But we need a backup plan, just in case we can't find him or he doesn't have it any longer. How well can you cut a rug?"

Her spoon stopped half-way to her mouth. "Come again?"

"Dance. How well do you dance? I think you and I need to attend that fundraiser this weekend. Part of the event is a ball being held in the convention center next to the building where Stafford lives. It also means you will have to find something else to wear. I mean, I love the whole wood elf garb, but I'm not sure you should wear it to a black tie event."

She gave me the finger, but smiled doing it. "You really think you can get us in?"

"All it takes is a fifty grand donation to the Democratic Party. Piece of cake. Let me call Kurt and tell him what I need."

I got my hacker friend out of bed, gave him the details, and set him to work. I paid our bill and we left the Waffle House. When we started we had no clue what we were after. Now we had targets and a working plan. I worried about what Elizabeth's disappearance meant, but shoved it to the side. Forward momentum is what I needed. We now had it and I wanted to make sure we kept it.

First things first, I called and booked adjacent rooms at the Hotel Monaco. The hotel, rated the best in Philadelphia, sat right downtown, with Independence Hall and the Liberty Bell across the street. To stay there, we would both need a step up in wardrobe. I hit the Brooks Brothers in town to pick up slacks, shirts and new shoes, claiming lost luggage as my excuse. Right down the street, we found a boutique to suit Mirsada's European sensibilities. Between the two of us, we racked up a clothing bill of several thousand dollars, but we were now dressed to the nines.

We hid our weapons in the weapons locker of my car, though Mirsada was not happy parting with her sword. When I pointed out you can't walk into one of the country's premier hotels packing a katana, she relented. But not easily.

Our rooms were not overly large, but both had king size beds and a view of Independence Hall. We made arrangements to hook up mid-afternoon. I then went to my room, took a hot shower and then went to bed for a quick power nap, asking the desk to wake me at one p.m.

It seemed I'd barely closed my eyes when I got the phone call to get up and at 'em, but I got dressed, this time in slacks, loafers and a polo shirt and headed to the lobby to wait for Mirsada. She came down a few minutes later wearing an all-white tennis outfit, shirt and shorts, with white Nike shoes. She'd braided her hair into a French braid. All she needed to complete the ensemble was the racket.

The change in outfits made her into a completely different woman. The warrior now became every man's desire and more than one head turned to watch her walk from the elevators to join me.

I offered her my arm and she slipped her hand around my elbow and we walked outside into the shimmering heat. Stafford's town home was only a few blocks down the street and we took our time getting there, window shopping and acting like a happy couple.

Stafford lived in the Founders Building, situated on Washington Square, a six acre park in downtown Center City. We strolled down paths winding in and out of the trees, while watching the comings and goings from the Founders Building. The Secret Service undoubtedly were already engaged in pre-visit planning and I wouldn't be surprised if someone was keeping track of us while we walked around. We sat on a bench for a bit on the other side of the park, Founders partially visible through the trees.

My phone chirped, I pulled it out of my pocket and answered. Mirsada crossed one long leg over the other, bouncing her foot and I tried hard not to stare.

"I'm on the scene," Winston said. "Kurt will be here on the next flight. I'll work to find our missing friend and let you know when I can track him down."

I'd asked Kurt to get a hold of Winston and set him on the trail of Stiles. Kurt did some digging and found a man with that name and general age owning a small home on the outskirts of D.C. Winston and Kurt would set up surveillance and see if it was our guy, while Mirsada and I would watch for him here in Philadelphia. I had to think he knew I had made it out of the train station by now, skin intact, thank the dear Lord, and would be coming for him. I hoped I saw him coming before he saw me.

"Good. Call me as soon as you know anything."

"Any word on Elizabeth?" Winston asked.

"Nothing, man. It has me worried. But all we can do is what we're doing. Happy hunting."

"Yeah. You, too. Try and stay alive."

We both hung up and I put my phone away, then filled in Mirsada on the part she couldn't hear. "Now we wait. With any luck, Winston and Kurt will be able to track down Stiles and then we can move on him.”

“And what do you and I do?”

“Pray for divine intervention.”

“Does that work for you very often?”

I laughed. “Almost never.”

And then it did. Across the park I saw a man I knew, walking past the Founders Building. A man I would never forget. Preston Deveraux strode down the sidewalk like a man without a care in the world.

Time for Fate to give Preston something to care about. And I was the man for the job.

CHAPTER THIRTY

It's hard for me to blend in with the crowd, considering I'm a good foot taller than anyone else and almost twice as wide. This meant letting Mirsada take the lead in following Deveraux, while I hung back even further and followed her. We were on the opposite side of the street and it gave me a chance to watch her at work, not to mention to admire her figure and the way she walked and moved through the crowd.

I'd never given any thought to there being other people who were the Hand of God. And if I had, I would never have considered one being a woman. That's not a sexist comment—at least I don't think it is. There have been times when the only reason I survived an encounter with a big ole' nasty was because I was bigger and stronger than the whack job I was up against.

For Mirsada to do what I do, day in and day out, that made her one tough lady. She didn't have my size to help out, which meant she needed to compensate for it in other ways. I thought back to her fighting Muramasa and how she did so with no fear, no doubt. She expected to kick his ass and gave it a good run.

I'd asked her earlier how many years she'd served as the Hand of God and she told me she'd been doing this for going on four years, a lot longer than me. The years gave her a hard look and I could only imagine how I would look after a few more years of doing this job, if I managed to stay alive. I remembered once seeing the before and after pictures of presidents and how the job aged them. I now understood how they felt.

And yet, the woman was beautiful in her own way. You would not call any one feature gorgeous, but the collection made her the kind of woman most men turned and gave a second glance. More than one man whistled while she strolled down the sidewalk. One of them pushed things a bit far and it was hard for Mirsada to ignore him, but she did to keep up with Preston. When I went by the asshole I pretended to stumble and slammed him into a light pole, giving him a little extra shoulder for good measure. Jerk.

Mirsada stopped at an ice cream shop and placed an order. When I finally caught up she gave me a cup filled with a double scoop of strawberry and a spoon, her cup filled with chocolate. We found an empty table in front of the shop and sat down, tearing into the ice cream, my back to where Preston had been walking.

"He met a woman in front of the coffee shop on the next block. I couldn't see her face because she wore a hoodie and kept her face hidden. The two shook hands and then walked inside together. Deveraux was smiling. It seemed like they knew each other well."

I ate my strawberry ice cream and considered what I wanted to do. My preference was to walk into the coffee shop, grab a handful of hair and then slam his face into a table a half dozen times. Not a good call in a busy city in the middle of the day, but that's what I felt like doing.

"He doesn't know me," Mirsada said. "Why don't I go inside and maybe I can even get a table close enough to them to listen in on their conversation."

"You only assume he doesn't know you." I glanced around, seeing a bookstore a little ways up the block. "Let's find a spot inside the bookstore where we can see the coffee shop."

She finished her ice cream, tossed the cup into a trash can and walked inside the bookstore with me right behind her. I found a magazine rack near the front window and browsed through a copy of the *Economist* while watching for Deveraux. I learned the Iranian revolution was over, politicians were moving to the center, which was utter bullshit, and European banks were looking for stress relief. Aren't we all?

A half hour later, Deveraux walked out and headed in our direction. But he was not alone. The woman he had met with came out on his arm, and the two of them were laughing like old friends. She tilted her face in my direction, and despite the hoody,

I could clearly see Elizabeth's face. I nearly ripped the magazine in half, watching as they walked past the bookstore and up the street. A clerk shot me a dirty look and I smoothed out the magazine, returning it to the shelf slightly more wrinkled than when I picked it up.

Mirsada appeared beside me, her anger barely in check. "Did you see who he was with? You don't get to keep me from killing her this time. Swear it."

I didn't answer, but watched until they were nearly a block ahead and left the store, Mirsada fuming at my heels.

I didn't know what to think about what Elizabeth was doing. There could be no doubt she found a way to get in Deveraux's good graces, but I didn't have a clue what the end game could be. In Columbus, they tried to kill her. Or had they? In the end, the most they did was shoot her with a tracer bullet. Did they do all that for my benefit? I couldn't see how it helped. Now my head really did hurt.

They turned left and walked down to another hotel, going into the lobby. When I got to the door, I waited a few beats and then went inside in time to see the door close on an elevator with the two of them inside, starting to kiss as the door closed.

I watched the numbers go up over the elevator, finally stopping on the ninth floor, staying there. I walked over and punched the button harder than normal and waited for my ride up. I don't know why her kissing Deveraux bothered me, but it did. Mirsada stood there, arms crossed, and the two of us looked like ticked off lovers.

It made me think of the first time Samantha kissed me in a small dive bar in Louisville, not out of love, but to cause a distraction hoping an Infernal Lord would not notice her. And Elizabeth first plying me with sex to get me to do what she wanted. It was a new world and I felt like I was walking in quicksand a lot of the time.

The elevator dinged, the doors opened and we got on and rode up to the ninth floor. It opened onto a quiet, red carpeted hallway, rooms stretching off in both directions. We stepped out and the doors closed behind us and we tried to decide which way to go. Then my phone chirped and I got a text from a number I didn't recognize which said "room 914."

A sign on the wall pointed me in the direction I needed to go and made my way to the right room. At the far end of the hall, I noticed a door leading to the stairway was closing. I stood to the left of room 914, and Mirsada stood on the other side. We listened for a moment, but heard nothing. The door was cracked open with a drink coaster.

I almost charged into the room, but made myself walk normal, trying to stay calm. I know most martial arts teachers will tell you to be an effective fighter, you must keep your emotions in check, the spiritual and the physical working in harmony. I've found, for me, the angrier I am, the more emotional I am, the more carnage I can create. I feed off the turmoil and it brings clarity to what I need to do. Weird, huh?

The room was large with a king size bed, full sofa, two armed chairs and a desk. I stopped by the bed, and looked around but did not see Deveraux. His suit coat and tie were folded on one of the chairs, but that was the only evidence he'd been in the room.

Mirsada shut the door behind me and said, "In the bathroom?"

I walked over to the bathroom door and opened it, finding Deveraux in the combination shower and tub, trussed up with what looked to be a phone cord, a wash rag stuffed into his mouth. His normally perfectly quaffed hair now stood on end. The man, at least, had put up a fight. But lost. He stared at me a moment, his eyes dazed, but then they focused and I could see intelligence return. And hatred.

I grabbed him by the shirt and lifted him out of the tub and sat him down hard on the toilet. "I'm going to remove the rag. If you start screaming I will put it back and then do things to you which might not help me get to heaven, but will make me feel a whole lot better. How the next few minutes go, is up to you. Understand?"

He nodded his agreement and I removed the gag. He spat out threads for a few moments, while he regained his composure. I could see a nice welt popping up on his forehead where Elizabeth clocked him with something, a nasty bruise marring those George Clooney good looks.

"Well, well, well. Victor McCain stooping so low he

needs to have a woman do his dirty work for him. Oh, how the mighty have fallen. First you use Samantha Tyler, then Elizabeth Bathory." He leered at Mirsada, "and now this gorgeous creature. Hiding behind skirts. Maybe you should be called the Wimp of God."

"So says the man tied up like a Thanksgiving turkey because he thought with the wrong head. But you're wrong, Preston. This woman is not an empty skirt. She's also a Hand of God. Where's Elizabeth?"

"Then my apologies, my dear. You must be Mirsada Vesela, since you don't look Asian. I've read about you, but never seen a picture, much to my sorrow. We knew there were two female members of your little club, one European and one Asian."

"Preston, I asked you where's Elizabeth? Don't make me ask you again."

"Obviously, not here and where she is now, I have no clue. She betrayed me, tied me up and tossed me in the tub, then left."

I let that go for the moment, because he was right. If she left him for me, he likely didn't know where she was going.

"How did she get to you? A few days ago you wanted to kill her. You sent Muramasa to cut her to pieces. Why the meet and greet?"

"She contacted me, said she wanted to turn you over. She told me you knew about the bomb and she wanted to be forgiven by the Lord of Light. She also told me if I tried to double-cross her again she would rip my throat out and eat it. I believed her. She suggested we meet in a public place, one with a lot of people, just the two of us. I agreed and you see how it turned out for me. You would have thought an ex-lover would treat me better."

"What the hell are you talking about?" The cold, dark anger which seemed to be a large part of my existence these days, began to fight for control of my brain. I didn't want to hear what the man had to say, but knew I would beat him to death if he didn't talk.

"Elizabeth recruited me when I was a young man, showed me the pleasures I could enjoy if I agreed to follow the

Lord of Light. She is greatly responsible for making me the man I am today. I owed it to her to at least listen. In Columbus, we weren't trying to kill her so much as punish her and kill you."

I looked at Mirsada and I could see doubt in her eyes. I didn't know what to believe myself. If Elizabeth and Deveraux had been lovers, it would explain the kiss in the elevator. Considering she murdered women and children to bathe in their blood, the fact she slept with Deveraux shouldn't make one bit of difference to me, but it did. I could feel my cheeks burning with Mirsada standing next to me, once again being proven right that the Infernal Lord used sex to get what she wanted. Did that include me? I liked to think when it came to me, it wasn't all about the sex. Idiot? Wishful thinking?

More immediately, if she was still on my team, then why didn't she wait for Mirsada and me at the hotel room? She must have seen us in the bookstore, since she sent me a text to tell me the room number. But why run and not wait for us? The closing stairwell door must have been her. It appeared Elizabeth was running her own game now and, for whatever reason, cut Mirsada and me out.

I shoved my anger and hurt down and tried to focus on the matter at hand. I needed to know what Deveraux knew.

"Time to cut this short, Preston. I need to ask you a few questions about what Cyrus Tyler has planned. When will he set off the bomb?"

"No clue. Not to change the subject, but I am curious. Have you ever wondered how your life would have been different if you'd killed me in that kitchen in Louisville, like I advised you to do? Not killing me lead directly to the death of Dominic Montoya, the capture of Samantha Tyler, and many other things you have no knowledge of, all because you didn't have the guts to do what needed to be done. You lost your soul because you were too weak to do what needed to be done. No wonder you have women doing your work for you now. I think—"

I grabbed him by the throat, cutting him off. "You know what, Preston? You're right. I should have killed you when I had the chance. That's a mistake I won't make this time."

I lifted him off the toilet, raised the lid and forced

Deveraux onto his knees. "I hope you find this a fitting way to die, Preston, because this is what your whole life means in the grand scheme of things."

I shoved his face into the water, pressing down as hard as I possibly could. I thought he would fight me, try and raise his head out of the water, but he didn't. Not at first. His body remained calm, almost relaxed, with the occasional air bubbles floating to the surface. Back on that night long ago he told me he didn't fear death because Satan promised him another shot at the big time and he would come back stronger and more powerful than ever. What kind of man wants to die bad enough so he can go to Hell, and then come back? Whack job.

Facing death bravely in thought, is one thing. Doing it is something else altogether. When the last of his air was gone, he started trying to fight his way free, his body's need for air overpowering his desire to die his way. His feet drummed the floor and he tried to twist out of my grasp, but I had strength and leverage on my side, and kept his face planted inside his porcelain grave. In the end, his struggles didn't make any difference. I held him down until I was sure he was gone.

I stood, breathing harder than I should have been. I could cross killing Deveraux off my bucket list, yet it didn't make me feel any better. And that surprised me. I finally had revenge for Dominic Montoya, a man I knew only for a few days, but for whom I felt great empathy. And for Samantha, who spent a brutal three months being ravaged by a fallen angel, thanks to this man.

In the end, his death meant very little in the grand scheme of things. None of our lives did, when it gets right down to it. But in the here and now, they were all we had. Hell, when did I become so maudlin?

Mirsada laid a hand on my arm. "We should be going, don't you think?"

"Yeah. We should. Let's toss the place first."

We did, but found nothing useful. We agreed to leave separately then meet up at the Hotel Monaco. She left first. I sat on the edge of the bed and stared at Preston through the bathroom door. I wondered if Satan would grant his request to return as an Infernal Lord. Wouldn't that be a kick in the teeth? Not for the first time I wondered how I'd die. One thing I promised myself: death by toilet would not be allowed to happen.

I gave myself a mental bitch slap to snap out of it, saluted the other man's dead body and left the room. Mikey and Deveraux were together again, maybe even nailed to the same wall. Sucks to be them.

Now it was time to add Cyrus Tyler to their growing old boys club in Hell.

CHAPTER THIRTY-ONE

Mirsada and I laid low for the remainder of the day, hanging out at the hotel and rested. She joined me for dinner in my room and then retired early to get some sleep. She didn't bring up what Deveraux told us about being recruited by Elizabeth, never said I told you so, and didn't rub it in my face. For that I was eternally grateful.

I almost asked her to stay with me for the night, but resisted the temptation. If I didn't reign in my libido, I would need to change my theme song to *I Get Around.* Perhaps I wanted to put Elizabeth and Samantha out of my mind. Who the hell knows? I think what bothered me more than anything else was Elizabeth not telling me about her past with Deveraux. We all keep secrets and I could intellectualize why she wouldn't tell me, but it didn't help.

I checked in with Winston and Kurt, but no sign of Stiles. Kurt did his best to find the man via cyber space, but Stiles lived off the grid. I suggested he used an alias for most things and we weren't likely to find anything, but for them to keep after him.

Several times while lying in bed, I picked up my phone and started to call Samantha, only to put the phone down each time. I needed to move on, but found it hard doing so. I wondered if it would be too late for me to join a monastery and live out my life reading esoteric texts and chanting Latin songs at sunset. Yeah, I think that ship sailed a long time ago.

The next morning, I thought for sure the death of Preston Deveraux would make the morning paper and the local stations, but there was no mention of him. Nor later that night on the evening news shows.

That was not the case for Dr. Collins and her daughter.

Their deaths were all over the news for several days. Senator Stafford issued a statement of sympathy for her family and promising to do something in the next session of congress to increase funding for drug treatment programs. If he only knew. The Speaker of the House, Cyrus Tyler, said this proved we had to get tougher on crime and to put an end to the movement to make illegal drugs legal.

What a sanctimonious son of a bitch. I almost threw the remote control though the TV set, it made me so angry. The man made the usual politician seem like an angel in comparison.

My phone shouted at me and a glance at the screen told me Winston was calling.

"What's up brother from another mother?"

"Man, we're bringing the circus to you,' he said.

"Tyler is coming to Philadelphia? Damn."

"Yeah, to a place called Washington Square. I've never been there, but with a name like that, I'm guessing it's not far from where you're holed up?"

"Very close. Stafford's fundraiser is being held at a building right off the square. Why's Tyler coming?"

"He's called for all good Republicans to show up in the park and protest the fact the President is holding a fundraiser while the country is having problems abroad and at home. They hope to get a couple thousand Tea Party members to show, make the news. Same old bull shit. You think he wants to be nearby when things happen?"

"Stride right into the rubble and take charge? With a bank of cameras and microphones already there? I think you can bet on it."

"Well, we are on our way. Save us a spot at the party. Still no sign of Stiles. He's gotta be there someplace."

He hung up and I went back to wanting to throw things. Over the next few days Mirsada and I toured the city in our down time. We visited Independence Hall, took in the Liberty Bell and ate our dinners at different restaurants around town. I got fitted for a tux for the fundraising dinner and ball on Saturday. Mirsada picked out a stunning blue Donna Karan dress. I only knew the name because she told me. I knew it was fancy by the price tag. Ouch.

I called a car company to arrange to pick us up at the appointed time and then we settled in to wait. Winston shadowed Tyler to a couple of different events, but found no signs of Stiles. Kurt sat in a van near the man's house, same result. Nada. Both Winston and Kurt would drive to Philly Friday night, then join the Tea Party crew with Tyler in Washington Square.

Time seemed to drag by until Saturday. Mirsada and I ate a large lunch at an outdoor café. One thing I can say about the woman, is she's not afraid to eat. We both took naps late in the afternoon, not knowing when we would get the next chance.

While asleep, I dreamed about Samantha, Elizabeth and Mirsada. They kept saying I overlooked something about Tyler's plan. They berated me for not seeing it and I pleaded with them to tell me what I'd missed. I tossed and turned, but when I woke up, I knew what they were talking about.

I got my phone and sat heavily in one of the chairs and called Kurt. When he answered I said, "Kurt, I need you to look at who works for Senator Stafford, the President and Vice-President, but I'm thinking you need to zero in on Stafford."

"I can do that, dude, but what am I looking for?"

"If they plan to set the bomb off tonight, then they need to do it when the three men are together. How will they know when that is unless someone tells them? They need a bird-dog to alert them to the right moment. Otherwise, the plan fails. Have your hacking buddies hit this hard. We've only got a couple of hours left."

"You got it, man." He hung up and I tossed the phone on the end table and took one of the longest showers of my life, trying hard not to think of anything, but thinking about everything.

An hour and a half before the event, we got dressed and met in my room for a last strategy pow wow before the car came to pick us up. Mirsada dazzled in the Donna Karan, her hair once again in a French braid, with a blue clutch purse to complete the ensemble.

She helped me with my bow tie. God how I hate ties. Suits and I rarely ever made an acquaintance and I hadn't worn a tux since my senior prom. I apologized for not getting her a corsage, making her laugh.

Once we were both properly dressed, we sat down on the bed to discuss the evening. I told her about my thoughts on the spotter, but admitted I didn't have anything else.

"I wish I could tell you what I had planned, but I don't have a clue. With any luck, we will see Stiles and can take him down. Or Kurt comes through and we find out who they have on the inside. If not, we need to try and get to Stafford. I still think if we tell him there's a bomb in his knee, one he won't believe us, and two, I can't afford to be that much in the spotlight. But we might not have any other play. Do you have any last minute insights?"

"I spend most of my time improvising when I am in situations like this, so I think we go, see what's what and then react the best we can."

"I'm beginning to think you are the female me. Besides, if you're like me, you work better when you're winging it."

We went downstairs and a man stood in the lobby holding a sign which read "Clay." Clay is one of my favorite undercover names and tonight Mirsada and I were Wilson and Audrey Clay, of the Kentucky Clay's. Henry Clay is surpassed by only Abraham Lincoln, when it comes to politicians born in Kentucky. Kurt created a good back story and documents for me some months back, for when I needed an alias. It didn't take much for him to do the same for Mirsada.

We introduced ourselves to our driver, and then followed him out to the car, a Cadillac limo. We got in and the driver started on the short drive to the Founders Building. The evening was warm, with a bright full moon hanging over the city. Things slowed when we turned right by Washington Square, with the traffic backed up due to people being dropped off for the event.

To my left, I could see the protestors in full swing in Washington Square. I could make out several protest signs, one saying "stop shredding our Constitution." Another said "English is our language, no excetions, learn it" with exceptions misspelled. Glorious.

In the distance I could see a stage and guessed that was where Cy Tyler and the other pols would be speaking. I texted Winston and asked if he was in position, getting a smiley face in response. Cute.

Our car made it to the curb at the Founders Building, and we got out. The driver gave me his card and told me to call when we were ready to be picked up. I thanked him and offered Mirsada my arm. She accepted and we walked inside.

We were required to first meet a hostess where my ID was checked, confirmed, and signed in. Then we passed through a security check. Despite my nervousness, we got through with no issues. People shot glances at us constantly. I am sure it was due to Mirsada looking so lovely and not because she walked with a man twice the size of everyone else there.

The ballroom at the Founders was huge and decorated in Early American, what else, with a nod towards modern sensibilities. Yeah, whatever. The main thing was a band played at one end, there was a spot for dancing and off to either side of the room, there was a large bar. I steered Mirsada to one of these and ordered a Fireball Whisky neat, while she asked for a Riesling.

When our drinks were served, we made our way to a table off to one side, allowing us to people watch. The President, Vice-President and Majority Leader would not make an appearance until much later in the evening. My watch showed seven p.m. and I knew from the email we received in response to my donation, the President and VP would show around eight, giving us an hour to figure something out.

About half way through my whisky, my phone vibrated in my tux pocket. A quick glance showed me it was Kurt.

"Tell me you got something," I said.

"Janet Marx. She's an assistant to Stafford's chief of staff, the one who makes sure things run on time and acts as the go-getter when anyone needs anything. One of the things we got from the Black Hat's computer was a list of Church members who could prove useful. Her name is on the list. She has be your girl."

He texted me her DMV photo and I thanked him and hung up. I put my lips near Mirsada's ear and whispered, "We have a name. Janet Marx. Aide to Stafford. We need to find her. Now."

I pulled up the picture and showed it to Mirsada and we both stood, leaving our drinks behind. At several spots around the room, there were volunteers wearing blue Democratic National Committee jackets. A young man wearing one of the jackets walked through the room near us, so I intercepted him.

I stuck out my hand. "Hi. I'm Wilson Clay, this is my wife Audrey. I was wondering if you could help us. I was told by a good friend of mine, once I got here I should speak to Janet Marx, an aide to Senator Stafford. Can you tell me where I can find her?"

"I'm not sure. One second, let me call someone and ask." He pulled out a phone of his own and punched in a number. While he did this, I glanced around the room and my eyes landed on a man across the room and I was rocked by a feeling of wrongness strong enough to make me take a step back.

Mirsada tightened her grip on my arm and hissed, "What's wrong?"

For a moment I couldn't answer. But I'd felt this feeling before. Several times. When coming face to face with a fallen angel. The man looked familiar, but I couldn't place him.

I raised a finger, asking Mirsada for a moment. The man locked eyes with me and even from this distance, I could see his eyes, for a brief moment, changed, and I knew there would be stars falling in them.

The young man put his phone away and smiled. "Ms. Marx will meet you at the north ballroom entrance." He pointed to double doors in the far corner of the room.

"Thank you. One more thing. Can you tell me who the man is over there, the one with the woman in the red dress?"

The young man turned to see who I meant. "Oh. That's Alex Dabney. He's the owner and CEO of Dabney Industrial Tech."

Holy hell. When I fought with and kicked the ass of the Watchers, one of them had already flown the coop, going rogue. None of the others knew where he'd gone. Now I knew. Gadriel had taken up residence in the mind of one of America's largest weapons makers. No real surprise there. I'd done some research on him in the months following my take down of Samyaza and the others. Gadriel was the angel who taught man how to make and use weapons, before his banishment until Judgment Day. I could only imagine what type of horror Gadriel could bring about in Dabney's body.

I thanked the volunteer and started towards Dabney. Mirsada said, "Victor, when I look at Dabney, I get a bad feeling."

"Yeah. Me, too. It's because he has a fallen angel in his head. Be ready, this could get nasty quick."

I also recognized the woman on his arm. She'd been on the cover of this year's *Sports Illustrated* swimsuit issue. Guess being a fallen angel had its perks.

When Dabney and I were face to face, the other people around us gave us some space. I'm not sure what type of vibe regular people got around one of these things, but the tension between the two of us could be felt, the air practically full of electricity. Mirsada stepped a few paces to the side, putting some distance between us and seeing to it if an attack happened, Gadriel would need to fight two fronts. Elsa, the super model, also moved back and away from the two of us. A supermodel with a brain.

I didn't offer him my hand. I wanted to keep them free in case he decided to attack here and now.

"Gadriel. We finally meet. Seems you found a fun place to call home."

Gadriel/Dabney set his drink down, freeing up his own hands. "And not one, but two Hands of Gods. I feel honored. How did you find out about me?"

"Luck. We're here on another matter. But I'll make time for you. After taking out the other eleven fallen angels, being able to say I'd kicked the ass of a dozen fallen angels would be sweet. Kind of like collecting the whole set."

He glanced around the room. "You mean to take me on here? In front of all these people? I don't think so," he shook his head. "And if you did, what about the real reason you are here? Think you would still be able to stop what is coming if you were fighting me? I don't think so."

He was right and it pissed me off. Fighting an angel, even a fallen one, could get ugly. And people would get hurt. Regular human beings are nothing more than cattle to the Divine. He would kill everyone in the room without shedding a single tear.

I leaned in close, our noses almost touching. "You'd

better find another body because when I'm done here, I'm going to hunt you down and rip you to pieces with my bare hands. I will send you to share oblivion with Samyaza and the rest of your old buddies."

He rubbed his chin with one hand for a second, then smiled. "I don't think so. I like this one. And Alex wants me to stay. He's found my knowledge to be…invaluable. The two of us can create weapons never dreamed of by common man. The two of us have grand plans. I think the one who needs to be careful is you, Victor McCain." He glanced at Mirsada. "And I'll know everything there is to know about you before the night is over. You'll be next."

"You are fallen for a reason," she responded. "And I will wipe the floor with your entrails before you could lay a hand on me."

Yep. No doubt, the female me. I reached out and adjusted Gadriel/Dabney's bow tie, then smoothed out his lapels. "When I put you in the ground for good, I'm going out to the farm where your body is buried and take a leak over the spot. I'm sure it will get down to you eventually. Enjoy what little time you have left."

He made no attempt to hold back the hate he felt, his mouth pulling back in a snarl. I gave him a wink, once again offered Mirsada my arm, and we left in search of Ms. Marx.

"Life keeps getting better and better," I said.

"Do you think he will jump bodies?"

"While I don't know for sure, I doubt it. Dabney is as close to perfect as a fallen angel can get. Rich, weapons making bachelor? Hell, he's Tony Stark without the Iron Man suit. I wouldn't want to change if I were him. Plus he has the resources to make my life difficult. So, no. I think he will come after us first. Better watch your ass when this is done."

She nodded agreement and we made our way to the north entrance. I can't begin to tell you how hard that was with a deadly fallen angel behind you, but we managed.

We only had to wait a few minutes, when the door opened and a woman matching Marx's photo ID walked out. Wearing a cream colored dress which stopped a few inches above the knees, and a string of what looked to be very expensive pearls, she smiled at us and offered her hand.

"Hi. I'm Janet Marx, and you are the Clay's?"

She had a firm handshake and a pretty smile. "Yes. Is there a place we can speak with a little less crowd noise? I would like to discuss contributing more to the DNC, but I have a few questions about how the money will be spent."

"By all means, follow me."

She turned, held the door open for us, and then led us down a long hallway to a conference room with a long table and a dozen chairs. She waved us to a seat. I took the chair at the head of the table, with Mirsada sitting on one side of me, Marx on the other. I got up and closed the door. Marx didn't seem to mind.

"What type of questions can I answer for you?" she asked after I returned to my seat.

"I'm afraid we got you here under false pretenses, Ms. Marx. We're not democratic donors. Truth be told, I could care less about politics. And my friend is not even from this country. She doesn't get to vote here."

She furrowed her brow, looking from Mirsada to me. "But you donated fifty-thousand dollars to attend this dinner. If you don't care for politics, then why—"

"To meet you, actually. We know you're the one who will tip off Cyrus Tyler when it's time to set off the bomb. We want you to tell us how you plan to do it. Phone call? Text? How?"

Her face went pale and her eyes fluttered so badly, I thought she might pass out.

"I don't have a clue what you're talking about. I would never—"

I slammed my hand down on the table, cutting her off and making her jump in her chair. "We know it's you, Janet. There's no use denying it. You have a choice: you can tell me what you know, or we can kill you here and now and end the threat. Up to you."

Her hand flew to her throat. "If you kill me, they will blow up the bomb anyway. It gains you nothing."

At least she was no longer denying her role in the plan. "We'd rather not kill you," Mirsada said. "But we will and take our chances. Answer the question."

Her eyes darted to the door, but Mirsada moved, blocking her way. Marx looked like a deer in the headlights, afraid to talk to us, afraid we'd kill her if she didn't.

Finally, she gave in. "I have a phone. I'm supposed to text "happy birthday" when Senator Stafford sits down with his guests."

"Are the President and Vice-President here yet?"

She shook her head. "They're running behind. They won't get here until closer to nine." Tears streamed down her face. "Are you going to kill me?"

I ignored the question. "Where's the phone?"

"In my purse, back in Stafford's spare bedroom."

"Here's what you're going to do. You're going to take us there and hand over the phone. If you so much as point a finger in our direction, then you are a dead woman. No matter what happens to us, we know who you are and we have people who will take you out. Do you understand?"

Again she nodded, ringing her hands. Mirsada opened her clutch and removed a tissue. She handed it to Marx. "Get yourself together, woman. You best introduce us as the huge donors we are pretending to be. And you'd best look the part. Stop crying, it's making your eyes look puffy."

Marx blew her nose in the tissue and steadied her breathing. She stood and I stood with her. She offered a wan smile, walked to the door and opened it when Mirsada stepped aside. We followed her out and she led us away from the ballroom, the fallen angel, and the other guests.

In a few minutes, I would be in the same room with a bomb big enough to blow up us and half the building. Nothing like ending the evening with a bang.

CHAPTER THIRTY-TWO

We stopped at a bank of elevators, with a security guard keeping watch. Marx told him we were with her and he used a key to open one of the elevators and we stepped inside. Marx pushed the button for the top floor and the doors shut with a whoosh.

Marx looked everywhere but at us while we rode to the top. I could only imagine what was going through her mind. Mirsada, for her part, seemed relaxed, almost happy. I think, like me, she loved the action, the adrenaline of getting it on with the bad guys. I knew the feeling.

The elevator came to a stop and the door slid open: open upon a scene from Hell. Marx started to scream, but I put a hand over her mouth, cutting it short. On the floor in front of us was another guard. He wore the same uniform the guard wore downstairs except his black uniform looked mostly red, smeared with his own blood. Someone had ripped out his throat. I knew this because it lay on the floor next to him. Blood covered one wall, where I could see the handprints of someone wiping off the blood from their hands.

The elevator door started to close and I blocked it open with my foot. The elevator opened onto a short hallway leading to a polished oak door. From here, I could see blood on the doorknob.

Mirsada quickly searched the dead man, finding his gun still in its holster. Whoever attacked him, caught him off-guard and killed him before he got the chance to react.

I turned to Marx and asked, "How many were up here when you left?"

Unable to speak, she lifted her hand and held up the

number three, her hand shaking so bad I had to ask her to make sure. I snagged the leg of the dead guard and pulled him across the elevator threshold to block it open. I didn't want to hit the emergency button and set off the alarm.

I took Marx by the arm and stepped over the dead man, dragging her with me. She pulled back, trying to break my grip. Mirsada stepped up and clipped her hard on the chin, and the woman crumpled to the ground, dazed.

"We don't have time for this," she whispered. "Problem solved. Let's get moving."

She took the lead towards the door and I nearly laughed. I could get to really like this woman. I fell into step behind her and when we reached the door, she reached out and turned the knob, pushing the door open with her foot, gun at the ready. She had to be the best dressed shooter walking the planet. Donna Karen dress and a 9 millimeter. Quite the pairing.

The door opened onto a small entryway, with a coat closet on one side and a mirror on the other wall. We moved into the apartment and hadn't gone far when we found a man on the floor, his head bleeding from a blow to the back of the head. I knelt and felt a pulse, but a weak one.

We could hear a voice coming from up ahead and to the left. The entryway gave way to a living room, with a kitchen and dining room on one side and two other doors on the other. One door was open and I could see a huge bedroom, but the lights were off. I could hear sounds behind the other door and we quickly crossed the living room. I was about to open it when I heard a man's muffled scream.

I turned the knob and threw the door open. On the bed lay Senator Stafford, a strip of duct tape across his mouth, dressed only in an Oxford button down shirt and underwear, his hands tied to the head board, his feet tied to the baseboard. Well, one foot tied to the head board. The problem was that the other leg was no longer attached to the rest of his body, having been severed a few inches above the knee.

Elizabeth stood with a meat cleaver in her hand, blood dripping from the blade, wearing a black cocktail dress. She looked like a scene out of *American Psycho*. I could tell from the end of the Senator's leg, it had taken several hacks to cut it off.

Elizabeth tossed the cleaver onto the bed, dropped the leg into a carry bag on the floor, then picked up a belt and strapped it around the stump, pulling it tight, using it as a tourniquet. The senator shook back and forth, his muffled screams continuing.

"Bloody hell, Elizabeth, what have you done?"

"Do you always ask such obvious questions? This man had a bomb planted in his body. I removed it. I would think you would be happy, no?" She picked up the bag and wrapped the leg in plastic, then zipped the bag closed.

Mirsada entered the room, moving off to one side, the gun pointed squarely at Elizabeth. "This is a monster's solution. Not that of a normal person. Victor, if I get off a couple of quick shots, I might be able to blow her head off."

Elizabeth rolled her eyes. "Oh, please, child. If we do nothing, the man blows to pieces. Now, he may live. I pulled the belt tight, stop the bleeding. Better than what was going to happen. We must get moving before they use code and blow up the bomb. Besides, if you try and shoot me, I will have to kill you, too. And I don't want to do that. I've grown quite fond of you."

"You left us. Why? We were supposed to be a team."

"Victor, if I'd told you what I plan to do, remove this man's leg, would you have agreed? I think not. I knew what needed to be done."

"And the wraiths," Mirsada asked, "you left us behind with those creatures?"

"What are you talking about? What wraiths?"

The look of confusion seemed genuine, but at this point it was irrelevant. She was right about one thing, we could not stay here. "Ah, hell. Let's go. We will sort this out when we are away from here."

The last thing I needed was Mirsada and Elizabeth going toe-to-toe. With my luck, the moment they did, the bomb would go off, killing all three of us.

I covered the Senator with a blanket, hoping he didn't fall into shock and die, then we left the room. Mirsada went into the other bedroom, found Marx's purse, and came back with two phones, and we left the apartment. I lifted Marx to her feet and rubbed her cheeks until she came around long enough to tell me which phone she was to use to send the text. She pointed to an iPhone in a green case.

I turned the phone on and went to the text messages.

"Which one?"

Marx pointed to the third one down, a number with the Philly area code. She got a text saying "it's my birthday."

"And all you do is type in 'happy birthday?' That's it?"

She nodded yes, and I turned the phone off and slipped it into my pocket. "We need to call an ambulance for Stafford. Despite your poor man's tourniquet, the man will die if not treated soon." I turned to Marx. "Do you know this building well?"

"Yes. We spend a lot of time here, especially since the surgery." She finally noticed the bag Elizabeth carried. "What's in the bag?"

"A leg of Senator," Elizabeth said. "Not quite a leg of lamb, but what can you do?"

Her attempt at humor only made Marx slump against the wall, but I held her up by one arm. "Get yourself together. We need to get out of here, but not by the main floor. Which way?"

She led us to the elevator and nearly screamed again looking at the dead security guard. I dragged the body into the hallway and we got in the elevator. Marx frantically punched the button for the fifth floor.

The door closed, leaving the dead guard behind. I tried to keep my temper in check, but it was hard. "Did you have to kill the security guard? He was only doing his job."

Elizabeth pouted for a moment, but answered me. "He started to pull his gun. I reacted on instinct. It's hard to break centuries of bad habits overnight. I am sorry for his death."

I wasn't sure I believed her, but what could I do? The elevator opened on the fifth floor and we got out, Marx in the lead. This floor featured business offices, all darkened on a Saturday night.

"This floor connects with the building next door. There are guards at the other end, but I know them, so getting out won't be a problem."

We made it to the other doors and then through to

stairways going up and down, but there was no guard. "That's strange," Marx said. "There's always a guard here."

"Always?" I asked. My spidey senses went off full blast and I shoved Elizabeth and Mirsada back inside. I was too late to save Marx, as a man wearing black fatigues leaned over the top railing and shot her with a quick burst from an automatic weapon, maybe a Heckler and Koch, but I didn't watch long enough to find out. The poor woman bounced against the stairwell, then fell down the next flight of stairs, dead before the first bounce.

"Gun!" I shouted to Mirsada, my hand outstretched. She tossed me the handgun, and I rolled next to the door in time to shoot the man coming down the steps. He fell next to the door, with two more guys right behind him. I fired off a couple of rounds, driving them to cover, reached over, snagged the dead guy and managed to drag him into the hallway with us. Bullets slammed into the door frame, shredding it in a matter of seconds.

Mirsada unslung the machine gun from around the guy's neck, while Elizabeth searched him for other weapons. When the shooting paused, I stuck my hand around the corner and emptied the clip. Mirsada then traded places with me and we waited. A moment later I heard the sound of metal hitting the ground and looked around the corner in time to see a grenade thrown in our direction. I didn't even think, but caught it and flung it back up and over the railing.

I started to shout grenade, but it was too late. I'd managed to turn my head when the grenade went off, but the flash was intense, the sound even louder in the enclosed space. I could hear Elizabeth scream. With hearing as fine-tuned as hers, I could only imagine how much pain it caused her. My own ears rang and you could have shouted in my ear from a foot away and I wouldn't have heard a thing.

Most flash bangs are set to a bit over a second. The fact I still had all ten fingers thrilled me to no end. Mirsada had dropped her weapon and lay on the ground, hands over her ears, curled up in a little ball.

I picked up the Heckler and Koch and bounded up the steps. One of the two men started to get up and I shot him with a quick three shot burst, sending him back down. I didn't bother on the other one. When I tossed the grenade over the railing, it must have gone off right in front of his face, ripping off his nose and turning the rest of his face to pulp. Uggh.

I hurried back to Mirsada and Elizabeth, got them on their feet and headed down the steps, saying a quick prayer for Marx. All the gunfire and the blast would bring people running soon enough and we needed to be far away when they did.

When we got to the last landing, I laid the guns on the floor and we hit the bottom at a fast walk, Elizabeth still carrying the bag. The stairwell emptied into a parking garage. We made our way quickly to the other side, then out onto the sidewalk full of people staring up the street.

There were blue lights galore in front of the Founders Building. Guess we didn't need to make a call about the Senator. The three of us crossed the street and into the park where even the Tea Party folks were no longer screaming and waving signs, but watching the unfolding scene across the street.

I texted Winston, asking where our friends were. He responded with "still on the stage." I asked him to meet us at the Tomb of the Unknown Revolutionary War Soldier. Five minutes later, Winston, Elizabeth, Mirsada and I were huddled together and I made the round of introductions and filled Winston in on what happened, including Gadriel running around in Alex Dabney's body. Kurt and his laptop were holed up in a car a few blocks away, keeping track of things in cyber space.

"Damn. This is one screwed up evening." Looking at Elizabeth and her bag, Winston asked, "And you have what I think you have in that thing? If so, we need to get rid of it and soon. What if they decide to set the bomb off?"

We all agreed, but before we could decide what to do, a man on the stage shouted into a microphone, asking for everyone's attention.

"Tonight, there has been an attack on Senator Stafford." Half the crowd cheered and the man shouted them down. "Stop that! We don't condone violence of any kind. Senator Stafford has been rushed to the hospital and we all pray for his steady recovery."

Amen to that, brother. I turned to say something to Elizabeth, but she was gone. I searched the crowd, but didn't see her.

Bloody hell. She'd taken the bomb with her.

CHAPTER THIRTY-THREE

Cyrus Tyler made sure to keep a look of great concern on his face, while at the same being filled with rage on the inside. Months of careful planning blown. With any luck, the President and VP would visit Stafford in the hospital and he could still pull it off, but he knew that was a pipe dream. Word reached him that Deloris came back to the room to find Stafford had been assaulted, but that's all he knew.

Tyler walked off the stage and over to a younger man waiting for him. "Randy, let's get out of here. I want to get to the airport and back to D.C. as soon as possible."

"Yes, sir."

The two men walked to a VIP lot and waited for the valet to bring his car around. When the car pulled up, Randy opened the door and Tyler got into the backseat. Before he could close the door, a woman stepped up to the car, stopping him from closing the door.

She stuck her head in the door. "Congressman Tyler, Preston Deveraux said if anything happened to him, I should find you."

Tyler thought for a second. "It's o.k. Randy. She can join me."

"Are you headed to the airport?" she asked.

"Yes. And you?"

"The same. Thanks." She tossed her bag to Randy. "Mind putting that in the trunk?"

Randy stepped out of the way and the woman slid onto the seat opposite him. Randy popped the trunk, tossed her bag in next to Tyler's bags, slammed the lid shut, got back behind the wheel and eased the town car out of the parking lot and onto south Sixth Street.

The woman wore a black dress which showed off her body to the max. When she crossed her legs, one foot brushed against his calf, lingering a second longer than would be normal. Twenty years ago, her flirting might have paid off dividends. Not now.

"Alright, young lady. You have my attention. Why did Preston Deveraux send you to me? Do you know who murdered him?"

"I do. It was Victor McCain. You may have heard of him. I warned Preston that McCain was in town, but he didn't take the proper precautions and it got him killed. McCain will come for you next."

"Sweetheart, McCain is in over his head. He should have died the other night, but he was rescued by—"

The woman smiled at him, waiting, and for the first time in years, Tyler felt fear. Real fear. He looked at the woman more closely, noticing a hint of red on the inside of her wrist. Blood.

She followed his gaze and when she saw the blood, she brought her wrist to her mouth and licked the blood away.

"Sorry. Seems I missed a spot."

"Elizabeth Bathory, I presume? Do you plan to kill me?"

"Heavens, no." She waved a hand, dismissing the thought. "Why would I want to kill you when you do such a great job of creating chaos in the world? I feed off chaos."

"We'd been told you were off the reservation, trying to switch to the other side."

"That's what I wanted people to think, so I could get in close to them, learn what they were thinking. I went undercover, something I did often for my former employers in Hungary."

Tyler sat thinking. If anyone else told him such a story, he would dismiss it out of hand and arrange for such a person to die a slow agonizing death. But when it came to an Infernal Lord, he was not always told what they were doing.

He needed more information.

"Stafford. Do you know what happened?"

"From what I can understand, when McCain showed up at the fundraiser, he found out Alex Dabney was possessed by a fallen angel. The two nearly came to blows in the middle of the ballroom and when McCain and another woman went to see Stafford, Dabney sent men after them, trying to take them out. Stafford was injured during the confrontation."

"And McCain? What happened to him and the woman?"

"I honestly don't know. I tried to get upstairs to see if I could take out McCain myself, but they were involved in a firefight, so I left, waiting in the park. I saw you and here we are."

Tyler relaxed a bit. He didn't feel any immediate threat from Bathory and he felt confident in his ability to read people.

"I want a full debriefing. I want you to tell me everything you learned in your time spent with McCain, his weaknesses, strengths, anything you can which will help me kill him once and for all."

Bathory stared out the window for a moment, then tapped on the glass between the passenger compartment and the driver. He rolled the window down. "Yes ma'am?"

"Would you pull over, please?"

He did as she asked, pulling to the curb a block before the entrance to the interstate. She then motioned for him to raise the glass back up, and he complied.

Tyler, back on edge, asked, "What's the meaning of this? I thought you said you were going to the airport?"

"The more I think about it, the more I think I don't want to be around you at the moment. McCain and his forces are going to come for you and I don't want to be near you when they do. If you survive the next few days, I will be in touch and tell you what you want to know. The Lord of Light will be very displeased your plan to blow up the President and VP failed. I think I will wait to see what happens."

She opened the door and stepped out of the car, but leaned in for a last word. "There are times when we all think we are indestructible. And we all find out we are wrong. Be careful, Cyrus Tyler, or you will find this out yourself, sooner than you think."

She shut the door and tapped on the passenger window. When Randy rolled it down, she asked him to pop the trunk so she could get her bag. He complied and the woman walked to the trunk, taking out her bag, then closing the lid.

She stepped to the curb, holding the bag and Randy

merged into traffic, then onto I-95 to the airport. Tyler stared out the window watching the city flash by, but not really seeing, his thoughts turned inward, thinking about what Bathory had to say.

They were half way to the airport when his blood ran cold. The bag. He pressed the intercom button. "Randy! Pull over! Pull—"

*****

Elizabeth removed the green iPhone she stole from Victor, flipped over to text messages, selected the third one down and typed in "happy birthday."

She tossed the phone and empty bag into a garbage can and walked down the sidewalk singing *I Feel Pretty,* until she disappeared into the night.

*****

I sent Winston to hook up with Kurt, while Mirsada, and I left the park. I called the driver, telling him we wouldn't need him as we'd walk to the hotel. We were almost there when a huge explosion rocked the night. A fireball rose high into the air, but because of the buildings surrounding us, we couldn't see where it came from.

Mirsada turned to me. "Oh my God. Victor. The phone!" I frantically checked my pockets, but the phone was gone. I looked at her and shook my head.

"It has to be her. Has to be. But where did she set it off?"

We hustled to our room and turned on the TV, horrified at what we saw. A large section of an I-95 overpass simply ceased to exist when a car bomb went off, turning the road to rubble. At least half a dozen cars were on fire or completely destroyed, having fallen into the street below. The TV talking heads were calling it an act of terrorism.

They said the attacks on Stafford and now the car bomb had to be related and authorities were treating them as such. I said aloud to myself, "No shit, Sherlock."

They reported Stafford was in surgery, after suffering a major attack in his own home. At least six were dead at the

Founders Building and adjacent property. Unnamed sources were reporting several para-military soldiers among the dead as well as a member of Stafford's staff, last seen giving a tour to a pair of wealthy donors who were also missing.

When we saw this, the two of us quickly packed, went down to the valet, got the car and left. We called Winston and Kurt and arranged to meet them outside of Harrisburg, Pennsylvania. If the authorities tracked down our IDs they would find them to be bogus. Kurt said he would take care of changing the photos attached to the IDs to keep our pictures off the TV.

We kept the car radio on the news channels on XM radio, trying to learn what the main target had been. We'd been on the road about a half hour when word came the car may have been that of Speaker of the House Cyrus Tyler. The Speaker left the park not long before the explosion and had not been heard from since. Shortly thereafter, a smartphone video surfaced of Tyler getting into his car with a woman. Mirsada went to CNN.com and checked out the video. It was Elizabeth. It also showed a young man putting a bag into the trunk, then getting into the car and driving off. Elizabeth's bag.

Speculation was rampant as to the identity of the woman leaving with the Speaker of the House, but to this point she was a mystery.

"Victor, do you think she blew herself up? Would she do such a thing?"

"I have no clue. From what I could tell, she was very self-absorbed. I find it hard to believe she would commit suicide. But maybe she thought this would get her into Heaven, taking out the top leadership of the Church."

Before I could say anything else, my phone rang. I didn't recognize the number, but assumed it was Elizabeth. I answered and my world fell away.

"Vic. This is Samantha. Where are you? My father, did you kill my father? Please tell me this wasn't you."

Samantha Tyler practically yelled her questions into the phone. Having lost her mother at a young age, Cy Tyler was the only family she had left in the world. The fact he was a scumbag murdering son of a bitch, made little difference. Samantha held out hope she could one day change her father's path. We both knew it was a false hope. But now that chance was forever gone.

"Samantha, you have to listen to me. Your father—"

"Don't you dare. Don't you even dare. You did it, didn't you? You're in Philly. And don't lie to me. You owe me the truth." The pain in her voice cut me to the core. And she was right. I did owe her the truth.

"Not directly. No. But I've been working with the person who did. The person who did this did so without my knowledge, but Samantha, he deserved it. He created the instrument of his own death. I wish I could tell you I was sorry, but I'm not. You don't know what your father had planned."

"It wasn't for you to judge." I could hear her crying.

"It is for me to judge. Your father chose his path, just like Mikey. Now he will live in Hell with the consequences for the rest of eternity."

She didn't say anything else. Not a word. The phone line went dead. I stared at it for a moment, then called Winston, telling him we needed to scrub it, and hung up. I rolled down my window and threw the phone out into the darkness. He would be doing the same thing. We wouldn't take any chances the government could filter our phone messages and find us. With an attack on the Speaker of the House, the Feds would be cranked up and while I was supposed to be immune to prosecution, I didn't want to push it.

Mirsada laid a hand on my shoulder. "Do you want to talk about it?"

I didn't. I really didn't. But over the next hour and a half, I talked about Samantha, how much I loved her and why we would never work out. I'd hurt her too much, allowed others to hurt her. I rambled on and Mirsada let me. She never interrupted, or belittled what I said.

When we approached the Harrisburg exit, she took my hand in hers and squeezed. "You are a good man, Victor McCain, but I have no words of comfort. You and I lead a hard life. One which will end in violence for both of us. We cannot make everything right, but we can make a difference. Honor her with how you live your life."

I got off at our exit and I found a dark spot and changed the license plate on my car. The hotel would have made a note of the old one and I kept several in the hidden compartment for such emergencies.

We met Winston and Kurt at a Holiday Inn Express and we checked in. We agreed to meet for breakfast the next morning before getting back on the road to Louisville. They went up to their rooms and I started to follow them, but paused to glance into the bar. I'd never needed a drink more than right at that very moment. It called out to me, whispering my name. A line from a Robert Frost poem came to mind:

The woods are lovely dark and deep,
But I have promises to keep,
And miles to go before I sleep,
And mile to go before I sleep.

I did have promises to keep. And I wouldn't be able to do them if I turned to a bottle every time life punched me in the face, since that seemed to be a near daily occurrence. I sighed, took the elevator up to my floor, found my room and collapsed on the bed, asleep in minutes. And like the night I murdered my brother, I did not dream.

CHAPTER THIRTY-FOUR

Breakfast was a solemn affair. Death totals for the bomb damage sat at nine, including four members of the same family whose minivan had been in the lane next to that of Speaker Tyler at the moment of the explosion. Injuries counted in the dozens. Elizabeth Bathory may have killed the deadliest man in the world, but she also robbed many innocent people of all they would ever be. If she was alive, she had not contacted me and the authorities said it could take weeks before DNA analysis could prove if she was still in the car when the bomb went off.

The ride to Louisville passed in a haze. Mirsada and I hardly spoke. I think she knew I needed time to think about what had happened. It took us nearly nine hours to get home and I couldn't tell you one thing about the trip. One moment we were on the road, the next we were at the Derby Mission.

Winston and Kurt went home while Mirsada and I went straight to J's office. Mirsada and I took turns filling in J on the events in Philadelphia. He listened, only interrupting to ask questions clarifying something we said. When we were through he steepled his fingers, pressing them against this lips and we waited for him to speak.

"It shouldn't take them long to find out if Bathory was in the car. There is no point on speculating any further until we hear one way or the other. As for Cyrus Tyler, he is now paying the ultimate price for selling his soul. With his death, along with that of Deveraux and your brother, Victor, this will leave a power vacuum at the top. I am curious to see how this affects the Satanist church. One school of thought is cut off the head of a snake and kill the snake. But this is more of a hydra than a snake. Cut off one, and perhaps several more grow in its place."

"Aren't you a ray of sunshine? Thanks, J. What a real pick me up this conversation is turning out to be."

To Mirsada, I asked, "You came to this country to hunt down and kill Elizabeth Bathory. Will you hang around until you find out if she's really dead?"

She shook her head. "I don't think so. I can always return. I think there is no doubt she tried to do the right thing, but being the creature that she is, she could not find it in herself to do it the right way. She murdered those other people when she set off the bomb. I am torn about what to do where she is concerned, and for people like you and me, such indecision leads to an early grave. The way I see it, as long as she stays in America, she is your problem."

"And the gifts keep on coming." I managed a smile. "Thank you, Mirsada, for all you've done. I wish you the best of luck back home."

"They need me there. We have evil much older than what you normally deal with here in the States." She stood and we embraced. At least this time she didn't threaten to run me through with a sword like our last meeting in this room.

She asked, "You're sure you don't need me to help with the fallen angel?"

We discussed it briefly on the trip home and she'd offered to stay. "Nah. Besides, keeping the two of us in the same place makes it easier to take us both out at the same time. I'll rest up a day or two and then come up with a plan to take him out."

"Then be well, Victor McCain. Good hunting."

She left to go to her room at the mission and to arrange her flight home. Lisa, J's assistant, would then take her to the airport.

"Samantha called me to get your cell phone number," J. said. "I assume she called?"

"Yeah, and as you can imagine, it didn't go well. She blames me for her father's death. I don't know if I will ever hear from her again."

Deep in my heart, I knew this to be true, but saying it out loud drove the dagger home. I did my best to push the thoughts of Samantha into a dark corner, and lock them away. Time would tell if they would stay there.

I left the office, went out to my car and drove to Molly Malone's. I found my regular table and the waitress brought me a Guinness. I spun the bottle around a few times, took a sip and set it to the side. I would nurse it through dinner. Time to institute a one drink minimum.

I was watching the news about the bombing on a TV over the bar when the door opened and Brad Stiles walked in, glanced around until he found me, then walked in my direction.

I reached behind me and found the grip of my gun, pulled it out and held it on the seat next to me.

He approached my table, hands out, showing me he didn't have anything in his hands. I motioned for him to lift his jacket. He did and turned around, lifting it up in the back, showing me he was unarmed.

I motioned for him to sit on the other side of the booth and he sat down heavily, keeping both hands on the table where I could see them. I waved to the waitress and she brought him a Guinness as well. He thanked her, took a long pull on the beer, then set the bottle down.

"You used me to kill Tyler, didn't you?"

"What? No small talk? No foreplay? You cut right to the chase? You're no fun."

"Well, it's been a rough last twenty-four hours. My gravy train is now in a million different pieces. Kind of kills the mood, pun intended."

"I know what you mean. But to answer your question: no. It wasn't me."

He nodded. "The woman getting into the car with Tyler was Elizabeth Bathory, wasn't it?"

I tipped my bottle in his direction, taking another sip of mine. The man seemed to have aged ten years and his suit looked as if he'd slept in it overnight. Good bet he had.

"Will they come after you?" I asked.

"I doubt it. The only one, as far as I know, who knew I was involved, was Tyler. You know, I warned them, Tyler and Deveraux, Bathory would be a problem when she found out about Isaac. She really had a thing for the guy. Out of all the men she ever met over the last few hundred years, she falls for a braniac. Go figure."

The last thing I wanted to discuss was Elizabeth's love life. "Why are you here, Stiles? Nothing personal, but the last time you and I talked, you'd hired a guy to peel the skin from my body. Doesn't make you one of my favorite people."

"You and I both know that was just business. They hired me to do a job, and I did it. That's one of the reasons I came here. I wanted to make sure you and I were square. I don't want to spend the rest of my life looking over my shoulder wondering when you're going to show up. Thought we could come to an agreement. A truce. I agree to never come after you, you agree to never come after me."

"I'm not sure I can make that promise. You work for some pretty bad dudes. You stay on their payroll, then I'll have to take you down."

He lifted his hands in defense. "No worries on that score. I think it's time for me to retire from the merc business. I have a buddy in D.C. who's offered me a job with a security company. I told him I'd take the job, asked for a week before I started. I wanted to see you first."

I thought about it for a moment, then did what I always do: trusted my gut. I stuck out my hand and he took it. He drained the last of his Guinness, set the bottle back on the table and stood.

"You said make sure we were square was one of the reasons you came. There's another?"

"Yes. I wanted to tell you, there's a contract out on you. I got the word from an associate. Wanted to know if I'd be interested in accepting the job. I told him no, I wouldn't."

"How much money?"

"Ten million dollars. Cash."

I whistled. "Wow. Thanks for the heads up, but as the Hand of God, there is no shortage of people who want me dead."

"Yeah, but for that kind of money, it will bring out the weirdoes and professionals alike. You need to watch your ass."

"My thanks. Anything else?"

He took a card out of his inner suit pocket and tossed it on the table. "As a gesture of good faith, I thought you might want to visit this address this coming weekend. A man and woman will be there on vacation. I hear they took you on a boat ride. Thought you might want to pay them a visit."

"Payback's a bitch. If I find out you're setting me up..."

"No, no. You'll find out I'm not. Take friends. These two are worse than a den of rattlers."

He offered a small wave, then left. I pulled the card to me, and read the address, a street somewhere around Lake Tahoe.

The waitress brought over my shepherd's pie and while I ate, I thought to myself, "Road trip."

CHAPTER THIRTY-FIVE

Eduardo drove the convertible down the winding road above Lake Tahoe. With the convertible top lowered, they watched the sun dip behind the mountains while taking in the fresh evening air.

Donut removed the scrunchie keeping her pony tail together, allowing her long black hair to blow in the wind. They were enjoying a bit of down time while trying to decide what job to take next.

Like everyone else, they were shocked at the level of destruction which took place in Philadelphia and were glad to be well removed from the East Coast.

Tonight, they ate at a little hole in the wall Italian place in town, then saw a movie. Even assassins needed time to recharge their batteries. Donut changed CDs, punched a button or two, and then they were listening to the new Darius Rucker album. Donut was on a country kick and Eduardo knew to go with the flow.

They rounded a curve and Eduardo locked up the Mercedes, skidding to a stop, and trying to keep from crashing into two other cars stopped in the middle of the road. He saw two men arguing with each other and could hear bits and pieces of the conversation, with one blaming the accident on the other.

Donut rolled her eyes and muttered under her breath. Eduardo got out of the car, making his way over to the two men.

"You guys need any help? If you don't get these cars out of the way, you're going to get someone killed."

One of the men, a large black man, said, "This MoFo done dented my ride, man. He can't drive for shit."

The other man, with sandy brown hair and a nice

California tan, said, "Dude. You're the one who crossed the line and hit me."

Eduardo stepped past them, looking at the two cars. "I don't see any damage. What's the big—" He never got out another word. The black man jabbed the syringe into his neck, pressing the plunger down. Eduardo reacted instantly, launching into an attack, but it only took a second for him to feel his knees buckle and then pitch forward onto the blacktop.

Donut, who'd been watching the sun reflect on the lake as it set when they attacked Eduardo, started to slide over into the driver's seat when a man stepped up beside the car and pressed a gun barrel to the back of her head.

"I would place both hands on the steering wheel. Now, if you please."

She did as the man asked. "You're the man from the boat. The one they had us take to Philadelphia, aren't you?"

"That would be me. I hope you don't mind, but I'm going to take the donuts you have in the back seat. I do love me some Krispy Kremes."

She thought furiously about what to do, then felt a needle stick her in the side of the neck. The man said, "I thought I would return the favor. This is for Dr. Collins and her daughter."

Her last thought, before blackness overcame her, was "I hope they got the dosage right."

She was dead before she finished the thought.

EPILOGUE

I got home from Tahoe feeling better than I'd felt since becoming the Hand of God. Maybe it was the fresh air of Lake Tahoe. Perhaps it was avenging the deaths of Dr. Collins and her daughter. I had no clue. Maybe I had begun to come to grips with the emotional state of my love life, or lack thereof. Who knows?

While we were gone the investigation into the bombing continued in Philadelphia. Forensics found DNA of three people in Tyler's car: his, his driver and Senator Hedley Stafford, but not the woman seen on the video getting into the car.

This meshed with the story Stafford told authorities following his brush with death. The EMTs got him to the hospital in time to save his life—though he died twice on the table before being stabilized. He told the police a woman knocked on his door, assaulted one of his staffers, and then forced him into the bedroom where she tied him up and then cut off his leg.

She told him his knee replacement contained a bomb and she intended to save his life. He thought she was nuts until the news about his DNA was found in the bomb debris. He also confirmed the bag she was seen walking to Tyler's car with was similar to the one she brought with her to his apartment.

The explosives used in the attack were traced to Dabney Industrial Technologies. They'd reported a theft of explosives to the A.T.F. some weeks prior to the events in Philadelphia. Alex Dabney promised to cooperate fully with the investigation and offered a twenty-million dollar reward to anyone who helped to identify the people involved.

A white supremacist group in Alabama claimed responsibility for the attack on Stafford, but nothing could be proven at this time.

I knew the truth, of course. I was happy Elizabeth hadn't died when the bomb went off, but I wasn't sure I should be. Being an Infernal Lord still meant it would be tough for her to make it to Heaven, but I believed she deserved the chance.

I got a cab from the airport and rolled into the Derby Mission in the early afternoon. I dropped my gear in my room and contemplated where I wanted to have lunch when the phone rang.

I picked it up and offered a very upbeat, "Hello."

"Victor, this is your mother. I need you to come over here, right now."

Her voice dripped with tension. "What's wrong mom? Are you feeling alright?"

My mom was closing in on her mid-sixties and, all in all, was in good health. But I worried about her living alone with dad gone.

"I'm fine. Victor, there are some police detectives here. They want to talk to you. Can you come now? Please?"

"Sure mom, I'm on my way."

I sat the phone back on the charger and thought for a moment. Brother Joshua told me the police wouldn't bother me for as long as I was the Hand of God. Why would they want to talk to me?

I went out to the car, hopped in and drove to mom's house. She lived in a small home in Anchorage, about a twenty minute drive from downtown Louisville.

I pulled into the driveway and parked next to a Ford Crown Vic. It seemed every police department in the world used Crown Vics.

I went inside and found my mother on the couch in the living room with a man and woman sitting on a love seat across from her. They both wore suits, and hers fit better than his. They stood up and the woman did the introductions.

"Victor McCain? I'm Detective Linda Coffey. This is my partner, Detective Sam Wallace. We'd like to ask you a few questions about your brother, Michael McCain."

Coffey, a woman of average height, with brown hair cut short and brown eyes, offered her hand and I shook it. Wallace didn't offer, and I guessed he must be bad cop, with a Marine buzz cut with white wall sides, and a gut which strained the buttons of his shirt. He opted for the cop glare.

My mother, a petite woman with hair gone gray, and smile lines around her eyes, gave me a hug and a kiss when I sat down next to her. She'd placed a tray of cookies on the table between her and the cops. They'd not partaken of any of them, but I grabbed two and started munching.

Around a mouthful of cookies, I asked, "What's this about Mikey?" I wondered if someone had found his body. I thought this unlikely, since I tossed it down a sinkhole in Eastern Kentucky.

"When was the last time you saw your brother," asked Detective Coffey.

"Hell, I haven't seen Mikey since last November, when his warehouse burned to the ground. Why are you asking? What's he done?"

Detective Wallace said, "If you know where he is and don't tell us, you know that's obstruction of justice, right? We can have your bounty hunter's license yanked."

"Well, golly gee Officer Krumpke, I ain't seen nothin'. I swear."

My mother slapped me on the arm. "Victor Riley McCain, you behave. Show Detective Wallace some respect."

I started to point out to my mother that Wallace started it, but Detective Coffey jumped in. "We're not accusing you of anything. We just need to find your brother and would appreciate your help."

"You still haven't told me why?"

"Do you recognize the names Ron Fisher and Gloria Small?"

I thought for a moment. I didn't recognize the last names, but I did the first. "I'm not sure. My brother employed two security guards at his warehouse who were named Ron and Gloria. Are you talking about them?"

"Yes. We are. Did you know them at all?"

"No. I only met them once when Mikey gave me a tour of the warehouse. What about them?"

"They're dead. Murdered," Wallace said.

"I'm sorry," I said, confused. "You think Mikey killed them? When were they killed?"

"Three days ago," Coffey replied

"How were they killed?"

"He broke both their necks. Each were found at home, with their necks nearly snapped in two," Wallace said.

My mother covered her mouth with her hands, and I put my arm around her. "Look, Detectives, there's no way my brother did this."

"Oh, and why not?" asked Wallace.

I wanted to say, "Because I killed him and dumped his body nearly a year ago." I decided that wasn't a good response.

"Detectives, there are Smurf's bigger than my brother. Hell, there are Yorkshire Terriers bigger than my brother. My brother couldn't snap a cannoli in half, let alone someone's neck. You're barking up the wrong tree here. Sorry, but you have to be wrong."

"I'm afraid not," said Coffey. "He left fingerprints on their necks from where he squeezed them to death."

I sat, stunned. This couldn't be. Mikey was dead. I killed him. I watched the light fade from his eyes. There was no way he was alive. Unless...

"Are you o.k., Mr. McCain?" asked Detective Coffey.

"He's o.k. Linda, he's finally realizing his brother is a murderer," sneered Wallace.

I got control of my emotions and resisted the urge to grab Wallace by the side of the head and drive my knee through his face.

I stood and so did they. "I'm sorry detectives, but neither my mother nor I know where Mikey is hiding out. We haven't seen him or spoken to him since last November."

Detective Coffey took out a business card and gave it to me. "If you hear from him, call us right away. It's best for him if we bring him in peacefully. We don't want him to get hurt."

I showed them to the door, then shut it behind them. I watched from a front window until I was sure they were gone.

Mom joined me and I hugged her.

"Do you think Mikey really killed those people, Victor?" She spoke quietly, afraid to hear my answer.

"I don't know mom. But I will find out."

I kissed her on the forehead, then left. I called Winston, who came in on the flight before mine.

"Listen, I need you to take a trip with me. Do you have any climbing gear?" I asked.

"Yeah. I do. We going climbing? I've had enough mountains after Tahoe."

"Just get the gear ready. I'm on my way over to pick you up."

I nearly flew to Winston's house and he was waiting in the driveway. When I pulled in, he tossed the gear in the back and got in on the passenger side.

I told him what the cops said and he listened, then reached the same conclusion I did.

"You don't think—"

"That's what you and I are going to find out."

We drove to the mountains of Eastern Kentucky. I parked in the same spot I'd parked in the previous year when I hiked over the mountain to kill my brother. The two of us followed the same trail until we came to the sinkhole, out in the middle of nowhere.

Winston tied off a long length of rope, knotted every three feet, to a large maple tree, and then tossed the loose end down and into the sinkhole.

"You want me to go down?" he asked.

"No. I have to see for myself."

I strapped on a miner's hat, and turned on the light. I grabbed hold of the rope, then started over the side, going down hand over hand. The sinkhole ended up being about thirty feet deep. When I got to the bottom, it didn't take long to look around. No Mikey. The bottom, covered in piles of leaves, broken sticks and the bodies of a few dead animals, showed signs of someone having walked around.

I used the light from my helmet to check around the walls. On one of them, I could see deep gouges where someone had dug deep into the dirt, finding hand holds and toe holds. They went straight up to the top of the sinkhole.

I could feel my breathing coming in quick, short breaths and my head swam with the consequences of what I was seeing, or in this case, not seeing.

Winston looked down from up above. "Is he down there?"

It took a moment before I could reply. "No. He's gone."

I took hold of the rope and struggled to the top. Winston offered me his hand, and helped pull me up the last few feet.

We stood for a moment, staring at each other.

"You know what this means, right?" he asked.

I nodded, but was unable to find my voice.

Bloody hell. My brother was an Infernal Lord. Killing Muramasa opened up a spot and Satan gave it to my brother. Mikey was back and he finally had what he'd always dreamed of: power, strength and immortality.

And I knew what he would want next.

Payback.

I looked for the last time down into the sinkhole where my brother should have stayed until his bones turned to dust, my light only penetrating so far into the darkness. By murdering the two guards in such a blatant fashion, he knew I would find out. Mikey was sending me a message.

The McCain boys were going to have a reunion. And this time, he planned to be the one tossing bodies down a sinkhole.

It was Cain and Abel all over again. More like the Brothers Grimm. At the end of this story, only one McCain brother would be left standing. The question being, which one?

On the drive back to Louisville, a quote I once read by Marlon Brando popped into my head. "If we are not our brother's keeper, at least let us not be his executioner."

Too late, Marlon. I killed him once and I would do it again. This time, permanently.

Acknowledgements

While writing is a solitary endeavor, producing a novel is not. I would like to take this time to thank those who helped drag me across the finish line, starting with my own Scooby-gang: Wendell Farrar, Donna Krieg Monroe, Brad Stiles, and Tom McNeil. And, of course, Bob Fulks, without whom this book would never have been written.

I want to offer a special thanks to Linda Coffey and Teresa Collins both of whom made donations to local charities in exchange for having characters named for them in *The Speaker*.

A large thank you to Dr. Daniel Maurer who did a superior job in performing my knee replacement and answering my technical medical questions for this novel.

Thanks to Starbucks Store # 2464 in Prospect, Kentucky who has yet to charge me rent—though I'm there more than a lot of their employees.

Thanks to my wife, Karin, who did the major edits on this novel. She loves the fact she gets to show me, time and again, where I'm wrong.

Special thanks to my daughter, Katy, who at the age of nine, suggested a major plot twist for the story. At nine. Years. Old.

A huge thank you to cover artist Karri Klawiter for another wonderful cover which hits it out of the park.

Thanks to Hydra Publications, and to my other fellow authors, who are quickly becoming part of the family.

Most of all, I'd like to thank all the readers who have made the Victor McCain thrillers a huge success. Your constant contact asking about your favorite characters, keeping track of when the next book will be released, and where you can find my work is what keeps me going. Thank you!

214

About the Author

Tony Acree is the author of the Amazon bestselling novels, *The Hand of God* and *The Watchers*. He lives in Goshen, Kentucky, with his wife and twin daughters. Visit his website at Tonyacree.com. You can find him on Twitter and Facebook. Email him at Tonyacree@gmail.com

www.ingramcontent.com/pod-product-compliance
Lightning Source LLC
Chambersburg PA
CBHW071151180726
48291CB00007B/2413